SAFER

ALSO BY SEAN DOOLITTLE

The Cleanup

Rain Dogs

Burn

Dirt

SEAN DOOLITTLE

Delacorte Press

SAFER
A Delacorte Press Book / March 2009

Published by Bantam Dell
A Division of Random House, Inc.
New York, New York

This is a work of fiction. Names, characters, places, and incidents either are the product of the author's imagination or are used fictitiously. Any resemblance to actual persons, living or dead, events, or locales is entirely coincidental.

Book design by Catherine Leonardo

Delacorte Press is a registered trademark of Random House, Inc., and the colophon is a trademark of Random House, Inc.

Library of Congress Cataloging in Publication Data
Doolittle, Sean, date.
Safer / Sean Doolittle.
p. cm.
ISBN 978-0-385-33898-1 (hardcover)
1. Married people—Fiction. 2. Domestic fiction. [1. City and town life—Iowa—Fiction.]. I. Title.
PS3604.O568S24 2009
813'.6—dc22
2008039208

Printed in the United States of America
Published simultaneously in Canada

www.bantamdell.com

10 9 8 7 6 5 4 3 2 1
BVG

For Jessica, again and always

The Bible tells us to love our neighbors, and also to love our enemies; probably because generally they are the same people.

—Gilbert K. Chesterton

It is evidently consoling to reflect that the people next door are headed for hell.

—Aleister Crowley

SAFER

Friday, December 16—9:25 p.m.

1.

MY WIFE, SARA, AND I are hosting a faculty party at our home when the Clark Falls Police Department arrives to take me into custody.

It's the last day of the fall semester. On campus, offices are darkened, final exams completed, lecture halls standing empty until the new year. Most of our colleagues, a few graduate students, and assorted companions have retreated here, at our invitation, to shake off the cold and brace for the holidays.

The house smells like mulled cider and catered food. Hickory logs crackle in the fireplace while conversation bubbles and alcohol flows. I'm at the foot of the staircase with Warren Giler, the chancellor's husband, where we've found common ground on Islay scotch, the '04 Red Sox, and a mutual ambivalence regarding faculty parties. Winter air threads its way into the festivities.

"I'm sorry?" I hear my wife say. She's standing at the front door in her dress and heels, talking to a man in an overcoat. I see two uniformed officers behind him, breathing clouds on our stoop. "Can you tell me what this is about?"

"Uh-oh," Giler says to me. "Those men look stern."

He's right. They do. "I'd better go help," I tell him. "You're not wanted, are you?"

"Not to my knowledge. Possibly the music is too loud?"

I chuckle and excuse myself. Sara gives me a worried look as I join her at the door. She looks terrific with her hair up.

"Evening, guys." I smile. "Cold tonight."

"Paul Callaway?"

"That's right." There are two squad cars parked in front of our house, plus an unmarked sedan in our driveway, behind the catering van. "Is something wrong?"

The man in the overcoat reproduces the badge he's just shown Sara, a gold shield seated in a black leather wallet. He stands medium height, trim and efficient-looking, gray hair neatly combed. Detective Bell, according to the ID card. "Mr. Callaway, we're here to place you under arrest."

"Excuse me?"

Bell hands me a folded document. "I'll give you a minute to find a coat."

Sara takes the papers out of my hand. "Let me see that."

"Guys," I say. "Obviously there's a mistake."

"I'll give you a minute," Bell repeats, "to find a coat."

Our guests are starting to pay closer attention. The simmering stew of conversation thins near the door. Sara, leafing through what appears to be a court-issued arrest warrant, takes a short breath and whispers, "Paul..."

"I'm telling you, I don't even have any parking tickets. Arrest me for what?"

"Suspicion of the sexual exploitation of a minor," Bell informs me, this time louder than strictly necessary. He produces a second document. "This entitles us to search the premises, as well as your office on campus."

"My office on campus?" I don't even have an office on campus. I have a mailbox and a table I like in the faculty lounge. In the pin-drop background, all conversation has ceased. I hear the silence rippling through the house, but I've had three rounds of scotch with Warren Giler and now I've lost my temper. "Let me see that badge again."

"I can instruct the officers to handcuff and Mirandize you right here on the steps if that's the way you'd prefer to accomplish this." Bell looks me in the eyes. "But I can see that you're having a party."

"Some detective."

Sara says, "Paul..."

In spite of the shock I know exactly who's behind this little production. But it still doesn't make any sense. Sexual what? I picture all of this from the point of view of one of our guests—say for instance Warren Giler, the chancellor's husband—and I realize that by reacting the way any reasonable person might, I'm only making things worse. In fact, I can see in the tense, readied looks on the faces of the two officers flanking Detective Bell that I'm possibly one good outburst away from getting Tasered in my own doorway.

"This has to be a joke," I say.

"Mr. Callaway, you have the right to remain silent." Detective Bell stands aside as one of the officers moves his hand to the cuffs on his belt.

"Jesus." I kiss Sara on the forehead, break away, and reach for the closet.

"Paul, this says..."

"It's okay." I nod inside the house. "See if anybody in there knows a lawyer who can make things as unpleasant as possible for Detective Bell and his teenage sons here."

"I want your badge numbers before you leave," Sara says. "All of you." She's taken her administrative tone, and something about the sound of it fills my heart with gratitude. It tells me—if I needed to know—that despite all we've been through these past few months, we're still playing on the same team.

For the moment, that's all I need to set aside the fundamental injustice under way here, swallow the hundred protests clanging in my head, and move this insanity away from our doorstep. I put on my coat and join the two officers waiting to escort me to the curb.

The night air is a bracing slap that leaves me hyperalert, yet strangely numb at the same time. On either side of me, I can feel the officers' hands on my elbows. I can feel the flagstones beneath the soles of my shoes. I can hear myself breathing, feel the hairs freezing in my nostrils, but none of it feels real.

At the curb, the cop on my left cuffs my hands in front of me and puts me in the back of the lead squad unit, behind the wire cage. The other cop finishes informing me, in case I didn't catch it the first time, of my right to remain silent. As to rights, I have a number of others, and he lets me know about those. Do I understand?

No.

I nod my head anyway. The door slams shut, muffling the world outside.

The officer who handcuffed me retraces his steps back to our front door, where he says something to Detective Bell, then something to Sara. Giving his badge number as requested, I presume. The silence around me is punctuated by the occasional soft crackle of the police radio up front. The car smells like peppermint and sweat.

After a few moments, the officer returns and gets in behind the wheel.

"I know you're just doing your job," I tell him through the wire cage, "but this is bullshit."

He makes a sound like it isn't a shift until somebody tells him that. How old is this kid? Except for the uniform, and the gun that goes with it, he looks like he could be a new freshman on campus.

"Out of curiosity, who am I supposed to have exploited? I'd really love to know."

The officer speaks a few words into his radio in a code-riddled language I don't understand, then fastens his seat belt and starts the car.

Our house is the first on the left as you enter the circle, making it the last house you'd pass as you leave. All of our guests' cars are facing my direction. But these cops came in backward, straight to our address, which means that we have to drive clockwise all the way around in order to exit, past each of our neighbors, one by one. Through the foggy backseat window, I see Pete and Melody Seward's porch light go dark as we roll past.

"I guess these cars don't go in reverse," I say, still too angry to be humiliated. We pass Trish and Barry Firth's house, now Michael and Ben's. I saw Michael not half an hour ago, in our kitchen, tutoring the caterers. "Why didn't you back up into the driveway, turn around—wait, but then you couldn't have paraded me around the neighborhood first. You're right, this is much better."

"Let's have a contest," the young cop finally says. "Whoever can be quietest all the way to the station wins. How about that?"

"Gee, I don't know, Officer." Condescending prick. "Who gets to judge?"

Sycamore Court is decked for the holidays. All around the circle, white light drips like icicles from the dormers and eaves. Tendrils of smoke curl from the chimneys, and all the trees twinkle in the cold. I see a wet glint in the dark as the cop's eyes flicker to the mirror again.

"That's a good point," he says. "I guess it'll have to be your word against mine. Sir."

We're almost all the way around now. Between the squat stone pillars on either side of the entrance, I see the black ribbon of newly topped asphalt that will take us around the tree line, down the hill, and into the thick of Ponca Heights, the newer housing development below.

I take a long look at my neighbor Roger's house as we roll past, directly across the circle from ours. His dark windows seem to be watching us. I sense the meaning in the cop's eyes, still fixed on me in the mirror: *Get the picture?*

For the first time, I feel a chill in my joints that has nothing to do with the weather. I get the picture.

Off we go.

2.

OUR NEIGHBORS SAY they can't believe how much Clark Falls has grown. They wonder where all the people are coming from.

Sara and I came from Boston, and to us, Clark Falls feels more or less like what it is: a pleasant little university town fifteen hundred miles from Boston. The city proper tucks up against a range of forested bluffs, which rise unexpectedly from the Iowa flatlands and run along the eastern bank of the Missouri River. We've learned that these bluffs are known as the Loess Hills, which explains the town slogan found on welcome signs posted at the city limits: *Clark Falls: Loess Is More.*

Forty-five thousand people live here, sixty thousand during the school term. According to the plaque on the front steps of the courthouse, the original township, built up around the frontier fur trade, earned its name for the modest tumble of springwater William Clark pointed out to Meriwether Lewis some months into their storied walk to the Pacific Ocean two hundred years ago.

We don't go up the front steps of the courthouse. Instead, I'm driven around back to a secured parking facility, then escorted into the adjoining building, which houses the Clark Falls Municipal Jail.

I realize that I've been anticipating the police station. I know what the inside of the police station looks like because Sara and I went there together, back in July, to leaf through mug shots. I've been thinking of the police station, not the jail, and that's the first thing that makes all of this start to sink in.

The officer who drove me here—C. Mischnik, according to the nameplate pinned to his fur-collared duty coat—stops in a frosty vestibule and checks his gun at a bank of small gray lockers. He takes the locker key in one hand, my elbow in the other, and pushes on through the next set of doors.

I'm led down a buzzing fluorescent corridor, past two officers on their way out, and into a grimy central pod for booking. A middle-aged desk sergeant with veins in his cheeks sits me down in a cold plastic chair. He asks me questions without looking at me, hunts and pecks at a plastic-covered keyboard. I'm entering the system.

"When does somebody explain this?" I shift in my chair. "Where's Detective Bell?"

"Address of residency," the sergeant says.

I can only imagine what the sergeant must be thinking. Wouldn't an innocent man have asked for an explanation already?

Or maybe the sergeant couldn't care less. Maybe he's just waiting for my information so that he can type it into the blank spots on his computer screen.

Why didn't I take the time to read the arrest warrant? There I was, marching out of the house with a righteous stride, and now I don't know the first thing about the charges against me. I feel like I've leapt off the end of a sturdy dock onto a frozen pond, and the ice is cracking all around me.

The sergeant is waiting.

"I'd like to make a phone call," I say.

"Address."

I take a deep breath and let it out slowly. Now the sergeant finally looks at me. He raises his eyebrows.

"Thirty-four Sycamore Court," I tell him, starting the gears of the justice machine turning again.

I know that Clark Falls isn't Boston. It can't be more than fifteen degrees outside, the local bars won't close for three more hours, and I have no frame of reference in the first place, but still: it must be slow in here for a Friday. Except for me and the desk sergeant, the intake area is bright and vacant.

A plate of crumbs and candy sprinkles sits in a puddle of red cellophane on a nearby table. There's a spindly artificial Christmas tree standing cockeyed in the corner; colored lights blink a few times, chase each other around the frazzled branches, then blink again.

I follow the faint crackle of radio chatter to a glass partition labeled *Dispatch,* where a young woman wearing a bulky holiday sweater and a radio headset sits behind a shoulder-high console, working the controls. I hear Officer Mischnik joking around with somebody down the hall. In a moment, I see him emerge with a foam cup in one hand, steam curling around the rim. He pauses to chat up the dispatcher through the glass.

Sitting here, hands cuffed in my lap, robotically answering these questions about the mundane nuts and bolts of my life, it strikes me that, on the right side of things, this is just a place where people work. They come here for a while and go home again. In between, they joke and eat cookies and earn paychecks.

There's no way to get comfortable in this chair. The desk sergeant pokes at the keys and squints at his screen. Hard steel gnaws at my wrist bones. I forgot to put on gloves before I stalked out of the house, and my hands are freezing.

I'm on the wrong side of things.

This is happening.

• • •

The officer who catalogs my personal belongings has a gunmetal crew cut and a faded gray Marine Corps tattoo on one leathery forearm. He tells me I shouldn't get too comfortable—I might not be staying.

Apparently, they've been having problems with the heat in parts of the facility; it's an old building, twelve beds and a drunk tank, used primarily to hold people who are waiting to bond out, sober up, or appear before a judge. If the housing area goes on the blink, I'll be transported to the county facility on the north edge of town.

I tell him that I doubt I'll get comfortable. If he hears me speaking, I wouldn't know.

They say that time crawls behind bars, but I wouldn't know that, either. My jail cell doesn't have bars. It has a steel door with a small square window, shatterproof glass threaded with wire. There's an oblong slot in the door at about waist level; beneath the slot is a gray metal tray. Bolted to the wall is an iron cot with a thin vinyl pad that smells like disinfectant. Bolted to the floor is a small steel toilet with half an inch of blue fluid in the bowl.

Time could be speeding right along for all I know, because the old cop with the Marine Corps tattoo took my watch. Along with my wallet and cell phone. My photo and fingerprints.

It doesn't matter. Lying on my hard cot in my quiet cell with my arm draped over my eyes, smelling the stuff they gave me to wipe the ink from my fingers, I can't muster the will to care what time it is.

At my request, I've been shown a copy of my arrest warrant, along with the sworn affidavit detailing the charges against me.

The charges include two counts of producing pornographic images of a child. According to the arrest affidavit this constitutes a class C felony, punishable by not more than ten years' imprisonment. I am charged with one count of promoting the pornographic images of a child, a class D felony, punishable by not more than five years' imprisonment. I am subject to a grand total of not more than $200,000 in fines.

By now, my computer has been confiscated from my office at home. My credit card, bank, telephone, and Internet account records have been subpoenaed. I expect that the party at our house is probably over.

The child named in the affidavit is Brittany Seward, our next-door neighbor. Our friend Pete's thirteen-year-old daughter. Our friend Melody's stepdaughter.

I wanted to know.

At some point, there's a hard rap on the door, followed by a muted jingle of keys. The lock tumbles, and the deputy in charge of the housing area steps inside my cell. He's a young horse of a guy, soft around the middle, with flaky red blotches on the backs of his hands. I don't remember his name.

"Visitor," he tells me.

I draw a breath and sit up slowly. My joints are stiff, and my head is pounding. Have I been sleeping? I don't even know. "What time is it?"

"Depends where you are," a second voice says. "Here it's 11:18 p.m. Which gives us just under twelve minutes before your legal visitation hours run out."

The man who enters my cell has the look of someone who has practice being pulled out of bed. He's shorter than the deputy but taller than me, somewhere in his fifties, casually well-heeled. He's wearing an expensive-looking suede overcoat, sweatpants, and cross trainers. He stands with his hands in the pockets of the overcoat, a brown leather messenger bag on one shoulder. "You're Paul?"

"Yes. Hi." I'm not sure what to do with myself, so I stand up too. "I'm Paul."

"Douglas Bennett." The man who apparently is my attorney

takes half a step and extends a gloved hand to me. "Nice to meet you, Paul."

I shake his hand. The glove is soft leather. "Thank you for coming. I—"

Bennett cuts me off with a nod. "We're all set, Deputy. I'll be fine now."

"I'll leave the door open," the deputy says.

"That won't be necessary, but thank you."

"The door has to stay open."

"Like hell it does." Somehow Bennett makes this sound nonconfrontational. "If the counsel room weren't a walk-in deep freeze I'd be able to counsel my client there."

"I can't help the heating system, Mr. Bennett."

"Of course not, Officer Gaines. We'll just have to make do. Now, I've been through the metal detector and you've searched my bag, so I think we're covered."

Deputy Gaines seems unsure how to handle this. "I need to check with the lieutenant."

"Maybe that's the best course." Bennett's smile remains perfectly collegial. "There must be some kind of waiver for me on file somewhere. Look under B for Ballbreaker."

Gaines purses his lips, debates a little longer, then sighs like he doesn't need the grief. He steps out, pulls the door shut behind him with a clang, and stands post outside the small window.

When we're alone, Douglas Bennett turns to me. "Warren Giler called me at home. Our kids go to St. Vincent's together, and I've handled all three of his DUIs."

Under normal circumstances, I'd probably find some grain of amusement in this information. Under normal circumstances, I wouldn't be talking to Douglas Bennett in a jail cell half an hour to midnight a week before Christmas.

"I'm grateful," I say, meaning it completely. "Thank you again. This is . . . I can't even tell you."

"Had better nights, I take it?"

"You could say that."

Bennett offers a commiserating grin. "I spoke briefly with

Sara on the phone. How are you doing? Have they treated you okay so far?"

Compared to what? "I guess so."

"Any problems?"

"Apart from the bogus felony charges, you mean."

This earns a chuckle. "So you didn't do it, then."

I can't stop thinking about the way Pete and Melody Seward's porch light extinguished at the sight of me. "No."

"Terrific. We've got that part out of the way."

Bennett unshoulders his satchel and gestures to my cot. I sit down eagerly. I'm ready to hear every word Douglas Bennett has to say. He takes off his gloves, unbuttons his coat, and sits down on the edge of the cot bolted to the opposite wall, four feet across from me. Under the coat, he's wearing a Western Iowa University hockey jersey. I didn't even know we had a hockey team.

"The first thing," he says, "is to get you out of here."

"Yes, please."

"Now the bad news. You'll have to spend the night."

Before he's finished that sentence, I feel the strength run out of my shoulders.

"Not what you wanted to hear, I know. The judge didn't allow for bail on your warrant, which is a load of horseshit, but I'll address that at your arraignment in the morning." He unzips the satchel, reaches inside, takes out a yellow pad and a glossy black pen. He uncaps the pen with his teeth and parks the cap on the butt end. "So. A couple things. Sara tells me we don't have any sort of prior record to contend with, which is good." He looks at me. "Is it true?"

"Yes, that's true. Like I told the detective, not even a parking ticket."

"Nothing floating around from the wild and crazy days? Something that your wife wouldn't know about, maybe?"

"My wild and crazy days were never all that wild and crazy."

"Fair enough." He makes a note. "How about the two of you?"

"Sorry?" For one crazy moment, I actually think he's asking about me and Brit Seward. "How do you mean?"

"Everything okay at home?"

Of course he's asking about me and Sara. I pause, maybe a beat too long.

In truth, these past weeks haven't been the greatest stretch in our nine years together, but Sara and I have been over rough spots in the road before. We love each other. We have a good marriage. Douglas Bennett looks up from his notepad and waits for me to say so.

I admit to him that there's been some stress lately. I consider delving into reasons, but the reasons seem irrelevant. Or maybe, deep down, I'm aware that the fault is primarily mine, and I'm too embarrassed to admit it. Or maybe I just don't like the thought of watching a man I just met scribble our reasons on a yellow notepad. "Normal ups and downs, I guess."

"Hey, I know all about the normal ups and downs. Believe me."

"Sara knows I wouldn't do a thing like this. She knows that."

"That was my feeling when I talked to her." It's almost as if Bennett suspects how much I want to hear that. He moves on. "You own your home?"

"We closed the papers in July. That's when we moved here."

"From Boston."

"That's right."

Beneath the words *No Record* he scratches down the word *July.* "Sara told me that you're on a lecture contract at the university?"

"She accepted her job contingent on spousal consideration for me." Truthfully, with the move to Clark Falls I'd looked forward to spending the academic year unemployed. Then one of the assistant professors in the English department drove her car into a drainage culvert on Labor Day weekend, an act that put her in a pelvic brace for the semester. The late-hour shuffle dealt me three sections of composition and a seminar on the Lost Generation, which happens to fall in my area. "They offered the contract in September."

"When does that contract end?"

"It just ended."

"Are you contracted for the spring term?"

"No."

Bennett scribbles some more and caps his pen.

"Okay," he says. "We're a little shaky in the ties-to-community department. Obviously no fault of yours. And I don't know yet what kind of evidence the county prosecutor will produce to substantiate these charges." He pauses a beat, glances at me briefly, and says, "If anything comes to mind on that front, feel free to educate me."

Will produce, he said. Not *might.* Not *try.*

They don't do it this way unless they have something, he seems to be saying. The implication is clear enough, but I don't know what to say in reply.

Bennett doesn't wait. "Last but not least, we'll be in front of a judge who has what you might call a leniency disorder. Not to mention young teenage daughters of her own. Emphasis on *her* own." He waves his hand. "But don't worry about that, I'll get your bail set. Our job tomorrow is to get out of there at a fair price."

"Wait a minute." It's as if the floor tilts beneath my bunk. "Are you saying there's a chance I might *not* get bail? Is there . . . is that a possibility?"

"Anything's a possibility, Paul. But it's not going to happen."

"Let's say it did. What would that mean?"

"That would mean you'd get to put on a powder-blue jumpsuit and ride a bus out to county lockup until your next court date. But like I said, it's not going to happen."

"Could you say that last part again?"

"Say what again?"

"That it's not going to happen."

"It's not going to happen."

I was wrong. Hearing him say it again doesn't make me feel better.

Bennett smiles. "I know your needle's in the red right now, but I'm pretty good at this, so I want you to try not to worry. The thing to do is take it all one step at a time. Okay?"

I exhale, long and slow. Rub my eyes. Nod weakly.

"Good. Tomorrow is Saturday. On Saturdays, felony cases and misdemeanors are arraigned together, felonies first. Which means we're in court at eight o'clock sharp. I'll be here in time for us to meet and go over our game plan. Let's call that Step Three."

I raise my head and look at him.

"Step One starts now." He repacks his satchel and stands up. "Sara told me that you've been having trouble with your neighbors. Is that right?"

"No," I say, louder than I mean to. But we're finally getting to the part that matters, and I want to make things clear. "One of our neighbors. That's what this is all about. His name is Roger Mallory, and he's saying... Christ, he's got Brit Seward telling the cops—"

"I've read your charge sheet," Bennett says. "And I'm familiar with Mr. Mallory."

He doesn't bother telling me what I already know. That Roger Mallory, who lives in the house directly across the circle from ours, is a retired Clark Falls police officer himself. That in his retirement, he runs an educational citizens' academy for the department, sits on various civic boards around town, built the citywide neighborhood watch program that has earned Clark Falls statewide media coverage, and is widely—understandably—considered an inspiration to this community.

Bennett doesn't point out that I am some childless East Coast liberal arts academic who moved here five minutes ago. That, jobwise, I don't even wear the pants in my house. He doesn't confirm what I can't help fearing, which is that I am fucked.

"Listen, there's a hell of a lot that affidavit doesn't say," I tell him. "I—"

"Let's deal with what the paperwork says for now. We'll have plenty of time to deal with what it doesn't say."

"But listen—"

"One step at a time, remember?" Bennett looks at his watch just as the guard thumps his fist on the door. "Right now our twelve minutes are up, and we're still talking about Step One."

It takes a great deal of effort, but I close my mouth and try to pay attention.

"After I'm gone, while you're stuck in here spinning your gears, I want you to think all of this through."

"I don't even know where to start."

"As your attorney, my advice is to start at the beginning," he says. "All the pieces—every detail, every last point between wherever that is and where we are now. Okay?"

I must be nodding, because Bennett nods back.

"You're an English professor, so you know what I'm looking for here. Clarity, logic, structure. A nice dramatic flow can't hurt, but we can work on that later. Have the Cliffs Notes ready for me in the morning."

Step One. My head is swimming. I can't see how to begin collecting my thoughts.

As the stranger who has agreed to defend me buttons his coat and pulls on his gloves, it occurs to me to ask him, "What's Step Two?"

"Sorry?"

"You said that tomorrow is Step Three and this is Step One. What's Step Two?"

"Right." A final nod. "That'll be the tough one. But it's important."

"Okay." At this point I'm prepared to hear just about anything.

"Try and get some sleep," he tells me.

While I sit there, trying to decide if he's being serious, Douglas Bennett makes an *OK* sign with his thumb and index finger. *One step at a time.*

Then he straps his bag over his shoulder and knocks back to the guard.

3.

THE VICTORIOUS WARRIOR WINS FIRST, and then goes to battle. Our neighbor Barry Firth said that. I remember because it cracked me up, coming from Barry. At least it seemed funny at the time.

This was only in September. Just three months ago. Pete and Melody Seward had invited the whole circle over to their place for a Saturday barbecue—Sara and me, Trish and Barry Firth, Roger, Michael Sprague.

I remember seeing my new pal Brittany Seward that night; she'd been stuck in charge of her kid stepsister and the Firth twins. I remember—fondly, no matter how that sounds to anyone now—that she'd been reading the beat-up Cambridge edition of *Gatsby* she'd borrowed from my library while the tots zoned into juice box comas in front of some talking animals on Pete's giant television inside the house.

Meanwhile, we cultivated adults had stayed out on the Sewards' back deck as daylight seeped away behind the trees, drinking margaritas and playing Risk, the old-fashioned board game where you build up your armies and try to dominate the world.

Upon capturing Madagascar and the South African peninsula, thus eliminating the Callaway team and our pitiable troops from the game, Barry had nodded sagely, joined his palms together, and that's when he said it.

The victorious warrior wins first. I still remember the flickering light from half a dozen citronella candles playing dramatically over his brow. *And then goes to battle.*

Poor Barry. Pudgy, earnest, nice guy Barry Firth. We'd hurt his feelings, cackling like tipsy teenagers, but it was that sort of evening, and we'd all assumed he was trying for laughs. How does anybody deliver a line like that with margarita salt on his eyeglasses and a straight face?

It wasn't until two or three pitchers later that Trish, to her husband's booze-blushed horror, had confided the truth to the group: Roger himself had given Barry the board game we'd been playing as a gift for Christmas the previous year, along with one of those popular business wisdom books titled *Suit Tzu: The Art of War from Battlefield to Boardroom.* According to Trish, Barry had been posting sticky notes with hand-scribbled quotations around the house for random inspiration ever since.

"And who got the Flint account in May?" he'd protested, sending us all howling again.

It strikes me now, in a way that it hadn't then, that we hadn't all been yukking it up at Barry's expense.

Not our friend Roger Mallory. Roger just grinned, chucked Barry on the shoulder, and said, "Keep at 'em, General."

Come to think of it, Roger hadn't been drinking margaritas, either. Within the next few turns he'd single-handedly overtaken the whole of Africa with one massive invasion force. Come to think of it, playing Risk that night, he'd outlasted us all.

• • •

I already feel defeated. How am I supposed to tell this story so that any reasonable person would believe it?

By tomorrow morning, Roger Mallory will have zipped up his side of this so-called case against me so tightly that nobody will be able to see the seams.

What am I saying? He's done that already. If I know Roger, he moved his pieces into place long before Detective Bell ever set foot on our doorstep.

I need to remember that if I've learned anything, I've learned that I've never really known my neighbor Roger at all. I don't know how he's managed to set this offensive into motion. I don't know how he's managed to put me here. But I still know this:

You can bounce a quarter off Roger Mallory's reputation in Clark Falls. You could bounce *me* off Roger Mallory's reputation in Clark Falls.

And that's exactly what's going to happen.

It's not going to matter how I tell my story. It's not going to matter what I claim. Douglas Bennett could be the Alan Dershowitz of Iowa, and it still wouldn't change the simple reality that no informed person within a hundred miles of this town would ever believe that Roger Mallory is capable of doing what he's doing to me.

Me.

What about poor Brit Seward? While I'm sitting alone in here, outlining the story I need to submit to my defense attorney in a few hours, what kind of nightmare has settled in for Brit Seward out there?

I want to see the evidence that allows the police to show up at my house, charge me with these crimes, and take me away in handcuffs without the first bark of warning. Pornographic images of the eighth grader next door? I want to see that evidence.

What am I saying?

Of course I don't.

Brit. Kiddo. What have you gotten yourself into?

What have I done?

There was some racket for a while earlier, as the detox cage filled up with refugees from the town bars. I could hear the incoming traffic and the fratboy laughter and the occasional drunken bellowing all the way down here in my cell. At one point, from what I could gather, someone threw up on somebody else. Later, it sounded like a fight broke out.

All of that quieted down some time ago. The drunks are sleeping, and I'm still awake. I guess what they say is true after all: time does crawl behind bars.

Enough.

Douglas Bennett doesn't want this rambling mess in my head. He wants clarity. Logic. Structure.

How about irony?

This isn't our first involvement with the local law since we've been here, after all. That's where I'll start with Douglas Bennett in the morning. He wants me to start at the beginning? I'll begin with our very first day in Clark Falls.

The police came to see us that night, too. A different detective, a whole different gang of uniforms, all shaking the bushes, looking for answers. We were on the right side of things then.

I wonder how they're coming along with *that* case by now?

Intruder

4.

IT'S THE PRIVATE QUANDARY of all untested men, my friend Charlie told me after the attack. It seemed like every bit the kind of thing my friend Charlie, an untested man, might say. He called it "the last question deep down in the stomach." *How would I handle a wolf at the door?*

According to Charlie, I had my answer. When it came down to the animal basics, Paul Callaway bared his teeth and stood his ground. *The victorious warrior wins first,* I should have told him.

But I can be realistic. My friend Charlie Bernard doesn't have a relationship with the animal basics. He has a PhD in English literature, just like me. The fact is, the guy who broke into our house that night could have split my head open, had his way with Sara, had his way with *me,* and made himself a sandwich if he'd wanted one.

Either I got lucky, I'd told Charlie, or our wolf hadn't really been hungry.

The university had called out of the blue that January, during the winter break. They were a third-tier state school with an undergraduate enrollment nearly three times that of Dixson College, where Sara had chaired her department and I had recently come up for tenure in mine.

"What do you think?" she'd asked me on the plane ride home from our first visit to campus in February.

"I think it's just like Massachusetts," I'd told her. "Massachusetts with more cows. Without the ocean."

But their graduate economics program had begun to make a promising splash in the national publications. A big donation had helped them to establish a heavy-duty faculty endowment, which had enabled them to offer Sara a no-nonsense salary hike. Next to Boston, the relative cost of living in Clark Falls, Iowa, seemed like a clerical mistake. And though she'd never mentioned it before that initial phone call, Sara confessed that she'd developed a private inkling toward an administrative position beyond department chair. We'd flown back to campus again in March, again on Western Iowa's dime.

Finally, in April, after one last, long discussion over two bottles of oaky red wine, Sara had called to accept the position of associate dean for graduate studies, duties to commence in the fall.

On the morning of July 12, the Associate Dean and I overslept at a Holiday Inn off the Interstate, drove fast through open cornfields for six more hours, and found the movers waiting for us in the driveway.

It was high summer in the Midwest, buggy and sweltering. While I apologized to the guys smoking cigarettes by the truck in the glaring noon sun, Sara christened 34 Sycamore Court by hurrying through the front door, moving directly to the main floor bathroom, and barfing in the sink.

The day grew longer from there.

"Paul?"

"I'm in here." Night. Living room. Utter upheaval.

"Look at this."

Her voice sounded like it was coming from the kitchen. I called back, "Tell me if it's good or bad."

"Jodi left us something."

A stack of business cards? The head of a competing realtor? I worked my way toward the kitchen, navigating the crooked city of unpacked boxes the movers had settled none too gently in the middle of the floor. Sara stood at the refrigerator, holding the door open against one slim hip. Had to be a head.

On the otherwise bare top shelf stood a bottle of champagne, a red ribbon tied around the neck in a bow.

"Huh," I said.

She handed me a card, which read, *Welcome Home, Callaways! Call me if you need anything. Jodi, Heartland Realty.*☺

Sara nudged me. "And you didn't like her."

"I never said I didn't like her."

"You said she sucked all the oxygen out of the room."

Had I said that? "Okay. Only most of the oxygen."

"Well, I think we can agree that this is a very thoughtful gesture."

"One of us could be alcoholic," I pointed out. "Or Mormon."

"Or knocked up."

She gave me such an odd look that we both cracked grins. It seemed as though only days had elapsed since her doctor back east had confirmed this unexpected bit of parting news, and though it had actually been closer to three weeks by then, I don't think either of us had fully absorbed it yet.

I still wasn't sure which had come as the bigger surprise: the little blue line in the little white window of the home pregnancy kit, or our mutual embrace of the result. Anyone who knows us—friends, family members, and the two of us included—would have found the idea of Sara and me getting into the parenting business, at our age no less, only slightly less plausible than the idea that we'd pack up and move to the middle of flyover country.

Yet here we were.

I stepped in and rubbed her shoulders; Sara sighed and sagged. The refrigerator door closed with a soft-seal thud.

"I'm done," she said. "Put me to bed."

I wasn't entirely sure where I'd last seen the bed, but I took her hand.

Someone from the university search committee had discovered the house, a big brick and timber Tudor on a wooded half-acre lot, the only place we'd seen in town that reminded us of home. Twice as much home as the home we'd left, at that: four bedrooms, three baths, two fireplaces. Flagstone sidewalks and hardwood floors. We'd already decided to use the upstairs master suite for the library.

While I worked in the larger of the two main floor bedrooms, Sara found the box with the sheets. I huffed and puffed, wrangled the box spring and the mattress into place, then sat on the edge and rubbed her feet for a while.

"Mmm." She stretched out, limp as a cat. "Do you do happy endings?"

"We should consult the local statutes before we get into all that." I kneaded her arches. "No telling what kind of trouble you can get into in this part of the country."

"Smart-ass." She closed her eyes. "I'm too tired anyway."

And looking green around the gills again. I mentioned the all-night supermarket we'd spotted nearby. "Want me to pick up some ginger tea?"

"I think I'm over the ginger tea."

"Something else?"

"Just sleep," she said, nearly there already. "Are you coming to bed?"

It should have occurred to me then that Sara had more on

her mind than the morning sickness, which ebbed and flowed throughout the day.

I rarely go to sleep the same day I wake up. She almost never stays up past 10 p.m. I should have recognized that she wouldn't have asked the question if she hadn't felt an uncharacteristic need for company. That she was feeling just like me: displaced, out of her element. Probably wondering if she'd made the right decision, accepting the job here. Wondering if we'd made a mistake.

But I didn't get it. It was hard to relax with our life in boxes, and my mind had already wandered. I thought I could at least unpack a few books.

It took me ten minutes to drive to the SaveMore on Belmont, pay for a six-pack of Goose Island, and drive back to the house. Ten minutes, maybe fifteen. Less than the amount of time it had taken me to hook up the TiVo machine. Barely enough time to feel like I'd been anywhere.

Here's the way I remember it:

I parked in the garage and came in the side door, through the kitchen. I know that I put the beer in the fridge and my car keys on the island counter, because that's where I found them later, after the police arrived.

Sara told me later that I'd called her name, but I don't remember doing that. I don't remember hearing anything, or seeing anything. I don't remember what it was that made me stop on my way from the kitchen to the bedroom to pull a golf club from the bag I'd almost left behind in Newton, which I hadn't otherwise touched in years.

I remember feeling silly doing it. I remember thinking how bare all the walls looked. Nothing about the house seemed like ours yet. I remember thinking: *I don't like those curtains.*

Then Sara screamed. Or at least she tried.

The man pinning her down on the bed had one hand clamped over her mouth. I remember a fat vein in his wrist. I remember the desperation in my wife's muzzled voice. The wild fear squirming in her eyes.

The academic in me would like to report that I recognized an intruder, period. I'd like to say that, in the heat of the moment, his ethnic makeup was not a detail that I noticed.

But I can't. I saw what Charlie Bernard later called *the liberal white male's secret horror:* a rough black hand creasing my wife's pale skin, a black fist tugging her waistband down. His eyes were bloodshot. His teeth were yellow. I could smell his sweat from the doorway. Or at least I remember it that way.

Looking back, I can hardly picture myself. It seems incredible to imagine how easily I might have hauled off with the golf club and accidentally hit Sara in the face. Or how easily Sara's attacker—taller, heavier, far stronger than me—might have taken the stupid club out of my hands and used it against me.

Which is more or less exactly what he did. Just not before I managed to land the first blow.

I don't exactly remember swinging, but I remember the meaty thud of the clubhead landing somewhere between his shoulder blades. My arms went rubbery, weak with fear and adrenaline, delivering little power. Still the guy grunted, arching his back. He stood straight and clawed at his spine, as if I'd planted a knife there.

Then he turned toward me.

"Mother*fucker,*" he said.

Before I could steady my balance, he launched himself over the bed, eyes blazing. On collision, my limbs turned to water. My feet tangled.

We went down together. I landed flat on my back, all his weight on top of me, hot breath in my face.

My own breath rushed out of my lungs. I felt my head bang the floor, saw a flash of light, and couldn't see anything after that.

A miracle: I felt the pressing weight lift from my chest.

But it wasn't a miracle. When my vision cleared, I looked up and saw how all of this would end.

The intruder stood over me, face twisted, my golf club raised over his head. His broad chest rose and fell. Thin ropes of foamy spittle connected his lips.

"Hit me with a fuckin' *golf* club, man?"

Sara's next scream rattled the windows. She went for him before he could finish the fight, scrambling across the mattress, her legs tangled in the sheets. I watched the guy change his grip, opening his stance to both of us.

I thought: *Don't hit her. Don't hit her. Please.*

"Man, fuck this."

The club hit the floor with a thud and a clatter.

He bounded over me on his way out the door.

Maybe we were more than he'd bargained for. Or maybe we just weren't worth the effort. But I knew we were safe then. Just like that, our wolf had decided to cut out and head for the trees.

For some idiotic reason, I reached out and grabbed his foot anyway. The guy stumbled, almost fell, braced himself in the doorway, and yanked his leg free of my grasp. He stomped my eye hard enough to make me wish I hadn't grabbed his foot.

Then he was gone.

Sara actually picked up the golf club and chased after him, her bare feet thumping on the hardwood, his heavier footfalls already fading toward the back of the house. I shouted her name and tried to get up, but I couldn't seem to clear my head. I heard the back door burst open on its hinges; somewhere in the distance, I heard the golf club hit the floor again.

By the time I'd made it to my hands and knees, Sara had already returned to the bedroom, hair flying, one hand pressed against her ear.

"Sara and Paul Callaway," she said, panting our new address into the phone.

5.

"FOR WHAT IT'S WORTH," the detective told us, "my feeling is that Sara wasn't this guy's goal."

His name was Harmon. He had a pleasant manner, studious eyes, and a card that said General Investigations Unit. We sat in the living room, Detective Harmon in my reading chair, Sara and I on the couch, boxes stacked all around us. Sara folded her arms and tried to smile.

"Cold comfort," he said. "I understand."

I said, "He looked like a guy with a goal to me."

"I'm sorry. Of course. What I mean to say is that I don't believe you need to worry about him coming back." Harmon nodded gently. "That's my feeling."

Something in the way the detective acknowledged my comment made me understand that he wasn't trying to minimize the circumstances. He wasn't trying to downplay our fears. He was simply doing his best, out of thought for Sara, to give us his opinion of the situation without getting into words like *predator* and *rape.*

Cold water trickled down my neck. Earlier, one of the patrol guys had taken the plastic SaveMore bag from my beer run, filled it with cubes from the automatic ice dispenser in the freezer door, and handed it to me.

Now, while I took the sack of half-melted ice away from the boot print on my face, Detective Harmon explained that his unit had investigated a handful of roughly similar cases in other parts of town last year. "Old-fashioned burglaries, primarily, except that our operators seemed to target move-ins."

"Move-ins?"

"Everything's already packed up in boxes. All ready to carry right back out." Harmon gave us an empathetic look. *I know. People. I could tell you stories.* "First night in a new place, almost everybody realizes they need to run out for something or other. Toilet paper, something for breakfast in the morning, what have you."

I remember thinking of my inessential six-pack and feeling a pang of embarrassment. Of course, nobody faulted me. No responsible American adult should need to feel guilty about a cold beer on moving day. Right?

"In theory, we think that one person finds a spot on the premises while a partner circles the vicinity in a vehicle," Harmon explained. "When opportunity presents itself, the guy on the ground gains access through a back or side entrance, finds the box marked *Grandmother's Silver,* whatever else he can grab in a hurry." He gestured at a few of the boxes containing our belongings. "He signals by cell phone, the partner rides in, and off they go."

"Nice," I said. I was thinking, *A spot on the premises.* I thought of men lurking in the woods behind our house, watching and waiting. I wondered where Sara's attacker had been hiding when I'd left. Had I actually walked right past him? The thought prickled the skin at the back of my neck.

Harmon shrugged. "Like I said, that's been our theory."

Sara sat quietly through all of this. I said, "I don't mean to be argumentative, Detective, but this guy wasn't hunting for silverware."

"If I can be honest, that's what troubles me." Harmon closed his notepad. "Our offenders logged a few wins before we came up with a vehicle description and put it out over the local news. They've been quiet ever since." He looked at us and shrugged again. "Maybe they're back in business, or maybe somebody new decided to get in on the act. Either way, this is the first assault we've seen. That changes the picture. Considerably."

I felt Sara tense beside me. I reached out, put my hand on her knee. She flinched when I touched her. Then she laced her fingers through mine and squeezed.

"Based on the way this played out, I'm still inclined to believe that in your case, the suspect made a mistake. Thought the house was empty." Harmon opened his notepad again. "Mrs. Callaway—Sara—you said that when you heard the subject come in, you assumed it was Paul, and you called a greeting?"

"I . . . Yes, that's right."

"My guess is that our subject came in with one idea and then, unfortunately, got another." Harmon let his tone imply the rest: *If he'd liked the second idea badly enough . . .*

A burly cop came through the room, gun belt creaking, nodding politely as he passed us. He wore a pair of latex gloves and carried my golf club by the butt of the grip, between two fingers.

"The good news," Harmon said, "is that we stand to retrieve prints from that club of yours. Hopefully elsewhere. And you're the first to provide a physical description we can work with. Nice short game, by the way."

I glanced at the uniformed officer, already on his way out the front door with the evidence. From where I sat, I could see that the club I'd grabbed was a Chi Chi Rodriguez sand wedge left over from the junior set I'd had when I was twelve. A kid's model. Everything about the situation suddenly seemed absurd to me.

"If I could do it again," I said, "I'd use my driver."

Detective Harmon chuckled. Sara squeezed my hand. I felt like a hero for a moment, and then it passed.

A stout limestone sign at the mouth of the cul-de-sac lets you know when you've found Sycamore Court. According to Jodi, our realtor, what seemed like an offshoot to the larger subdivision down the hill had actually existed before the rest, a woodsy enclave on the northwestern edge of a town that had grown out to meet it.

There were four other homes situated around the circle; any one of them, in a similar neighborhood, in almost any New England city of comparable size, would have doubled the mortgage we'd signed on to pay here in Clark Falls.

Standing on the front walk with Sara, the heat of the day still hanging in the air, I watched the ripple effect of our incident as officers moved from house to house, climbing steps, knocking on doors. Flashlight beams arced in the surrounding woods as cops in uniform spoke to people in bathrobes.

Eyes turned to the new couple on the block. I wondered what people would be saying about us over the backyard grapevine in the morning. Then I remembered that I'd never cared what the neighbors said in Newton, or anywhere else. Sara calls me a nonjoiner.

We'd noted, the first time we'd looked at the house in May, that the center of the circle had been developed into a plot of community space. There were iron benches and ground lights, a swing set and a teeter-totter, a jungle gym made of safety logs—all funded and built, Jodi the realtor had told us, by the residents of Sycamore Court.

Over by the jungle gym, I saw a man in a T-shirt and

pajama bottoms speaking to one of the officers. After a few minutes, they shook hands. The man clapped the officer on the shoulder and headed toward us in his slippers.

That was how we first met Roger Mallory.

"Hell of a welcome," he said, coming up the walk. I put him several years older than us, but still in the vicinity of middle age. About my height, thicker across the beam, with a weathered face and a friendly charisma that reminded me a little of my friend Charlie Bernard back home. "You folks all right?"

"A little rattled," I said. "But we're okay." I slipped an arm around Sara's waist and extended my hand. "Paul Callaway. This is my wife, Sara."

"Roger Mallory. I'm the house right across." He nodded at my eye as we shook hands. "That looks like it hurts."

It did hurt. "Nothing too serious."

"I hear you've got a damned handy chip shot, though."

"A Rottweiler might have been handier."

Roger Mallory offered a rueful smile and said, "Sara, how are you? Can I do anything?"

"I'm all right, Roger. But thank you. We're sorry for all the commotion."

"For Pete's sake, don't apologize." Standing there in his pajamas, Roger Mallory seemed personally wounded that we'd had to move all the way to his little corner of the Midwest just to experience home invasion and attempted rape in the same evening. "I don't know what to say. This kind of thing doesn't normally happen around here."

I wasn't sure what to say, either. "I guess anything can happen anywhere."

"I guess that's the truth."

On the other side of the common, two men broke away from the same officer I'd seen talking to Mallory a moment ago. They walked toward us, both wearing bright green vests with reflective striping, flashlights and walkie-talkies on their belts. I assumed they were with the police department until they came close enough that I could make out the badge emblems printed on their vests. Framing the logos, top and bottom, were the words *Ponca Heights* and *Neighborhood Patrol.*

As they approached, Roger winked sideways at us and said, "Some program you people are running here."

"I can't believe we didn't see anything," the shorter of the two answered. "Cripes. We were just coming back up the hill. He must have slipped right—"

An easy pat on the back from Roger seemed to settle him. "I'm busting your chops, Barry. Can't expect to be everywhere at once."

"I still can't believe we didn't see anything."

"Paul, Sara, meet Barry Firth."

"Two houses up," Barry Firth said, gesturing toward the gabled Colonial with the ivy on the chimney and the big juniper trees in the front yard. He gave us a sheepish look. "Boy. This is embarrassing."

The taller guy rolled his eyes and stepped forward. He had athletic shoulders and a firm grip and turned out to be Pete Seward, our neighbor next door. "What Deputy Firth here means to say is, are you two okay?"

"We're fine, we're fine," Sara said. Her voice was steady, but as she rubbed my back, I could feel the lingering tremble in her fingers. "Thank you. We're just sorry we have to meet like this."

"Don't worry about that," Roger said. "We'll give you folks a proper welcome after you've had a chance to catch your breath." He nodded at Pete and Barry. "For now, you know where we are. Need anything, Sara, Paul, please. Just holler."

"We will," I said.

Sara drew in a breath, nodded, and exhaled. She said, "Thank you, guys."

Roger Mallory touched each of us on a shoulder, then turned and headed across the common to rejoin the officers now rounding the other side. Barry Firth fell in behind. Pete Seward sighed, shook his head for our benefit, and followed along.

As they cut across the common, I saw Pete pull his flashlight from his belt and play the beam along the ground in front of Barry Firth's feet, as though trying to trip him. I thought I heard Barry Firth tell him to knock it off.

After they'd moved beyond earshot, I said, "Wow. I feel safer already. How about you?"

"Be nice," Sara said.

But she smiled. It wasn't much of a smile, and it didn't last long, but it was something.

I pulled her closer; she put her head on my shoulder. I noticed that I'd placed my free hand on her stomach without being aware that I'd done so. She'd covered my hand with hers.

As we stood together, watching the activity around us, listening to the summer cicadas making their strange windup buzz in the trees, I found myself imagining a little Callaway bopping around the playground over there. It seemed funny to think that we'd both considered the playground an eyesore when we'd been here in the spring. Everything seemed to look different to me now.

Most nights, I sleep like a dead man. That night I lay blinking in the dark until long after the police had gone. Sara collapsed into a depleted, motionless pile almost the instant we'd finally turned in. For her sake, I was thankful for that much.

I don't know what time I finally gave up trying. We hadn't unpacked any clocks yet.

But there was still a six-pack of Goose Island sitting untouched in the fridge, so I slipped out of bed without waking Sara, opened a beer, and took it with me to the same chair Detective Harmon had occupied earlier.

There I worked on distracting my overcooked brain with a paperback novel someone had left behind in the hotel room where we'd stayed the night before.

The beer helped. The next one kept helping. By the time the first shades of daybreak lightened the curtains, Sara hadn't yet stirred, and I was almost finished with the beer and the book both.

The main character in the novel was a guy who drifted from town to town fixing people's problems. It was a hell of a story, and I couldn't stop turning the pages. In the course of the final chapters, the hero had killed four men, rescued the child, made powerful love to the widowed housewife, and hitched a ride out of town at dawn. At no point in the story had he been stomped in the face by a house burglar.

I don't remember closing my eyes, or finally falling asleep, but I remember dreaming that I was a guy who drifted from town to town selling used golf clubs from the trunk of his car.

Times were tough. Folks were mistrustful of strangers. It seemed like anything could happen anywhere, and with all the trouble in the world, it was hard for an honest fellow to make a go of it the old-fashioned way. There just wasn't much security in golf clubs anymore.

6.

THE NEXT DAY, Saturday, the Ponca Heights Neighborhood Association called an emergency meeting to discuss the break-in at 34 Sycamore Court. Sara and I learned of the meeting, and of the Ponca Heights Neighborhood Association, when Roger Mallory, the president, dropped by to invite us.

"Figured it might be time to circle the wagons," he said. He told us that word of our trouble had gotten around twice by now, and people liked to worry. "Hell, you haven't even unpacked yet, I wouldn't expect you to come, but I wanted to make sure you knew you were welcome. Sara, how are you feeling?"

"I'm fine, Roger. Come in."

"You two look like you're up to your necks," he said, "and I've got a few more calls to make anyway. But if you ask me next time, I promise I'll accept. How's that eye there, Paul?"

I said, "You mean it's noticeable?"

"Not if you're a prizefighter."

"I guess not if you're a very good one."

Roger chuckled at that, clapping me on the shoulder in a way that seemed almost proud. It was a disproportionately chummy gesture, having known each other then for all of ten minutes combined, and I felt silly that it boosted my ego. From the start it was hard to dislike Roger Mallory.

"I think we should go," Sara said after he'd left.

I assumed she was kidding, but she wasn't. I made some joke about bringing a covered dish, knowing as I did it that I was making the wrong play.

"Yes, funnyman. I get it." She bent at the knees, picked up the box, and headed toward the hall closet. "You don't want to go."

"Not really, no," I told her. "I'm surprised you do. Let me carry that."

"It's about us." Sara transferred our old towels to their new shelf and handed me the empty box over her shoulder. "The least we could do is show up."

"How can it be about us? We just got here." I broke the box down flat and added it to the nearest stack. "Nobody knows us yet."

"If only we could find some kind of an opportunity to introduce ourselves to people."

This general line of discussion led to more needless sarcasm on my part, followed by a period of stiff silence. It wasn't the first of the afternoon. I'd been in poor form since lunch, and I knew it, but knowing it didn't seem to help.

Before anybody gets married, my father used to say, they should paint a room together. Forty years as a service technician for Honeywell had made him a man of diagnostics and sensible gauges, and in his view, the simplest home improvement project teaches most normal people their snapping point. I once repeated this idea to my friend Charlie Bernard, who advised me that academics, who are not normal people, should never marry each other, period.

The overeducated believe themselves to be intellectually superior to childish arguments, Charlie said. This leaves fewer opportunities to indulge common insecurities and elementary pettiness, which in the long term promotes acrimony, bitter contempt, and avoidable bloodshed.

Even at the time, I'd pointed out that Charlie Bernard's longest marriage on record—to Sara—had lasted only ten months. I pointed out that he'd been the one who had set the two of us up with each other in the first place.

The bottom line:

Sara and I aren't rookies. We're not amateurs. We were looking at our thirties when we met, and we'd both been married before. We can argue like five-year-olds. We know how to paint a room together.

There are times when the trick isn't knowing how to paint a room, or how to have a good mean fight. Sometimes the trick is in having enough faith to leave each other the hell alone for a minute, and that's what I was making a piss-poor job out of doing that Saturday.

I wanted Sara to slow down for five minutes. I wanted her to take it easy. We'd had a hell of a thing happen, and I wanted to talk about it.

She needed to be busy. She wasn't ready to talk yet. It was exactly that simple.

Leave it to the guy with the PhD and the hangover to make it complicated.

We resolved the matter of the emergency meeting of the Ponca Heights Neighborhood Association by not discussing it again for the rest of the day. When the time came, Sara still wanted to go, and so she went. I still didn't, so I stayed home. I felt like a jerk but I stayed home anyway, indignant over being made to feel like a jerk.

In my defense, I didn't miss anything that I wouldn't see later on the ten o'clock news.

7.

"MR. CALLAWAY?"

"Yes?"

"Maya Lamb," said the young woman at the door. "Do you have a few minutes?"

It was just past eight o'clock, daylight still holding, the shadows of the trees growing longer on the ground. The young woman stood on our front stoop in a sharp beige suit, a collared blouse laid open at the neck. She had dark pretty eyes, a megawatt smile, and held a microphone at her side like a billy club.

"I'm sorry," I said. "Who are you?"

"Maya Lamb, Channel Five Clark Falls. Sorry to barge in—Sara told me I could find you at home."

"Sara told you that?"

"Is this a bad time?"

I finally looked past the edge of the door and saw the guy in faded blue jeans and a Channel Five T-shirt standing at the bottom of the steps. He had a massive television camera perched on his shoulder, a Channel Five ball cap turned backward on his head. For now he held the camera's bazooka lens at a downward tilt toward the sidewalk. When our eyes met, he lifted his goateed chin and said, "Hey."

"Hi," I said. Back to you, Maya Lamb. "When did you talk to Sara?"

"We just came from the meeting over at the school."

"The meeting?"

"The neighborhood watch meeting, yes. We're running a piece."

"A piece about what?"

"About your break-in."

"You're kidding."

"I'd love to get a comment," she said. "Do you have a few minutes?"

"I don't think so." I had any number of minutes, but none I felt like sharing. I was sweaty and tired. Cranky. By then I'd gotten over my earlier frustration with the Associate Dean, and for the past hour I'd been feeling like a grade-A chump. Wishing I'd done a better job of being supportive, wishing I'd done a better job of just about everything that day. Wishing I hadn't drunk all my beer the night before. I'd been on my way out to restock when Maya Lamb rang the doorbell. "Actually, I was just leaving."

"We'll be quick, I promise."

"I said I don't think so. Sorry."

She dialed down the telecast smile. "I know. Last thing you need, right? I wouldn't want to talk to me either." She glanced over her shoulder at the camera guy, then leaned in closer and lowered her voice, as if we were conspirators. "Look, I won't bullshit you. I've got an inside tip that there's a network job opening up in Chicago. I'm trying to get a decent clip file together. Know where I'm supposed to be right now?"

"Miss Lamb—"

"Covering the garden show at the Kiwanis Center."

"I don't know how I can make this any—"

"A home invasion in Roger Mallory's neighborhood is a great angle, that shiner of yours is going to read great on camera, and if I don't get this cut to tape inside the hour my news director is going to flame-broil my ass. Five minutes? Help me out?"

"Go away, Miss Lamb."

Her face fell, but I was unsympathetic. What made a home invasion in Roger Mallory's neighborhood a great angle? At that point, I didn't care enough to ask. She'd said that Sara had sent her here, and I doubted that very much.

Maya Lamb stood there a moment, as though considering an alternate approach. Finally she sighed and nodded. "Of course. I'm sorry to disturb you."

"No harm done. Good night."

"I mean, some guy breaks into your house with a knife your first night—"

"Sorry?"

"I'm just saying, I understand. Your first night in a new town, and some guy—"

I stopped her there. "Nobody had a knife. That's not what happened."

"It's not?"

"No. Who told you that?"

"I thought... Wait a minute. You're saying he didn't have a knife?"

"That's what I'm telling you."

At first I couldn't tell which disappointed her more: the fact that I didn't want to be interviewed, or the possibility that her story didn't have a knife-wielding maniac in it after all. Somehow, over the course of the next minute or so, I found myself explaining the circumstances in spite of myself.

I barely noticed Maya Lamb's subtle gesture to the cameraman, the subtle rise of the microphone in her hand. I was headlong into setting the record straight on the knife rumor once and for all when I became aware that both the microphone and the camera were now pointed directly at me.

"Still, you must have been terrified," she said. "What went through your mind when you returned home from a short trip to the nearest grocery store to find your wife, Sara, struggling with this man?"

I'd been suckered so easily it was embarrassing. Maya Lamb actually winked. *Your move.* Behind her, the camera guy fine-tuned his lens with one hand and waited to see what I'd do.

Looking back, I suppose I could have raised hell, or shut the door on them, or done any number of things. On the other hand, any self-respecting third grader could have seen that trick coming. I had my pride to consider.

The truth was, squinting against the light from the rolling camera now shining in my eyes, I couldn't find the energy to be angry. It had been a long, not-so-great day, and something about getting outfoxed by a twenty-something local television reporter seemed to give me all the permission I needed to lighten up. I had to hand it to her.

"It all happened so fast," I said. "One minute you're minding your own business, the next you've been ambushed in your own home."

"I can only imagine," Maya Lamb said.

Our story led the local segment on *News Five Clark Falls.* Sara and I watched the broadcast sitting up in bed. At the sight of me in my television debut—a one-eyed raccoon caught in the headlights of an oncoming car—she laughed a little, patted my leg through the covers, and said, "Sorry. I was still pissed at you."

"It did occur to me that I should have gone to the meeting."

"Then you wouldn't have gotten to be on TV."

We weren't fighting anymore. By that point we'd learned

what made a home invasion in Roger Mallory's neighborhood a great angle.

As it turned out, Roger Mallory wasn't just the president of the Ponca Heights Neighborhood Association. He was also the head of the Safer Places Organization, a citywide coalition of citizen patrols he'd founded himself half a decade ago.

In her report, Maya Lamb provided the broad strokes. Sara had come home from the meeting with more specific details, most of them supplied by Melody Seward and Trish Firth, whose husbands we'd met the night before, in their neighborhood patrol vests.

Ten years ago—while Sara and I were still getting to know each other in Boston—Roger Mallory had lived right here in Sycamore Court. He'd had a wife named Clair, a son named Brandon, and the rank of sergeant with the Clark Falls Police Department. One crisp autumn afternoon, a Wednesday in the middle of November, twelve-year-old Brandon Mallory stepped off the school bus at the corner of Belmont, a six-minute walk from home. He never got there.

When Brandon hadn't arrived in time for supper, Clair Mallory began making phone calls. By 10 p.m. the following evening, the local authorities—all of them Roger's colleagues from the police force, many of them close personal friends—had canvassed the area. They'd spoken to Brandon's friends and their parents. They'd spoken to his teachers at school. They'd spoken with every kid who had ridden Brandon's bus that day, along with every available resident of the burgeoning Ponca Heights subdivision.

Within the week, Brandon Mallory's broad-daylight disappearance had become a statewide news story. Search parties had moved by land and air into the surrounding woods—nearly two thousand acres of state preservation land that, then as now, begins at the backyards of the homes in Sycamore Court and spreads west to the river, north into the bluffs.

On the first day of the organized search, party members

had found Brandon's backpack at the base of a towering old pin oak just inside the refuge.

The backpack, and that was all. Nobody had seen anything. Nobody could help. It was as if Roger and Clair Mallory's only son had climbed the tree and vanished into the sky.

The first blizzard of that long cold winter had rolled in on Thanksgiving Day, covering Clark Falls in a foot of snow, effectively shutting down the search effort once and for all.

Five months later, after the spring thaw, hikers discovered a shallow grave deep in the preserve—the same woods Sara's attacker had likely used to make his escape from our bedroom just twenty-four hours earlier. The grave had been uncovered by animals and had contained the decomposed remains of a young human male.

On the day the Clark Falls Police Department released its official findings to the media, Clair Mallory had run a warm bath, climbed in, swallowed several weeks' worth of prescription antidepressants, and opened her wrists with a kitchen knife. By the time Roger had gone up to check on her, the water in the tub had already cooled.

"The whole time they're telling me this," Sara said, "I just kept thinking, *My God, that's horrible.* And then it just kept getting worse."

I didn't say anything. *Horrible* seemed to cover it.

"Poor Roger. I can't imagine how I could keep living in the same house all alone. Can you?"

"Not really." A brief image flashed in my mind, and I wished I could unthink it. "No."

"Melody Seward told me that when the weather is nice, Roger takes a walk back in those woods nearly every day."

I thought of our conversation last night. *I guess anything can happen anywhere,* I'd said. I thought of the way Roger had agreed.

"Wow," I said.

"I just don't know how you could bear it."

I didn't know either, but thinking about the tiny bunch of tissue growing in Sara's belly, I couldn't imagine a whole world of things.

I couldn't imagine what it was going to feel like, the day this little surprise life joined ours. At thirty-seven years of age, I'd only just begun to imagine myself as a father; in no way could I claim to imagine what it would feel like to stand over the grave of my murdered child.

As the sports segment cut to commercials, something made me look at the television. The moment I did, I recognized what it was that had drawn my attention: our new neighbor's voice.

Before you and your family leave to enjoy your summer vacation this season, Roger Mallory said, *remember to ask a neighbor to pick up your mail.*

Roger stood on the front steps of a cozy brick house between a flower box and a mail slot overflowing with circulars and bills. He looked good on camera: comfortable, casual, authoritative.

Or, arrange for your post office to stop delivery while you're away. A growing pile of mail can send a message to criminals looking for an easy target. He pointed to the camera. *For more summertime security tips, log on to www.saferplace.org.*

The screen cut to a variation on the neighborhood watch logo most everyone knows, the familiar "not-allowed" symbol over a prowler's silhouette. An announcer's voice said, *This neighborhood safety message is brought to you by the Safer Places Organization.*

Sara sighed and closed her eyes. She looked like I felt: exhausted, overwhelmed. I sensed a slight change in her posture, a new tension. When I squeezed her hand, she said, "I'm okay."

"Can I do anything?"

She shook her head, but not in answer to my question. It was the same reflexive gesture I'd performed myself a moment ago, thinking of Clair Mallory, at my own mental picture of finding Sara lolling in a tub of bloody water.

"I swear," she said, scooting closer, "every time I stop moving for five minutes, I remember what that guy's breath smelled like."

Besides being near just then, she'd wanted only one thing from me that day. It really hadn't been much. We weren't even fighting about it anymore.

But I still wished I'd gone to the meeting with her.

8.

OVER THE NEXT FEW WEEKS, as we settled in, found places to put everything in the new house, found a doctor for Sara, and found our way around town, we came to know our neighbors in Sycamore Court.

Pete and Melody Seward had celebrated their eighth wedding anniversary that June. Like us, they'd both been through divorces. Once upon a time, Pete had played football for Iowa State. Now he was a marketing VP for the local cable company. Though we insisted that we didn't watch much television, he set us up with the premium channel package as a housewarming gift. Melody worked in the human resources department at the First State Bank of Clark Falls. She introduced Sara to her yoga instructor.

Trish and Barry Firth both worked for her father's business, a commercial glass distributor, Trish in the employment office, Barry in sales. They had twin toddlers: a girl named Jordan and a boy named Jacob. Upon discovering that we were expecting—a fact Trish somehow intuited long before we'd chosen to mention it to anyone—Barry delivered to our house, under cover of night, four unmarked plastic storage tubs packed full of gender-neutral infant wear. He winked at Sara, chucked me on the shoulder, and said, "Congratulations, you guys. Mum's the word."

Michael Sprague lived in the rambling Craftsman between the Firths and Roger Mallory. He'd spent some time in our neck of the woods, having studied at the Culinary Institute in Hyde Park, New York. He'd returned to Clark Falls five years ago to take care of his ailing mother, stayed after meeting his partner, Ben, and now ran the kitchen at The Flatiron, an upscale restaurant on the riverfront.

We learned that Ben worked as a corporate trainer, and that he'd recently taken some kind of temporary contract job in Seattle. That was all we knew about that.

Michael had converted their backyard into a roaring vegetable garden; he kept the whole circle in fresh produce through the summer, plus a dozen different colors of squash in the fall. Visiting one night, he hugged each of us and thanked us for moving in.

"Don't get me wrong," he said. "Everybody's terrific. You'll like it here. I'm just saying that if we'd tilted any farther to the right my house might have fallen over."

Sara invited Roger Mallory over for dinner to thank him for our new alarm system, brought to us courtesy of Sentinel One Incorporated, a local home security company. One call from Roger, and a crew showed up with spools of cable and power drills. They left us fortified with enough special wiring to lock down a minor military position, installing the whole works free of charge.

"Stop thanking me," he told us, polishing off the last of the kebabs. "The owner and I were on the force together. I send him plenty of business. Besides, I got him free ad space in the Chamber of Commerce brochure. He owes me one."

On a given night, you could leave our front door and find somebody out visiting with somebody else. You could watch the Firth twins playing in the common with little Sofia, Pete and Melody's four-year-old. You could always have a chat with Roger, who seemed to preside over the goings-on in Sycamore Court like everybody's favorite uncle.

We found ourselves doing all of these things, and it didn't take long before we felt at home.

Nobody is going to care about Michael Sprague's vegetable garden. Nobody will care what our neighbors do for a living, or how many channels we get on our television. Nobody will care that Sara and I lost a baby in August.

From here on, the only thing anybody will care about is me and Brit Seward.

"Are all these boxes full of books?"

That was the very first question she asked me, the Monday morning after the emergency meeting of the Ponca Heights Neighborhood Association. Melody, who didn't work Mondays, had sent Brit over to deliver a hand-labeled DVD containing our news broadcast, which Pete had somehow procured through the cable company. Sara had gone to campus to meet with the dean; I was at home, still unpacking. I'd only asked Brittany inside because the guys from Sentinel One were busy working on the front door.

"All books," I said.

"*All* of them?"

"That's exactly what the movers said."

She put her hands on her hips and scanned the rampart of boxes stacked four high along the length of one dining room wall. "OMG."

Oh my God. The teenagers in Iowa spoke the same language as the ones in Boston. "LOL," I said.

She laughed out loud. "Cool."

"That's not what the movers said."

"I *love* to read. What's your favorite book?"

"You mean out of all of them?"

"I used to be into Harry Potter when I was a kid. Now I'm kind of all over the place."

"Oh yeah? What's the last book you read?"

She thought about it. "I just read *Bridge to Terabithia*. That was pretty good. Except I already saw the movie two years ago, so I knew the end. The book was better. Did you read *Da Vinci Code*?"

I couldn't say that I had.

"Me either. I'm reading this book now, I checked it out from the library. The title made me think of Ponca Heights."

"*Wuthering Heights?*"

"That's it! Have you ever read that one?"

"Once or twice."

"It's sort of hard."

"And a little depressing," I said. "But stick with it. It's pretty good."

"Talk about depressing, I'm grounded all week. That's depressing."

I was happy to talk books, but I didn't know what to say to that. Thankfully, the foreman of the Sentinel One crew stepped into the house and waved me over. I excused myself and went to answer his question, which involved the placement of the "master console" in the entryway. I told him that he was the expert. He agreed.

When I returned to the dining room, I found Brittany Seward peering into an open box, head tilted, scanning book spines.

"Well," I said. "It was nice talking to you, Brittany. Let me know when you finish with Heathcliff and Catherine."

If she heard me, she made no indication.

"Tell your mom we said thanks for the DVD, okay?"

Still nothing. She appeared to be lost. I liked her already. But what was I supposed to do with her?

Looking again at the daunting stack of boxes along the wall, thinking for maybe the hundredth time about how little I relished the thought of dragging all of them upstairs, unpacking them, realphabetizing everything I'd packed out of order in the first place, I had a flash of inspiration.

Roger Mallory had stopped by first thing that morning to check on the workers from Sentinel One. He'd brought with him a copy of the Ponca Heights Neighborhood Directory, which consisted of a few photocopied pages of telephone numbers stapled together in a booklet. It had local fire, police, and emergency contact information organized up front, a Safer Places logo printed on the back cover. "We'll get these updated if you and Sara want to list your number," he'd said.

I looked up the Sewards' phone number. Sara had introduced me to Pete and Melody the previous morning; she'd gone jogging with Melody before sunrise, then invited the two of them over for coffee afterward. We'd all seemed to get along fine, certainly well enough that I felt comfortable looking up their number and dialing it.

"Hello?"

"Melody," I said. "This is Paul Callaway."

"Oh! Hi, Paul. I just sent Brit to your place. Is she not there yet?"

"No, she made it," I said. "Thanks for the disc."

"We thought you might like to have a copy."

I didn't need a copy, and I doubted Sara did either, but it seemed like a thoughtful gesture. "We appreciate it. Thank Pete for me, will you?"

"I sure will." A four-year-old voice clamored for attention in the background; Melody's voice disappeared, then returned. "Sorry, it's a little nuts here, as usual. Say, Paul, when did Brit leave?"

"Actually, she's here now."

"Really? Still?"

"That's why I'm calling." I moved a few paces into the kitchen, out of sight of the dining room, and quickly recounted our *Wuthering Heights* conversation. "She's a big reader?"

Melody chuckled on the other end of the line. "We went to the Grand Canyon last summer, but I doubt she could tell you what it looked like. She had her nose in a book the whole trip."

She'd just described me as a teenager. "Well, talking about books," I said, "I've got a couple thousand of my own that still need unpacking over here."

"Did you say thousand?"

"A couple thousand, yeah."

"Wow."

"She's been browsing titles for the past ten minutes or so."

"Paul, I'm sorry. She's not exactly shy. Just tell her I said to come home, will you?"

"No, not at all, it's perfectly fine, I was just going to ask. Does she have a summer job?"

"She watches her little sister in the mornings," Melody said. "And she sits Trish and Barry's twins whenever they ask. But that's about it. Why?"

"Well, I was thinking I'd be willing to pay her if she wanted to help shelve this mess. That is, if you and Pete think it would be okay."

"Really?"

"I'm sure she's got better things to do with her summer."

"Not this week, she doesn't. She's grounded."

"So I heard. Maybe it's a bad idea?"

"I think it's a great idea, Paul. We're pulling each other's hair out over here. *I* should pay *you*."

After hanging up, I ran the idea past Brittany, who said, "You'd pay me?"

"Absolutely," I said.

"How much?"

"How much do you charge?"

She seemed to think about it. "Twenty bucks an hour."

"I was thinking more like five."

Brittany narrowed her eyes. "Five bucks an hour, and I get to borrow whatever I want."

"Done."

She had a pretty smile. "Cool."

As she was leaving, I said, "Hey, Brittany. Do you mind if I ask you a personal question?"

"Brit," she said. "What's the question?"

"How come you're grounded, anyway?"

She waved her hand in the air like the whole thing was too boring for words. "I bought this bikini with my allowance. Dad and Melody told me to take it back, but I didn't. Melody caught me wearing it at the pool."

Melody, I thought. As in, not *Mom.* I said, "Oh."

"Yeah. What's the big deal, right?"

It didn't seem like an especially big deal, but I wasn't the one to say.

"Melody thinks I can't wear a two-piece until I'm sixteen. It's super-cute, too. They're so uptight."

That made me pause. I said, "Can I ask you another question?"

"Sure."

"When do you turn sixteen?"

"In forever," she said. "I'll be fourteen in January."

Jesus, I remember thinking. *Poor Pete.*

My mother would have called Brit Seward an early bloomer. Bikinigate suddenly made a whole new kind of sense. I'd already noticed the way the Sentinel One guys had traded grins and glances when Brit arrived, her sun-lightened hair up in a ponytail. She'd been dressed for hot weather that day: denim cutoffs, flip-flop sandals, a snug-fitting tank top which stretched in ways that create problems for everyone. I'd noticed the way the workers kept stealing glances.

Had I stolen a couple myself?

"Do me a favor," I said.

"Sure, maybe."

"Don't buy any swimsuits with the money I pay you, okay?"

She laughed. "Are you serious?"

"Your dad looks like the kind of guy I wouldn't want mad at me."

She rolled her eyes. "He's totally harmless."

"If you say so."

"Melody's the one you don't want mad at you."

"I don't want either of them mad at me."

"Fine," she said. "I promise I'll only use the money you pay me to buy drugs."

"Terrific," I said.

"And condoms if I run out."

"I appreciate that."

She grinned. I grinned. We seemed to understand each other. Brittany went home, and I went back to work.

By the time Sara returned from her meeting on campus, Sentinel One had finished installing the new alarm system, which included magnetic strips on all the windows, pressure plates on all the doors, keypads wired directly to the Sentinel One response center, and motion-activated exterior lighting all the way around the house. Which now seemed, we both agreed, like a much safer place than it had before.

Saturday, December 17—7:05 a.m.

9.

I WAKE UP IN A PANIC, disoriented, unsure where I am. I've been startled by a noise, but I don't know what I heard.

For a moment, I sit paralyzed by the vague yet urgent sensation that I'm in immediate physical danger. When my chest begins to ache, I realize that I'm holding my breath.

On exhale, the fog in my head begins to dissipate. Little by little, my pulse recedes, and as my surroundings slowly bleed into focus, I become aware of the hard iron bunk frame behind my knees. I'm awake. I recognize, my sense of irony apparently intact, that in terms of immediate physical danger I really couldn't be safer.

My cell looks just the way I remember it. Actually, that's not true. A deposit has been made. This must have been what woke me up: the sound of the hinged plate covering the food slot in the door pushing open, dropping closed again. I see a gray plastic tray waiting for me on the shelf.

I feel like I've slept on a sidewalk. There's a hot stitch in my neck, a deadened nerve in my hip, muscles knotted in the middle of my back. My bladder is bursting, but I also smell food. Aiming my stream into the steel bowl of the toilet feels a little bit like taking a whiz at the breakfast table. I haven't eaten anything since lunch yesterday, and even over the rising smell of warm frothy urine, the smell of breakfast makes my stomach growl.

Breakfast turns out to be a fried egg sandwich that comes in a grease-spotted take-out sack from Petrow's, a '30s-style train car diner across the square from the courthouse.

Something about this amuses me, even lifts my spirits. What are they eating for breakfast at the big county facility north of town? Briefly I imagine sweaty guards dragging tin cups along jail cell bars. I imagine bleary-eyed men in denim shirts shuffling into a chow line at dawn. It doesn't matter that I'm picturing something straight out of *Cool Hand Luke;* the point is, they must not even have a kitchen here. This isn't where they keep the real prisoners. I'm only at the temporary jail.

I can't remember a fried egg sandwich ever tasting as good as this one. In the bottom of the sack there's a hash brown potato patty shaped like a football. It's cold by the time I get to it, and a little on the stale side. I could eat four more just like it.

Next to the sack is a lidded paper cup filled with lukewarm orange juice, still foamy on top. After using the toilet I'm inclined to leave the juice where it sits. I could use a cup of black coffee instead, or a gallon bucketful.

But things are looking up.

It's morning. A brand-new day. I've got a regular pit bull for a lawyer, and he's on his way now to get me out of here. Pretty soon I'll be able to see Sara. We're going to fix this.

• • •

Because the city jail and the courthouse are connected, travel to my arraignment involves a semiconvoluted indoor walk through a gradual shift in surrounding décor. A uniformed guard leads me along a gritty tile corridor, up a concrete stairwell, through a steel door, down a polished marble corridor, up a wrought iron stairwell, and through another door made of dark old wood, retrofitted with a modern security card reader.

Because the courthouse is a historic building that presides over a historic town square, I'm mildly surprised by the remodeled, carpeted, vaguely corporate look of the courtroom. Because it's Saturday—which means, as Douglas Bennett already informed me, that felonies and misdemeanors are heard in the same session—I'm the only person in the room with handcuffs and an armed escort.

I count perhaps a dozen people scattered around the general seating area, which consists of several rows of auditorium-style chairs separated from the front of the courtroom by a waist-high partition. On my entrance, all eyes turn toward me. It's equally easy to imagine that I'm walking in to teach an early-morning class on campus, or that I'm Hannibal Lecter being wheeled in on a handcart.

I spot Sara immediately, seated in the front row, just behind the partition. The look on her face when she sees me—unshaved, shackled, led in by the arm—isn't one I'm likely to forget. Almost as quickly her eyes cloud, then register confusion.

I try to communicate in some way, but I don't know how. Somewhere on the periphery, I hear the sound of my own name called out by the bailiff. The guard leads me to the nearest of two tables facing the judge's bench. I see a man in a dark brown suit already waiting at the other table, file folders stacked in front of him. While all of this is happening, my desperation mounts.

An hour ago, I couldn't wait for this moment. Now here I am.

Where the hell is my lawyer?

The judge looks down at the docket in front of her, then looks down from the bench at me. Like the courtroom itself, she's not what I expect, insofar as I've been led to expect anything. She's blonde, late middle-aged, attractive, and though she appraises me over the top of a pair of bifocal reading glasses, the frames are fashionable, making her look more stylish than stern. She may well be the mother of young teenage daughters, as Douglas Bennett has told me, but she exhibits no outward evidence of a leniency disorder.

"Good morning, Mr. Callaway. Am I to assume you'll be standing without representation?"

"No," I say. The word hops out of my throat like a yelp. "I mean no, Your Honor. I have an attorney."

She glances at the officer standing next to me. She glances to the man in the suit at the other table, who I gather must be the county prosecutor. She looks at me again and raises her eyebrows. "Is your attorney present?"

I'm grasping, craning for a look over my shoulder, as if my attorney might be hiding behind the potted ficus in the back. "I guess I don't see him."

"I guess I'll take that as a no."

"He said he'd be here." My voice sounds feeble even to me.

He said he'd be here early, I want to tell her. *We were supposed to go over our game plan.* Now I don't have a game plan. This is just some guard from the jail beside me, not my pit bull lawyer. I'm not ready. "Is there any possibility for a recess?"

The judge sighs in the manner I imagine she reserves for people who have watched too many courtroom dramas on television. "If this were a trial or a grade school," she tells me, "I might consider recess. Since this is your arraignment, I'll ask if the People object to an informal continuance until the end of the misdemeanor docket. Perhaps that will give defending counsel time to change his tire or come out of the bathroom or whatever it is that seems to be keeping him."

For a moment, when she says *the People,* I think of the audience behind me and wonder why the hell it should matter whether they object or not. Are they standing here in handcuffs with no game plan?

Then the county prosecutor speaks up from the other table. "The People have no issue with that, Judge."

"Fine. Mr. Callaway, we'll give your attorney some more time. If he hasn't arrived before the conclusion of the session, you'll be remanded to the custody of the county and this proceeding will be rescheduled for Monday morning. Do you have any questions?"

I have so many questions that I can't decide which to ask first. Just then, the doors open at the back of the courtroom. My heart does a flip and relief floods my chest at the sight of Douglas Bennett hurrying up the aisle, carrying his leather satchel by the handle, his overcoat rippling behind him like a cape.

"My apologies, Your Honor," he says. "Good morning."

"Good morning to you, Mr. Bennett." The judge glances at the large round clock on the wall directly above the bailiff's head. "Cutting it a little close, wouldn't you say?"

The jail guard turns over his post to Douglas Bennett, who takes his place beside me at the table. "Yes, Your Honor. Unintentionally so."

"Is everything all right?"

"Yes, thank you. Just a little winter engine trouble."

"It's cold out there."

"Again, apologies to the court. We're ready."

We who? How can we be ready? I have a hundred things to tell him, and we haven't even spoken yet.

In fact, Douglas Bennett still hasn't looked at me. I'm staring at the side of his face, practically begging for eye contact. I want to see him make an *OK* sign with his thumb and forefinger, the way he did last night on his way out of my cell.

"Fine." The judge folds her hands in front of her. "Let's proceed."

"Thank you, Judge. We're ready."

"As you've said."

Bennett offers the court a slightly harried grin, places his bag on the table, and fumbles with the straps. I can't help noticing his general disarray. If I woke up feeling like I slept on a sidewalk, my attorney looks like he slept in the nearest doorway. His tie is crooked, shirt collar skewed. His hair, neatly groomed last night, now looks dull and uncombed, matted flat on one side. His eyes are red-rimmed and puffy, and there's a general blotchiness in his complexion.

"As Your Honor knows, my name is Douglas Bennett, here on behalf of the defendant, Tom Callaway, a respected professor of literature here at the—"

"Paul," I whisper, derailing his already wobbly rhythm.

Bennett finally glances my way. He leans over, lowering his voice to a private level. "What?"

"My name is Paul."

"What?"

Jesus. As I lean closer, my spirits sink to a new low. The sour tang of alcohol hangs around my attorney like a cloud. There's no hiding it. No way to mistake it. It's twelve minutes past eight in the morning, and Douglas Bennett smells like a gym sock soaked in bourbon.

"You said *Tom,*" I tell him, still whispering, but what's the point? Any optimism I'd developed after three hours of sleep and a fried egg sandwich has drained away like so much dishwater. "My name is Paul."

"Paul Callaway," Bennett clarifies for the court. He straightens himself and clears his throat. "As I said, Dr. Callaway is a respected, as I said, professor here at the university. He is a resident of the . . . ah . . . of the Ponca community, where he and his wife . . . the Ponca Heights community, where he and his wife Brenda own a home."

I close my eyes, willing myself to wake up. Surely I'm still back in my jail cell, having some kind of terrible dream. Where is the legal gunslinger I met just a few hours ago? The guy filed under B for Ballbreaker? Who is this shabby, stammering wino in the expensive suede overcoat beside me?

I hear a fluttering sound. When I open my eyes, I see Douglas Bennett stooped at the waist, scooping up a file folder and a fan of papers from the carpet.

"At this time," Bennett says, laboring to return to an upright position, clutching what I assume must be the contents of my case file in his arms, "the defense waives a reading of the charges and we respect . . . that is, we request . . ."

"Mr. Bennett," the judge says sharply. She leans forward and narrows her eyes. "Have you been drinking?"

"Excuse me, Your Honor?"

"I asked you a direct question. Have you been drinking?"

There's a ripple of chatter behind me: a few whispers from the gallery, a low chuckle or two. I can hardly believe it. This is actually getting worse.

Douglas Bennett pauses as though he, too, can hardly believe it. He produces a facial expression that seems to indicate that he's heard the question and it has taken him aback. Or maybe bending over to pick up my case file has altered his equilibrium. Either way, he's swaying noticeably on his feet.

He does his best to camouflage the imbalance, taking a moment to arrange his snarl of papers. He taps the file folder on the table, squaring away the edges. While he's doing all this, he glances at the clock above the bailiff, shakes his head like he's heard a good joke, and says, "Judge, I think we'd agree that it's a bit early in the day."

"We would most certainly agree," the judge says. "And you haven't answered my question."

"I believe that it goes without saying—"

"Counselor, are you, at this moment, inebriated in my court? Yes or no?"

"Absolutely not, Your Honor."

At this point, the prosecutor pipes up from the other table. "Your Honor, the People can smell defense counsel from here."

The judge sends a warning glare toward the newest babble of laughter from the seating area. When things quiet down, she says, "The court appreciates the field report, but the People have not been called to speak."

"Sorry, Your Honor. The People withdraw the observation."

More laughter. Louder now.

"All right, that's enough." There's a crack as the judge snaps her gavel. She waits for silence, then says, "Mr. Bennett, approach the bench."

"Your Honor, with all due respect, I can assure the court that—"

"Mr. Bennett, with all due respect, you are clearly stewed."

"Your Honor—"

"And now you've lied to me."

"Your Honor, in no way have I—"

"Counselor, stop digging. Your hole is deep enough."

Standing there in my handcuffs, watching this pileup unfold right in front of me, I wish I had a hole that was deep enough. A hole and a shovel. I'd crawl in, lie down in the bottom, hand the shovel to the guard, and ask him to cover me over. Or maybe I'd just bury Douglas Bennett.

"Mr. Bennett, I don't need to point out," the judge continues, "that your client stands charged with troubling crimes. But I *will* point out that if defense counsel has attended this proceeding under the influence, the court may infer that said charges aren't being taken seriously. In fact, the court may be apt to regard such a circumstance as frank and direct contempt."

"Your Honor, I've been a member in good standing of this state's bar association for twenty—"

"We joined the bar the same year, Counselor. I don't need your background information."

"Well, I think that—"

She holds up her hand, palm forward. *Save it.* After a moment, she removes her glasses and places them on the bench in front of her.

"I'm not interested in embarrassing you, Doug. Or harming your reputation, or otherwise making a mountain out of what I choose to assume must be an isolated case of regrettable judgment on your part. But I'm not going to sit here pretending to ignore your slurred speech, either. So." She leans back, returns her glasses to the bridge of her nose, and folds her hands again. "You can approach the bench so that I can evaluate you, or you can submit to a formal breath test, if that's what you'd prefer. Either way, we're not moving forward until I'm satisfied that you are fit to represent your client."

Douglas Bennett reacts to his choices with more silence. He looks down at the table. He's quiet for so long that if I couldn't see that his eyes are open, I'd suspect that he's fallen asleep on his feet.

At last he exhales, lifts his head, and says, "That won't be necessary."

The judge nods once. "All right, then. This appearance is rescheduled for eight o'clock Monday morning. Officer, you can take Mr. Callaway—"

"Your Honor," I blurt without thinking. That's not true. I'm thinking: *No no no.* "This isn't... May I speak for myself?"

The judge glances toward the prosecutor, who shrugs. She returns her gaze to me. "You have the right to speak for yourself, Mr. Callaway. I don't recommend it."

"I'd like to speak for myself."

"I assume you've heard the one about the lawyer who had a fool for a client?"

I've heard the one about the lawyer who had a fool for a client. Is there one about the client who hired a fool for a lawyer? All I know is that I want to go home, not to the regular jail.

"I'd like to speak for myself."

"Very well. The court will note that the defendant elects to proceed without benefit of counsel." She looks at me as if to say, *I tried.* "Go ahead, Mr. Callaway."

My heart is pounding. I feel like I've managed to stop a

falling axe but the blade is still hovering inches over my neck. I take a deep breath to steady my nerves. It doesn't help.

Here's what I know:

When the police come to your house to arrest you the way the police came to my house to arrest me, you should remain calm, collect yourself, and take a moment to peruse your arrest affidavit. Here you will find details the police have used to establish probable cause for the warrant itself.

I don't know what a typical arrest affidavit looks like. My own is the first I've ever seen. It's two and a half pages long, written more or less in plain English, more or less neatly typed.

The affiant, meaning the cop who prepared the document, is Detective William C. Bell, Clark Falls Police Department, Sex Crimes Unit. The victim, meaning just what that term commonly means, is Brittany Lynn Seward, age thirteen, resident of 36 Sycamore Court. The accused, resident of 34 Sycamore Court, turns thirty-eight next May.

According to the narrative, Detective Bell was contacted at his home, by telephone, on the evening of December 14, by a former colleague, retired Clark Falls police sergeant Roger A. Mallory. Upon receiving this call, Bell proceeded to Mallory's residence, where he conducted an interview with Mallory and the victim in the presence of the victim's father.

Supposedly, this interview revealed that the victim had received an e-mail earlier that day. The e-mail contained a short, unsigned message—*When can I open my Christmas present?*—along with a link to a private Web page hosted by a popular online photo-sharing service.

Here the victim discovered digital images of herself "posed in a sexually provocative manner, each photograph portraying the subject in a further state of undress." The e-mail had reportedly been sent via a rented computer terminal at a coffee shop near campus. The e-mail contained no sender information but originated from an Internet account registered by the accused. Also in my name: the credit card used to pay for the account at the photo site.

The receiving address belonged to a free, Web-based e-mail account the victim had established for herself in order to circumvent the parental software used to monitor her regular account at home.

According to the affidavit, the reality of starring in her own Internet peekaboo show caused the victim to "view previous consensual interactions with Callaway in an altered light." Fearful of her parents' reaction should the photographs become known to others, the victim turned for guidance to Mallory, a neighbor and close family friend.

To Mallory, the victim confessed the nature of her relationship with the accused, a professor of English literature and five-month resident of Clark Falls. Said relationship began with the borrowing of books on the part of the victim, progressed to a reading mentorship initiated by the accused, and developed over time to a state of sexual intimacy. According to the victim, this phase of the relationship included photographing sessions that produced the images in question.

Everything I know, the judge knows already. It's her signature on the arrest warrant. Everything after *Go ahead, Mr. Callaway* already feels like a blur. I remember talking to the judge, but even now I don't remember what I said on my own behalf. I remember the prosecutor talking to the judge, but my brain shut down at the words *Our evidence will show.*

I must have been convincing. Or did the judge look at me and conclude simply that I was too pathetic to be considered a legitimate flight risk? Did the county's attorney somehow fumble the ball? All I know for sure is that I don't have to stay locked up until Monday morning.

My bond has been set in the amount of $200,000, the potential amount of my fines if convicted. Because I live next door to the victim, I've been ordered to vacate my residence before 1 p.m. this afternoon. I've been instructed that if I'm discovered within five hundred feet of Brittany Seward at any time prior to my pretrial hearing, which has been scheduled to take place a week from Monday, I'll be arrested again, this time without the possibility of release.

For showing up stinko, my defense attorney has been found in direct contempt of court. He's been ordered to pay a fine of his own, and he's been warned that a second offense will result in mandatory enrollment in an approved substance-abuse program of his choosing.

The guard leads me through the same door he brought me in, a downcast Douglas Bennett trailing several feet behind. On my way out, I take one last look over my shoulder. First I see Sara, hurrying away toward the big double doors in back, cell phone to her ear. To my knowledge, she has no bail bondsmen on speed dial. I wonder how long this will take.

That's when I see Roger Mallory standing silently in the back of the courtroom.

Sara is so intent on the task at hand that she walks right past without noticing him. He doesn't stop her. He makes no attempt to catch her attention. His hands are tucked into the pockets of his coat, and his face is passive.

But I see him. He sees me. Our eyes meet for what seems like a long moment before the guard pulls the door closed behind me.

Out in the hall, Douglas Bennett comes up on my left. He keeps his own eyes averted. "Tom. I owe you an apology."

"My name is Paul, goddammit."

"I'm sorry, Paul."

"You're fired, Doug."

If Bennett had a tail, it would be tucked. He nods, still without looking at me.

Watching him shamble away down the corridor, satchel slung over one humped shoulder, I realize that I'm observing a man with problems of his own. For a moment, I almost feel sorry for him. Then I remember that I'm still the one wearing handcuffs.

I say to the guard, "Know any good lawyers?"

The guard doesn't look at me either. He was pleasant enough before, on our way to the courtroom. Now that I'm a pornographer and a pedophile, he seems to wish that he had some other kind of job.

I almost feel sorry for him, too.

10.

IT'S A HARD, colorless morning outside. Frost climbs the flagpoles in the courthouse square like fragile bark. The sky is a dark stone ceiling overhead.

Two uniformed officers escort me home the same way I left twelve hours ago: in the back of a squad car. We pass the downtown branch of the First State Bank of Clark Falls, where Melody Seward works during the week. The time and temperature sign outside the bank is trimmed with all-weather garland and oversized clumps of plastic holly. It's half past ten in the morning, according to the sign. Twenty-six degrees.

The streets seem unusually vacant for a Saturday. At the stoplights at Armstrong and Belmont, a white van from Channel Five Clark Falls passes us, pulls ahead in a cloud of exhaust, and disappears over the hill. By the time we turn in to Sycamore Court, the van is waiting for us at the curb in front of my house.

I see a familiar figure bundled in a sleek, belted winter coat, microphone in hand, apparently running through a quick sound check with the cameraman.

"Congratulations," the cop at the wheel says over his shoulder. "You're famous."

"Real celebrity," the other cop says.

"Lucky us, right?"

They seem to enjoy opening the back door and waiting for me to climb out of the car. As I emerge into the frigid air, Maya Lamb gives a go sign to the camera guy and hurries up the sidewalk toward us.

"Professor Callaway," she says. "Can you comment on the—"

"No," I say.

She veers from her course, angling for an interception spot several feet ahead of me. The cameraman hustles around for position, all the while tweaking the barrel of his lens. The cops make a show of moving me toward the house.

"This morning you've been arraigned on counts of sexual misconduct with your twelve-year-old neighbor," Maya Lamb says into the microphone. "What's your relationship with the alleged victim, Dr. Callaway?"

Without thinking, I almost blurt, *She's thirteen.* As soon as the words form in my throat, I realize how they'll sound if they come out. I realize that this is a version of the same trick Maya Lamb used to get me talking when *I* was the alleged victim.

I also realize that the facts don't matter at this point. This is Maya Lamb's story now, not mine. It's all completely beyond my control.

Sara, a minute ahead of us, has already parked her car in the garage. She meets us in the driveway, stepping between me and the officer on my left, taking my hand. Her eyes are dry, and except for the cold-weather flush in her cheeks, her face is like pale marble. She looks strong and confident. But I can tell that she's been crying.

"Dr. Callaway," Maya Lamb says, then seems to realize

that she'll need to be more specific. "Mrs. Callaway, do you believe your husband to be innocent of these charges?"

Sara covers my hand in both of hers and looks at the officer on my right. "Can you get them out of our way, please?"

While the cop moves Channel Five back down to the sidewalk, I see a bright blue numeral 8 emblazoned with peacock feathers strobing through the bare trees along the hill. A few seconds later, a second microwave truck rolls into the circle, this one from the local NBC affiliate. Following Channel Eight is a dark BMW sedan.

What is it with this town? Did nobody crash a car or rob a liquor store or crash a car into a liquor store at any point between last night and this morning? Is there nothing else in all of Clark Falls that passes for news? Who the hell do these people think I am, the Boston Strangler?

No. Of course not. I'm the out-of-work university professor who lives across the street from Roger Mallory, that's who I am. For all I know, Roger faxed out a press release himself, first thing this morning. On Safer Places letterhead.

The first cop stays behind to manage traffic. His partner accompanies us up the driveway, around the corner of the house to the side door, just out of view of the media.

At the steps, Sara turns to him and says, "Where do you think you're going?"

"I'll just step inside, ma'am."

"No, you won't."

"As soon as your husband collects his things, we'll be out of your way."

"And you can wait outside while he does."

The cop attempts to be civil. It seems like a challenge, but he's a professional. "Mrs. Callaway, for the safety of myself and my partner I'll need to be—"

"Is my husband under arrest?"

He straightens his shoulders.

"Is he?"

"No," the cop says. "Your husband isn't under arrest. But he's still under our—"

"Then you can wait outside," another voice says.

Everybody turns to look, but I recognize the voice the moment I hear it. As Douglas Bennett joins us on the steps, I look toward the street and realize that the BMW now parked there belongs to him. I'm starting to wonder if dramatic entrances are his thing. He still looks like a rumpled mess, but his eyes appear brighter than they did in court two hours ago. He's combed his hair.

The cop says, "And you are?"

"Mr. Callaway's attorney." Bennett holds out a business card. "At this time I'll remind you, or inform you as the case may be, that the court's order to transport my client doesn't specify permission for you to physically enter these premises."

"No kidding." The cop glances at the card, then seems to smile with his eyes. "So you're Bennett."

"That's correct."

"Funny, I just heard a story about you."

"Marvelous. Then further introductions won't be needed." Bennett rises to the step immediately behind me and gestures Sara onward. "I'll accompany my client from here. When he's finished, we'll permit you to step inside and conduct a brief search to ensure that his shaving kit and his supply of clean underwear contain no threat to you or your partner."

The cop gives Bennett a long look. A tight grin pinches the corner of his mouth. He finally glances to the BMW and says, "Counselor, is that your vehicle?"

"It is."

"Did you drive here?"

"I believe you saw me do so."

"I believe that's my vehicle right there." The cop points to the squad car at the end of the driveway. "If we went and looked, I believe we'd be able to find a breath kit on board."

"Since department patrol guidelines require you to carry one, Officer, that wouldn't surprise me."

"How'd you like to step over to the street and blow into the tube for me?"

"I wouldn't like it."

"I'll bet."

"But naturally I'd comply, as soon as Mr. Callaway is finished gathering his belongings," Bennett says. "Unless you'd prefer to conduct the test now, while Mrs. Callaway and my client conduct their business."

The cop smiles. "Oh, I think I can wait."

"Then excuse us, please."

Up the steps we go. Once we're inside, out of the cold, Sara lets go of my hand and walks straight to the island in the middle of the kitchen. She stands there a moment, her back to me and Bennett. She finally puts her purse on the counter and takes off her coat.

I look at Bennett. "Didn't I fire you?"

"Yes. Well." He shrugs. "I'm not billing. Sara, it's nice to meet you in person. You have a lovely home."

Turning finally, Sara says, "I don't know whether to thank you for your help out there or kick you back out with everyone else."

Bennett nods as though he understands. "I realize that there isn't much I can say on my own behalf."

"No, there isn't."

"But I'd like to do what I can to help get you two through the rest of the morning. At least until we're clear of police interaction. In light of circumstances, I'm prepared to insist."

"With all due respect, Mr. Bennett, I'm not sure you're the—"

"In light of what circumstances?" I get the sense that he's talking about something other than this morning's fiasco at the courthouse.

Bennett's glance acknowledges that he's heard my question,

but he doesn't address it. "Once Paul is settled, I can offer you a referral to another defender, if you'd like one. Of course, I wouldn't blame you."

Through this entire exchange, Sara hasn't yet looked at me. I finally leave Bennett standing inside the door and walk over. She flinches when I put my hand on her back. When I step closer, she stands there stiffly, arms crossed, staring at the counter.

"Sara."

She turns without a word and walks out of the kitchen, leaving me standing with my hand in the air where her shoulder had been.

I listen to her footfalls on the hardwood floors. In the distance, I hear the bathroom door close quietly. After a moment, I put my hand down.

Douglas Bennett clears his throat gently. "The court order allows you twenty minutes inside the house." He looks like he wishes he didn't have to tell me that.

Twenty minutes.

Sara has emptied our savings account to pay the bond premium that allows me to be standing here in the first place. All of that buys me twenty minutes.

"I'm sorry, Paul."

At least he's finally getting my name right.

The house feels strange. Familiar and foreign at the same time.

There are blackened hickory logs left over in the fireplace, smelling faintly of ash. Around the floor I spot the odd cocktail napkin, a dropped toothpick here, a scatter of crumbs there. The remnants of last night's party lend a peculiar, lonesome quality to the air; it's almost as if the festive clatter still hangs somewhere in the silence.

Upstairs, my office looks like a looted office supply store. Disconnected cables drape my desk where my computer used to be. The drawers are pulled, contents jumbled. File cabinets stand open and emptied, library bookshelves randomly decimated. Even the telephone is gone.

I force myself to set aside the indignity, the sense of violation. For the moment, I'm only interested in knowing one thing.

I take a few moments to paw through the rubble of my middle desk drawer, already scavenged by the police. I'm looking for the spare credit card I keep there for the purpose of ordering merchandise over the Internet: books, gifts for Sara, the occasional box of cigars. I don't expect to find it, and I'm not surprised that it's not there.

Only in confirming this suspicion do I realize that the confirmation tells me nothing. The police have surely confiscated the card as evidence. I don't even know if that MasterCard account of mine is the account referenced in my affidavit—the account I'm said to have used to rent an Internet session at the coffee shop, and to pay for the online photo gallery starring Brit Seward. Standing here in my wreck of an office, there's no way to know much more than I knew sitting in my jail cell.

I take a small suitcase from the storage space in the alcove and carry it back downstairs with me. A few changes of clothes. Toothbrush. Alarm clock. Electric razor. At a thousand dollars per minute, I've got about ten grand left on the twenty-minute meter.

Sara is in our bedroom, sitting on the edge of the bed. She looks up when I come in. Her eyes glisten, and she says, "I'm so sorry."

"Sara..."

"I didn't believe you," she says. Her voice hitches. "You tried to tell me. And I didn't believe you."

I sit down beside her. She puts her head on my shoulder and covers her face and says, again, "I didn't believe you."

Nine minutes. Eight.

"If you believe me now," I finally say, "then you know that this is a lie. You know that, right?"

I feel her nodding her head against my shoulder. But she doesn't speak.

Mrs. Callaway, do you believe that your husband is innocent?

"Sara, look at me."

She does. Her eyes are red, streaming tears.

"None of this happened. These photos they're talking about . . . they can't be real. Please tell me you know that."

"Of course they're not real." Eyes closed again. "Of course."

"None of it happened."

"Then *why*?" She stands up and paces a few steps away. "Why is she *saying* these things?"

"It's Roger, goddammit." We're down to our last five thousand bucks. I grab as many clothes as I can cram in the suitcase, making enough room in it for the short pile of half-read books stacked on my night table. "That twisted son of a bitch is behind this."

"But Paul, *why*?" she says. "To retaliate somehow? Do you think that's really possible?"

I think about grabbing the charging cord for my cell phone, then remember that my cell phone has been confiscated as evidence.

"All of that happened weeks ago," Sara says.

A little over two weeks, actually. That's all. I don't bother pointing this out.

"You apologized," she says. "Why now?"

There are things that I haven't told Sara. I know that I'm going to have to tell her those things now. The thought makes me sick to my stomach.

"Forget about why," she says. "*How?* Paul, it doesn't make any sense."

I zip the suitcase. I can buy a new toothbrush and razor.

"We'd better go," I tell her. "Before they start lobbing tear gas through the windows or something."

Douglas Bennett is waiting for us in the kitchen, sitting

where I left him at the island counter: a pot of coffee on a trivet within reach, a chipped Dixson College mug in front of him. The pot of coffee was half full fifteen minutes ago. Now it's empty. Littered around the mug is a handful of what look like empty candy wrappers.

"Perfect timing," Bennett says, crunching something in his teeth. "I'll go tell Officer Breathalyzer we're ready."

I watch him stand, scoop up the twists of waxed paper, and crumple them all together. "A little late for mints, isn't it?" I ask him.

"Well past the point." He smiles. "That's why I stopped at the drugstore to buy these charcoal tablets."

Over the years I've heard students trade any number of dubious-sounding recipes for beating a roadside breath test, but I haven't heard this one. "Do they work?"

"I have absolutely no idea." Bennett hands Sara another business card—same as the card he handed the cop outside, except this one has a scribble of black ink on the back. "Sara, on the chance that I'm arrested, will you call the number written there and let them know the situation?"

"All right."

Bennett thanks her and buttons his coat. "Paul, I've instructed my office to book you a kitchenette suite at the Residence Inn downtown. The firm will cover your expenses there for the duration of the court order. If that's acceptable."

I'm not sure what to say. Is it acceptable? I still want to know about the "circumstances" he mentioned earlier.

Sara says, "That's good of you."

"Hardly." Bennett pops one last charcoal tablet and drops the empty wrapper into his coat pocket with the others. With the other hand, he gestures to the door. "Shall we?"

The cop outside is raising his gloved fist to knock when Bennett pulls the door open. Bennett smiles and says, "You may come in."

• • •

In the past twenty minutes, Sycamore Court has become a one-ring circus.

Roger Mallory appears to be holding his own little press conference on the other side of the common. Because the other major affiliates broadcast out of Sioux City, Channels Five and Eight represent the full roster of network news stations in Clark Falls. I'm quite a story.

Along with the news trucks, a second squad unit has arrived. One more uniform on scene. Two houses up, I can see Barry Firth standing on his porch, watching. Across the circle, Michael Sprague stands at the end of his sidewalk. Even from this distance, he looks physically pained.

The court order mandates that I'm to be conveyed by the police from here to the kitchenette suite Bennett mentioned earlier. So it's back out into the cold, back to the squad car—this time pulling a wheeled suitcase behind me, Sara on one side, the cop on the other, Douglas Bennett once again bringing up the rear.

Halfway down the driveway, Maya Lamb and her competing Channel Eight reporter begin yelling questions in my direction. Is it true that I play golf with the victim's father? How much did I pay the victim to work in my home? When did the university decide not to renew my employment contract? Why did I leave the volunteer neighborhood patrol?

All at once, over their barking voices, Sara yells, "Hey!"

I feel our hands part. By the time I look, the cop has taken her by the shoulders. He's already moved her several feet away, back toward the house.

I hear one of the cops at the end of the driveway say: "Sir?" At first I think he's talking to me. "Sir, I need you to stop right there."

That's when I see Pete.

He's come from his house, and now he's almost to mine: head low, shoulders hunched, strides long across our adjoining lawns.

"Sir." The cop holds out his palms. "Let's just turn it around. Okay?"

A few feet from our driveway, Pete breaks into a steady jog. His eyes are bloodshot. Jets of frozen breath pulse from his nose and mouth. He looks like a bull hunkering down to charge.

Our cop stays with Sara. The new guy stays with the media crews. The remaining cop, the one who drove us here, takes several quick steps up the driveway, one hand still warding Pete off, the other drifting to the baton on his belt. "Sir."

"Pete! Stop it!" It's Melody, running down the sidewalk ten yards behind her husband, hugging her arms.

Another voice calls, "Pete. Go easy." This time it's Roger, on his way across the circle, hands in his coat pockets. He doesn't appear to be hurrying.

Pete ignores them both. Or maybe he doesn't hear them. He feints left and goes right, leaving the cop flat on his feet.

"All this time?" He's four steps away from me when he says it, and I can practically see flames in his eyes. "All this time?"

No, I want to tell him. *Pete, Jesus, no.* But he's closed the distance between us before I have a chance to say anything.

The next thing I see is hard gray sky. Then pavement.

I'm not even sure which is which. It's as if all my organs just exploded; I feel like I've been hit by a car. Once upon a time, Pete played football for Iowa State. Middle linebacker, if memory serves. Now he's pressing the side of my face into my own driveway with his forearm.

"All this time?" Flecks of warm spit hit my face. Pete lifts his arm, and at first I think he's going to drag me to my feet. He drives his elbow down instead, and there's a burst of color as my head bounces on the concrete. *"All this fucking time?"*

Somewhere on the distorted periphery, Melody is shouting for him to stop. Sara is shouting at the cops. Pete is shouting at me.

I see shoes. I hear grunts and curses. I feel the cops hauling Pete off me. When I open my eyes, I can't see much at first. My eyes don't seem to be working together.

I catch a gauzy glimpse of Sara, trying to get past the cop holding her back. My vision clears. I see Douglas Bennett; from somewhere he's produced a small, handheld video camera, and he's recording all of this, right alongside every major broadcast news outlet in Clark Falls. I see Roger, standing clear of the action, observing the scene quietly.

The last thing I see is Pete, eyes full of violence, face twisted by pure thwarted rage. He lashes out with his foot as they drag him away.

Five months after the fact, there's still a small knot on my cheekbone left over from my tangle with our wolf the night we moved in. You can't find it by looking, but you can feel it with your fingers. It's smaller than a pea, but it hurts if you press on it.

By flailing luck, Pete manages to catch the faded injury dead-square with the toe of his shoe. The odds are ridiculous. I can't imagine that he could have aimed a truer kick if he'd tried. Even through the blinding, lightning-strike pain, I feel vaguely embarrassed. There's a sense of humiliation in being thrown to the ground and kicked like a dog.

But what choice is there? Even if I could marshal the will to defend myself against my friend Pete, I'm no fighter. Seeing his sneaker whistling toward me, I don't even have sense enough to roll out of the way.

I'm not the guy from the paperback thrillers I've grown to enjoy. I'm certainly not the suburban everyman who fought off his wife's attacker with a golf club, the way Maya Lamb's previous news story portrayed me. Not really.

I'm an academic. A teenage book nerd in a grown man's body. Before setting foot in Clark Falls, the closest I'd come to a physical confrontation in my adult life involved an attempt to shepherd Charlie Bernard out of a South Boston neighborhood bar we both should have known better than to patronize in the first place.

As it stands, I've now been kicked in the face on two

separate occasions in five months' time. By two different people. Both times in the same eye. On my own property, no less.

Being an academic, I have time to note the uncanny unity of these plot points before the sensation of falling carries me into the dark.

11.

I MARRIED A DANCER in my early twenties. Her name was Elinor, after her paternal grandmother, but everyone called her Ellie, which seemed a better fit. We met each other through a complicated network of roommates that extended from the East Village apartment I'd shared with four other guys to a brownstone on the Upper West Side, which Ellie's parents rented for their only daughter and two of her Connecticut prep school friends.

I'd just begun course work on my master's degree at NYU. She'd just been hired to play The Sister in an off-Broadway revival of *The Catherine Wheel.* She had terrific calves and a staggering smile. I told jokes that made her laugh.

Ellie and I dated each other for just under seven months, during which time, in a spectacular display of Manhattan natural selection, all six members of our combined roommate pool disappeared from the picture, for one reason or another, like houseguests in an Agatha Christie novel.

She'd invited me to move in, and I couldn't afford anything else. When Marshall Lockhart, of the Bridgeport Lockharts, caught wind that his little girl had shacked up, he threatened to withhold further housing subsidy until such time as the matter had been resolved.

I'd proposed marriage almost as a joke. She'd accepted almost the same way. Our wedding cake had a waterfall in it; our divorce featured no waterworks to speak of. By the end, we'd wearily agreed to consider it a miracle that we'd lasted two years.

By the time the English department in Boston hired me as an associate professor in twentieth-century American lit, I was in my late twenties and divorced for half a decade. Sara, at my age, was already a full professor in the economics department, closing in on early tenure, and three years divorced herself.

If you ask Sara, she'll say that she was too impetuous in her twenties, and that her marriage to Charlie Bernard is evidence in support of that claim. We met at Charlie's annual intramural faculty softball kegger, both of us sweaty and streaked with infield dust, Economics having trounced Literature twelve runs to two. After driving a profoundly inebriated Charlie Bernard home that day, we'd ended up showering together.

Not even my mother understands how I can remain such good friends with my wife's ex-husband. I've tried explaining that I was already pals with Charlie before I met Sara. That it was, in fact, Charlie, in his strangely sage way, who had done the matchmaking between us. None of this makes sense to people like my mother, and I've given up trying to explain it. The truth is uncomplicated: we were grown-ups when we met, Sara and I. We had histories. And we were nuts about each other anyway.

Tall. Intelligent. Impatient. Kind. Affectionate. Resolute. Vegetarian. All these words describe Sara, and there are more.

It's been my favorite book since day one, this deepening concordance of our life together. I still love her the way people in sappy love stories love each other.

And now it's time for me to tell the part of our story that has led us here, to this dark paneled office of an alcoholic Midwestern defense attorney, where we sit in a pair of matching leather chairs separated by a table with a lamp on it.

We came here directly from my new temporary home, the kitchenette suite at the Residence Inn downtown. I've refused a trip to the ER to make sure I haven't sustained a concussion or something. Douglas Bennett has managed to avoid arrest, and has demonstrated something by risking it. Exactly what he's demonstrated I still haven't decided, but for the moment, Sara and I seem mutually content to accept his counsel. Part of me wishes I were still unconscious in our driveway.

"A few weeks ago, Paul accused Roger of spying on us," Sara says. "That's what this is about. I'm certain of it."

"Spying on you," he says. "Spying on you how?"

"I caught him going through our garbage."

"You saw Roger Mallory going through your garbage?" Bennett looks at me carefully. "When was this?"

"I didn't actually see him," I say. "I found one of our credit card statements inside his house. I always tear them up. He'd fished it out of our trash and taped it back together."

"Roger claimed he'd found the pieces in his yard on garbage day," Sara said.

"And taped them back together."

Bennett puts one foot on the slate-top coffee table. "And you confronted him, Paul?"

"You could say that."

"What happened?"

"I called the police," I tell him. "They came, and they listened to both of us talk, and then they asked him if *he* wanted to press charges against *me*."

"He's not telling the whole story," Sara adds quickly. "There were other things besides just our credit card statement. That's why Paul called the police."

Douglas Bennett says, "What other things?"

"Roger Mallory is a goddamned lunatic." I lower the cold gel pack Bennett handed me when we arrived. Why does a defense attorney keep ice packs in his office? Why am I always the one needing them? "The guy's got video cameras trained on all of our houses. He's got whole file cabinets full of stuff in there."

"When you say stuff..."

"I mean *intelligence* files. On our neighbors. On us." I toss the gel pack to the table, where it lands with a slap. "He's got background checks and phone records and photographs. He's got fucking video footage. It's all organized by address. Everybody in the circle has their own little file. We're under goddamned surveillance over there."

The look on Sara's face as I'm speaking is one of apprehension approaching embarrassment. As though she realizes how all of this sounds. As though she's waiting for the same response from Douglas Bennett that I received from the police. The same response you'd expect from almost anybody.

But Bennett just listens. He sits and absorbs. After a moment, he tilts his head my way. "Back up a bit."

"Back up where?"

"To the part where you found your credit card statement." He leans back in the settee, deep brown leather creaking under his weight. "How did you come to find your credit card statement inside Roger's house?"

"That's the question I wish I'd asked myself before I'd called the police."

"We know how crazy this sounds," Sara says. "Roger managed to leave Paul looking..."

"Foolish?" Bennett says.

"Like an asshole," I say. "Roger managed to leave Paul looking like a paranoid asshole."

"Paul," Sara says. "That's not what I was—"

"With a grudge. A paranoid asshole with some kind of

grudge." I look at her and offer the closest thing to a smile that I've got. It doesn't feel like much, so I offer my hand across the lamp table. Sara reaches out. We sit there awkwardly, elbows locked, fingers laced.

She looks at Bennett and sighs. "We know how crazy it sounds."

But we haven't even touched crazy yet. Even Sara knows that much.

How can I do this to her?

Bennett sits quietly. He seems to be looking at something in the distance.

After a long stretch of silence, he stands and crosses the office. In an alcove shelved to the ceiling with legal volumes sits a big walnut desk. Bennett stops at the desk and reaches toward a group of picture frames crowding one corner. He chooses one frame in particular, turns it over in his hands, and gazes at it for a moment. Then he returns to the sitting area.

"My son," he says, handing the frame to Sara. "Eric."

Sara takes the frame. Bennett lowers himself back into his chair.

"That's out of date. He's only thirteen, fourteen there. Probably just a little older than Brit Seward."

"He's very handsome," Sara says.

"My wife says he looks like me. Maybe that's why he's been in and out of trouble since before that photo was taken." Bennett watches Sara tilt the portrait my way, then place the frame carefully on the table, faceup. "Drugs especially."

"I'm sorry," she says. "That must be very difficult."

"For the past five months he's been serving time in a youth offender program in Colorado. One of those boot camps for teenagers. A last chance before prison, in Eric's case. He'll be eighteen soon, and I've pulled all the strings I can reach. Believe me."

Sara glances at me, but I'm watching Douglas Bennett. Wondering why he's chosen this moment to tell us about his son.

"Hard as nails," Bennett says. "This place where we sent him. He wrote us hate letters for weeks."

Sara nods politely. "Those couldn't have been very pleasant to read."

Bennett acknowledges Sara's kindness with a nod. "Cheryl cried for two months straight. But we're past that now. These last three months... We visited in September. He seemed to stand a little straighter. Look us in the eye. The instructors say he's been studying, volunteering for things. Talking about college when he comes home. I don't know." He looks again at the outdated photo of the young boy with braces on his teeth. "Maybe they got him in time."

I'm honestly glad for Eric Bennett. I'm not unhappy to listen to this story, which sounds like it has a chance to move into happier chapters. But I'm still waiting.

"Despite innumerable ways in which I may have failed as a parent," Bennett says, "and in spite of whatever impressions I may have given the two of you in court this morning, the fact remains that I'm among the two or three highest-paid defenders in Clark Falls."

Sara says, "Mr. Bennett—"

He holds up a hand. "Doug. And don't mistake my meaning. I'm not sounding my own horn. I'm only providing context."

Just then he seems uncomfortable with the photo staring up from the table in front of him. He returns it to its place on the corner of his desk. Then he comes back and sits down again.

"Being the son of a highly paid defense attorney, in a town the size of Clark Falls, Eric's troubles are well-known in the legal circle here, as I'm sure you can imagine. The cobbler's children go without shoes, et cetera."

"I don't mean to seem uncaring," I finally say. "But why are you telling us this?"

"Twenty years ago—before Eric was even born—I successfully defended a client. The details of the case aren't important, but during that trial, a patrol officer named Van Stockman delivered what was considered to be key testimony for the prosecution. Unfortunately for the prosecution, I was able to turn Stockman's own procedural mistakes during the arrest, and the handling of evidence, into an acquittal for my client." He waves his hand. "I only tell you this to explain how I first came to know Van Stockman. And how I know that Van Stockman's training officer, in those days..."

"Was Roger Mallory."

Bennett seems impressed to hear me say this.

Sara seems shocked. She looks at me. *How did you know that?*

At the mental image of Roger in his former life, decked in his patrol gear, just like the young cop who handcuffed me in front of my house last night—the skin tightens at the back of my neck.

"I've met him," I tell her.

"When?"

I leave it there for now, except to explain that Stockman had been Clair Mallory's maiden name. That Roger had married his patrol partner's big sister, making Van Stockman not only his subordinate, but also his brother-in-law. Eventually, his son Brandon's uncle.

"That's right," Bennett says.

"What does Stockman have to do..."

"Last night, after meeting with you at the jail, I was followed to within a mile of my home by a Clark Falls patrol unit."

"Followed?"

"And eventually pulled over. On North River Road, where there are no streetlamps, and very little traffic at that hour. The officer who approached my window held a light in my eyes and asked for my license and registration."

"You were followed."

"After reviewing my license he apologized for the inconvenience. He indicated that he recognized me. He speculated that perhaps I'd just come from a late-night meeting with a client. He told me to drive home safely." Bennett leans back in the chair. "Then, as I was raising my window, he asked about my son."

I feel Sara pull her hand away and sit up a little.

"He turned off his flashlight, at which point I recognized him. Sergeant Van Stockman, now. He's put on twenty years and forty pounds, and apparently he's never moved out of a radio car in twenty years' time, but I recognized him. Which I believe was his intent."

"Jesus."

"He said that he'd heard Eric would be home soon. He said, 'I hope he doesn't run into any more trouble.' "

"Jesus."

"He told me that it would be a shame if some kiddie raper—his words—managed to end up roaming free while a young man like Eric somehow ended up in the state penitentiary." Bennett folds his hands in his lap. "Then he asked me to have a good evening and strolled back to his car."

"Jesus." I look at Sara. All the color seems to have drained from her complexion. "You've got to be..."

"I was angry at first. Not angry. Enraged."

"What happened when you filed the complaint?"

"The complaint?"

Is he kidding? "Jesus, Bennett, you can't just let—"

"Let me ask you," Bennett says to me. "What happened when you called the police after you found your personal documents in Roger Mallory's house?"

I don't bother answering the question. Bennett knows the answer already.

"So we agree," he says, "that in spite of our respective educations, we understand the way the world actually works."

This is unbelievable. "But you're telling me that..."

"What I'm telling you is that I hadn't had a drink in two years," Bennett says. "Two years and twenty-seven days, to be accurate. But I keep a bottle of Johnnie Walker Black in my office at home. A gift from a client that I've never opened.

Sentimental reasons." He looks at me. "The truth, Paul, is that in spite of my anger at being openly threatened—at this threat against my son, a mile from my home—I'd already decided to drop your case before I cracked the seal on that bottle. The truth is that I hadn't planned to come to court this morning at all."

Now he looks at Sara.

"And my point," he tells her, "is that from this moment forward, you don't have to worry about how crazy anything you tell me about Roger Mallory will sound."

For the first time since the police showed up on our doorstep last night, Sara looks genuinely frightened. I don't know that I've ever seen this look before. Not even the night a stranger came into our house and attacked her in our bed. Not quite like this.

"My God," she says.

I can't think of a thing to add.

Bennett says, "Tell me how you came to find your credit card statement in Mallory's house."

I feel numb.

"Paul?"

"That's not what started this," I tell him. I want to beg Sara's forgiveness before I say another word.

"What happened?"

My turn.

Voluntary Spies

12.

INSTEAD OF "HELLO," Charlie Bernard said, "Let me see if I heard this correctly."

"Hey, Charlie." I held the phone with my shoulder while I tied my shoes. "Heard what correctly?"

"When I phoned last evening, I was told that you were unavailable."

"Sorry I missed you, buddy. Sara said you called."

"Specifically, that you were—again, I'm confirming—out on patrol?"

It sounded funny even to me. But what could I say?

"I wonder," he said. "What in holy hell does that mean?"

"I joined the neighborhood watch. Didn't Sara tell you?"

"The neighborhood watch."

"I've got a vest and everything."

"Surely you must be shitting me."

"A vest and a walkie-talkie. And a hell of a nice flashlight." Before our break-in, I'd have been right alongside Charlie mocking the idea of patrolling a suburban cul-de-sac with a picture of a badge printed on my chest.

Even after our break-in, it still felt vaguely absurd. But after our new neighbors had rallied to make us feel welcome, it had seemed awkward to not join the neighborhood association. And after joining, I could either join the volunteer patrol or commit to being the only jerk in the circle who couldn't be bothered to serve like all the other husbands. After moving halfway across the country, I'd found that I didn't have enough energy left over to be a worthwhile jerk.

"One day," I told Charlie, "I hope to make shift leader."

Silence. Then: "This is Dr. Charles Bernard. I'm calling for my friend Paul. Callaway. Has he been at this number recently?"

I laughed. "Okay. I admit it. I go for a walk and smoke a cigar a couple nights a week."

"With your walkie-talkie close at hand, I presume."

"It's not so bad. We check in on the older folks, run the teenagers out of the park after ten. If it's midnight and somebody left their garage door open, we ring the doorbell, let them know."

"Paul Callaway," Charlie said. "Is he there?"

"Hang on, I'll see." I took the phone away from my ear, then put it back. "He says to call back when your wife's been assaulted."

"I keep no wife."

"Oh yeah."

"It was that woman you married who ruined me."

"She can be pitiless," I agreed. "You probably shouldn't have slept with her grad assistant."

"I had no choice in that instance. My hands were tied."

"Some things can't be helped."

"Handcuffed, to be accurate." His voice grew wistful before returning to the point. "Speaking of which, tell me, do you get to carry special neighborhood watch handcuffs?"

"I don't know, I'm still in training."

"How about a firearm? Surely you'll need to shoot someone eventually."

"I think we're just supposed to hit them with the flashlight and call the authorities," I told him. "We're only volunteers."

"You joke now," Charlie said. "What happens when you go up against some scumbag all hopped up on Frappuccinos, refusing to cut his grass? What's a fancy flashlight going to do for you then?"

"They tell me every situation is different, Charlie."

There came a long sigh from the other end of the line. "And every man is surrounded by a neighborhood of voluntary spies."

Quotations. With Charlie, always the first sign of a conversation in decline. "Who said that?"

"Jane Austen."

"I thought you hated Austen."

"Which only emphasizes my point."

I checked myself in Sara's mirror and felt completely ridiculous. Khaki shorts, a polo shirt, a pair of beat-up sneakers. I'd had to go out and buy the shorts and the shirt. My legs hadn't seen sunlight since the Dixson English department softball team disbanded six years ago. "Well, this has been compelling," I said. "But I've got a tee time in half an hour."

"Did you just say that you have a tee time?"

"At the club." I couldn't help myself. "Couple guys from my patrol unit are members. I'm playing as a guest."

Another pause.

"Sweet Christ," Charlie finally said. "You've drunk the fucking Kool-Aid, haven't you?"

"Call you back," I said, and hung up grinning.

For the past three weekends in a row, Roger Mallory had attempted to convince me that I should come play golf with him, Barry Firth, and Pete Seward. The three of them held memberships at Deer Creek Country Club, a ten-minute drive from Sycamore Court, where they played eighteen holes together every Saturday. Apparently, Ben Holland, Michael Sprague's partner, had been their fourth up until he'd taken the contract job in Seattle.

So far, each weekend, I'd declined the invitation. While recent events had left me more or less thankful that I'd never gotten rid of my clubs, I'd given up the actual game of golf—my parents' and their parents' game—as futile in my twenties. The last time I'd played, my own mother, a beautician by trade, had cleaned out my wallet in a friendly two-dollar Nassau round in which she'd fronted me, because it was my birthday, sixteen strokes per side. Hole after dispiriting hole, my father had convinced me to press the bet. They'd laughed together afterward.

When I told Roger this story, he laughed and said, "Hell, don't worry about that. Barry needs a little competition."

Partly as a joke on me, partly because she liked our new neighbors and wanted me to try harder to be sociable, Sara had been encouraging Roger while my back was turned. *He's been dying to play again. He just won't admit it.* A ridiculous lie.

Partly out of nostalgia, partly in hopes that my performance on the golf course would end the invitations once and for all, I'd finally relented. And so I met Roger in his driveway that morning, a few minutes before noon.

"There he is," Roger said, scratching Wes between the ears. Wes, Roger's ailing German shepherd, swatted Roger's leg feebly with his tail. As I reached the driveway, the old pastured watchdog limped over to take the cold ballpark frank he couldn't smell, and could no longer see, but knew I'd bring.

"Good boy," I said, letting the dog lick my fingers. "Don't tell Roger."

Roger took one look at my cracked leather bag of clubs, most of them handed down to me by my grandfather, and said, "You two wait here."

Already I felt like a dope. The only clubs I owned that didn't belong in a museum were a duct-taped 5-wood I'd found near a water hazard fifteen years ago and the junior-model sand wedge that had been confiscated by the Clark Falls Police Department in July.

"Tell me the truth," I said to the dog. "How dumb do I look?"

Before Wes could weigh in, Roger returned carrying a big, black-and-gold bag that looked like it belonged to a PGA Tour pro. "Here. Had these specially made for you."

I looked closer and understood the joke: they were Callaway brand clubs, a full set of them, probably worth more than my first car. The irons gleamed in the sunlight; the woods all had matching head covers with the Callaway logo stitched in white thread. My ancient persimmon driver had a gym sock with holes in it.

"Roger, I can't use your golf clubs."

"These? Hell, I gave up on these two seasons ago."

"I wouldn't even know what to do with all of them."

"I've got three other sets in the garage," he said. "Want to come pick out a different one?"

"No," I said. "No, that's not... I'm sure these work fine. Thank you."

"Here." He handed me two Partagas cigars, both sealed in screw-top tubes. "You'll need these."

Across the circle, Pete Seward's garage door opened; Pete emerged around the back end of his SUV with his golf bag on his shoulder. As if choreographed, the same thing happened at Barry Firth's place. Barry saw us and waved.

Roger waved back and took Wes into the house. In a moment he returned, twirling the keys to his own SUV, a GMC Yukon that could have carried my Honda hybrid on its luggage rack. "What do you say we go hit the hell out of some golf balls?"

"I hope you've got plenty."

"Come on," he said. "You can ride with me."

• • •

We'd play a team scramble, it was decided on the practice green. This meant dividing into opposing twosomes and keeping a "best ball" score, meaning that the members of each team would choose the best shot between them and play the next shot from that spot. The losing team bought steaks at the clubhouse grill after the round.

Pete Seward had suggested the idea—in honor, he'd said, of my long hiatus from using a golf club for anything beyond home security. I knew that he'd done so more out of consideration of my last known handicap, the maximum recommended under USGA rules, but I appreciated the gesture anyway.

"Perfect," Roger said.

"I'll take Roger," said Barry Firth.

Pete grinned and gave me a nod. "It's a lock."

On the first tee box, with new-guy honors, I looked down the lush green fairway of a short par four. Dogleg left, trees on both sides, sand traps at two hundred yards.

"Fore, please," Roger said. "Paul Callaway now driving."

"This won't be pretty." I pulled the cover from the number one wood. Compared with mine, the driver Roger had loaned me looked like a Volkswagen Beetle on the end of a stick.

"Just tee it high," Roger said. "Nothing to it."

"Okay," I said. "Here goes nothing."

I used the ball to push the tee into the turf. When I straightened, the setup looked like a dimpled white lollipop growing out of the ground at a crooked angle.

Roger grinned. "Maybe not that high." He stooped to correct the situation, then backed off and nodded. "That's better. Let her rip."

"Sprinkle some whoop-ass on it," Barry said.

Pete: "Nice and smooth."

I arranged my grip on the club, hunched my shoulders, and addressed the ball. "Somebody watch where this goes."

Barry: "There is no ball."

"Jesus," Roger said. "Would you two let the man swing?"

Nice and smooth, I thought. I remembered my father's advice: *just give it seventy percent.* After a few tense moments, I took a breath, drew the club back nice and slow, thought of the bunkers way down there in the fairway, and gave it all I had.

The follow-through spun me off balance. Something pulled in the middle of my back. The vibration at impact rattled up the club and into my hands, numbing my fingers.

When I opened my eyes, I saw that I'd driven the tee straight into the ground like a nail. The ball dribbled five or six feet to the right and rolled to a stop. Everybody stood around for a moment.

Eventually, Pete pointed at the ball and said, "There it is."

I nodded. "I'm guessing we won't be using that one."

"Hell," Roger said. "With Pete you never know."

Barry laughed.

Pete grinned, stepped up, and pounded a towering drive over the trees, cutting the dogleg and rolling his ball into the rough on the far side of the fairway, fifty yards from the green.

"Medium rare," he told Barry. "That's how I like my rib eye."

"Guess you'd better learn how to putt, then."

Roger chuckled and teed up, hanging a smooth little draw along the curve of the fairway, landing his ball softly in the middle of the short grass. Barry took half a dozen practice swings and pulled a screaming hook into the first fairway bunker.

"Damn," he said. "I gotta get this thing regripped."

Pete nodded. "That's probably it."

"Drive for show, jocko." Barry stooped to pull his unbroken tee from the ground. "Putt for dough."

As Pete and Barry headed for the gleaming, gas-powered, GPS-equipped carts parked on the path, Roger tossed me my duffed ball, a clean new Titleist, which he'd supplied in the first place. "Glad you could make it, Doc. This'll be fun."

Apparently, I already had a nickname. Doc? After thinking about it, I realized that I'd been named after my academic credentials. It hadn't occurred to me before then that this was how my neighbors saw me. "Famous last words," I told Roger.

He chuckled and clapped me on the shoulder.

Off we went.

Growing up, golf with my parents had always occurred on the trampled public courses of Morristown, New Jersey, generally with a pocket full of scuffed secondhand balls from the rusted bucket my father kept in the garage.

In his retirement, with his investments and his pension from Honeywell, I imagine that he could have afforded to treat himself and my mother to at least a partial membership at one of the plush private clubs in the area. But he'd never done so. *You find the same assholes everywhere,* he once told me. *Why pay more?* In his view, you could learn everything you needed to know about a person by the way they played a friendly round of golf.

By the time we'd finished the first nine holes at Deer Creek CC, where the range balls were in better shape than the ones in my father's rusty bucket back in Jersey, I'd learned the following things about my new neighbors in Clark Falls:

Pete Seward was the big hitter. He boomed the ball off the tee, sending it on a slow climb into the sun, and we'd find it either three hundred yards down the fairway or we'd never see it again. His short game was streaky, but he seemed secure with his skill level. He didn't brag or bemoan. If he had a temper, so far I hadn't seen it flare.

Barry Firth liked to talk. After nearly every shot, no matter how promising or poor, he'd send verbal instruction after his ball like commands to a spaniel: *Sit down. Turn over. Run. Bite.* After a good shot, I couldn't help noticing the way he subtly checked for Roger's approval. After a bad shot, he took a moment to repeat his swing in slow motion, eventually nodding to indicate that he'd identified the flaw.

Roger Mallory, who had ten years on all of us, was easily the most reliable ball striker in the group. Neither as spectacular as Pete nor as erratic as Barry, he played a quiet, conservative game from tee to pin, hitting fairways and greens, avoiding trouble, and shaping the flight of the ball to produce the safest result.

"Dang, Rodge," Barry said on the ninth green, after Roger lipped out a two-foot putt for par. I'd just rolled in a shocking, improbable twenty-footer to card a team birdie for Pete and me. "Haven't seen you miss one of those all year."

Roger shook his head and smiled. "Yanked it." His tap-in for bogey took us into the turn all tied up.

On the way to the tenth tee, from my spot in the passenger seat of the cart, I turned to Pete and said, "He did that on purpose, didn't he?"

"Who did what?"

"Roger," I said. "That putt. In nine holes he made four or five same as that one like he was falling off a log."

Pete manned the wheel and smiled a little.

I had my answer. "Why do you think he'd do that?"

"I'd only be guessing."

"Let's say you're guessing, then."

"I'd guess that Roger is working to promote a sense of solidarity amongst the troops."

"Ah."

"Or maybe he just yanked it." Pete goosed the cart up the hill, clubs clattering behind us. "Don't worry, we'll keep his ass honest on the back side."

13.

"I DON'T KNOW," Michael Sprague told me, the next night, while out on patrol. "Losing on purpose doesn't sound like Roger."

"Pete said he was trying to foster group unity."

"Actually, that does sound like Roger. He's big into the unity."

"Sure," I said. "Can't have a community without the unity."

"God, that's terrible. I'm stealing it."

We strolled through the playground at Washington Elementary, a ten-minute walk down the hill from our circle.

I'd grown to look forward to drawing Michael as a shift partner; the Ponca Heights Neighborhood Patrol, whose ranks had swelled in recent weeks, operated on the buddy system, and so far I'd mostly been paired with Roger, or sometimes Pete.

Roger maintained the rotation amongst the volunteers—about twenty men and about ten women—so that nobody had to go out more than once or twice per week. Michael and Sara had become fast friends, and though he visited our house often, I hadn't really gotten to know him until our first spin around the neighborhood together, two weeks earlier.

Nothing shaking at the elementary school. No teenagers making out or smoking joints in the shadows beneath the log gym. No skateboarders out after dark, trying to land their decks on the hand railings. The playground swings hung limp and vacant in the still, muggy night air.

Michael keyed his walkie-talkie. "Peter, this is Paul and Mary. We're all secure at Washington. Repeat, K through 6 is secure. Over."

A crackle. A beep. Then Barry Firth's voice: "Come on, guys. We're supposed to keep the channel clear. Cut it out."

"That's a roger, Barry. Where's Roger? Over."

Crackle, beep. "Seriously. You promised."

Michael laughed and clipped the radio back on his belt. "God, I love that guy. So what's with Pete, do you think?"

"I don't know." Normally, Pete would have joined in with the juvenile nonsense on the radio, assuming he hadn't started it himself. But he hadn't seemed himself, at least to the extent that I knew him, since yesterday's round of golf. "But I have a story."

"Do you now?"

"A small one."

"I'm all ears."

I told him that we'd all walked off the eighteenth green around five the previous afternoon. We'd repaired to the clubhouse together, where we'd spent the next four hours eating steaks and drinking scotch and smoking cigars.

"As men will do," Michael said.

"So I'm told," I said. "Nine, nine-thirty, I head to the manly men's room. I'm there awhile."

At the time I'd been exhausted, sunburned, full of bloody

red meat, half full of eighteen-year-old Lagavulin, and thinking that I might like to throw up. I managed to hold down my stomach, but there had been a touch-and-go moment.

"When I come out I take a wrong turn, go through the wrong set of doors, and end up outside instead of back at the table."

The accidental gulp of fresh air had seemed to clear my head, so I'd decided to take a short walk around the lodgepole-swank clubhouse before going back in and rejoining the others. On the far side of the building, with its decks and its tall windows overlooking Deer Creek Valley, I'd heard voices above me and looked up to see two fat cigar embers flaring in the dark.

Time to end it, Pete, I'd heard Roger say, in his calm, unmistakable baritone. Stern, but not angry. Like a fatherly friend giving hard advice.

Or what, Roger? Pete's voice had an edge. *You'll tell on me?*

Just end it.

Michael said, "End what?"

"That's what I wonder."

Michael thought about it and sighed. "He'd better not be sleeping around on Melody."

"That's what I wonder."

"What else did you hear?"

"That's it," I said. "I went back around the other way and pretended I hadn't heard a thing. Pete hardly talked after he and Roger came back, but he ended up getting lousy drunk. Barry had to drive him home."

"Pete." Michael shook his head. "Pete Pete Pete."

We walked along the empty sidewalks of Walnut Street, winding our way through its neighborhood in progress. With the nature preserve to the north, most of the new development occurred here, expanding Ponca Heights to the south.

We passed a row of new houses, all with the same rooflines, the same baby trees staked out front. We passed a row of nearly finished houses with the same weedy gaps between their sodless dirt yards. At the corner of Walnut and Cedar, a framed two-story faux Colonial sat wrapped in Tyvek.

The farther south we walked, the more skeletal the neighborhood became, until Ponca Heights South finally petered out into a group of bare lots, sleeping bulldozers, and a sign that said, *Future Site of Spoonbill Circle.*

"Do you figure these bulldozer guys ever stop and look around and think, "*You know, we're tearing out* these *trees*"—I pointed at the grove of old-growth oaks and elms bordering the future site of Spoonbill Circle—"...*so they can plant* those *trees*?" I pointed at a line of young Japanese maples tethered with wire, their wrist-sized trunks clad in protective plastic tubes. As soon as I said it, I wondered what Sycamore Court had looked like sixty years ago.

"Maybe it's something with Brit," Michael said, as though he hadn't been listening. "You know she's grounded again."

I nodded. "Melody told us." Apparently, a couple of nights ago, the parents of Brit's best friend, Rachel, had caught the two of them sneaking out with a four-pack of wine coolers. "Borrowing privileges at the Callaway branch library are once again temporarily suspended."

Michael grinned. "That girl's getting to be a handful."

"She seems like a smart cookie."

"Thirteen going on twenty-three," Michael said. "Maybe he was giving Pete a pep talk? Roger."

"A pep talk."

"You know, spare the rod or whatever." He wagged a finger, deepened his voice. " 'You've got to put your foot down, Pete, they need tough love at that age. Time to nip it in the bud.' " He checked for my opinion. "Right?"

"Maybe," I said.

"I could see that."

"Except for the 'tell on me' part."

Michael nodded. "That part."

"I didn't get the feeling it was a pep talk."

"What did Sara think?"

"Same thing you thought."

"Pete, you fink." Michael sighed again. "Well. I guess it's none of my business."

"That was my thought exactly." In the beam of my flashlight, I caught a glint from somewhere over in the darkened construction site. I swept the light back and found what looked like half a dozen crumpled beer cans in the scoop of a front loader. "My other thought was, *What makes it Roger's business?*"

"Aha."

"Don't get me wrong." As long as we were there, we walked the extra hundred yards, collected the empty beer cans, and tossed them into the excavation contractor's waste bin. The sound of the twisted aluminum cans clattering off the steel walls of the bin sounded loud in the stillness. "I like Roger. He did a hell of a lot for Sara's peace of mind, after the break-in. And what happened to his son . . . Christ, I'd be curled up in a gutter somewhere. You know?"

"I wouldn't claim to," Michael said. "But I can imagine."

"The truth is, I admire the guy."

"Blah, blah. Yes, we all admire Roger. But?"

"I get the feeling Roger sees himself as the sheriff around these here parts."

Michael smiled at that. We turned back and walked along in easy silence for a while, back up the hill, the neighborhood gradually filling in around us again as we cut north up Poppleton.

After a few blocks, Michael finally said, "You and Sara haven't met Ben."

"Not yet. We're looking forward to it."

"You'd like him. Not as much as you like me."

"Naturally."

"A word about Sycamore Court." Michael twirled his flashlight on its hand strap as we walked. "Pete and Melody, they've always been great. Trish and Barry, we got a few looks from them at first, when Ben moved in. Nothing malicious. More like . . . cautious curiosity."

"Right."

"But Roger was the first to reach out," he said. "The day Ben moved in, Roger and Wes came over, made Ben feel welcome. When Roger found out that Ben had played college golf, he went out and wheeled and dealed him some kind of VIP membership rate at the club."

"No kidding."

"Honestly, it always seemed a bit transparent to me. But not in a bad way. More like he was . . . I don't know."

Promoting a sense of solidarity amongst the troops, I thought. I said, "Leading by example?"

Michael touched his nose. *Bingo.*

"There was a time when I'd have found it demeaning. But that ship sailed long before I ever moved back to Clark Falls." He shrugged as we turned up Wildwood Lane. "The fact is, I still love him for it. And he and Ben seemed to genuinely like each other, which frankly surprised me more knowing Ben than knowing Roger."

"You're right," I said, almost wishing that I hadn't brought it up. "I'm probably being an ass—"

"Now ask me why Ben took the job in Seattle."

I looked over.

"You're supposed to ask me why Ben—"

"Why did Ben take the job in Seattle?"

"It's funny you should ask," Michael said. "I'll tell you why. He wouldn't admit it if you asked him the same question, but I know it's the truth."

The long, gradual climb uphill back toward Sycamore Court now had my shirt sticking to the sweat on my back beneath my safety-green vest. The air around us felt like a steam bath. Even the cicadas seemed to be laboring to keep up their rhythmic buzzing in the trees. As the surrounding woods thickened, the mosquitoes turned out in clouds thick enough to make me wish I'd brought that second cigar Roger had given me for the golf course yesterday.

I stopped noticing all of that as Michael began telling me an anecdote about a same-sex marriage initiative that had come up for referendum to the state legislature the year before. One day, he said, Ben had brought home yard signs that encouraged voters to "Vote Yes to Prop 42."

"I thought they were an eyesore, to be honest. But they seemed to make Ben happy. So we had these signs in our yard."

I thought I saw the general direction of the story taking shape. But Michael seemed to enjoy the telling, so I walked along and listened, flashlight clipped to one hip, walkie-talkie clipped to the other.

"After a couple of days, Roger came over." Michael nodded crisply. "I always gave him credit for being direct. No passive-aggressive mincing around, no smiley Hey Neighbor bullshit. He just came out and asked us to take the signs down."

"Really."

"He was polite about it. Very respectful. But he wasn't exactly asking us if we'd consider thinking about *maybe* taking them down, either."

"And this was Roger's job because..."

"Oh, he said it was nothing personal. He told us that he thought we were class A neighbors. His words. In fact, he said that based on some of the family values he'd seen in his time on the force, as far as he was concerned, we had as much right to marry each other as anybody else. Probably more than some. His words."

"So what was the problem?"

"Politics can be divisive," Michael said. "That was his reasoning. He said that in his experience, public displays of politics create tension where none existed before, and that's usually about all they accomplish."

"Public displays of politics."

"That's what he said."

"Welcome to America. What's the point?"

"Roger's point was that we had seven votes in our little circle. Everybody already had their own thoughts on the issue. And if knowing us personally didn't influence their opinion, a couple of yard signs weren't going to do the trick."

If pressed I'd have been forced to admit that I more or less agreed with that analysis. But that didn't mean I wanted anybody telling me what the hell I could or couldn't do with *my* yard.

"Roger said that everybody in Sycamore Court had always just sort of agreed to keep their politics to themselves. And that things seemed to work out pretty well that way."

"What did *you* say?"

"Me? I stayed the hell out of it. Like I said, I thought those signs were hideous anyway."

"Right."

"And after spending a Friday night keeping my staff from murdering one another with the kitchen utensils, more drama isn't what I'm looking for. You know?"

"Sure."

"Ben was livid," Michael said. "It was Chernobyl at our place after Roger left that night."

"Politics can be divisive."

"I've heard that."

"So what happened?"

"Ben kept the signs right where they were."

"Good for Ben."

"One morning, they were gone."

"Gone?"

"Like they were never there." He made a motion with his fingers. *Poof.* "Ben got some new signs. The next morning, *those* signs were gone. So Ben got more signs."

I had to chuckle. I liked this story, even if it did seem to support my new theory about Roger Mallory.

"Oh, it was completely ridiculous. Those two. Stubborn as a couple bighorn sheep on crack, the both of them." He shined his flashlight over to the curb near the corner; two silver coins glowed briefly in the dark, then disappeared as a fat raccoon squeezed itself down the storm drain. Michael clicked the light off again. "I swear, Roger must have had a basement full of those things by the time the vote came and went."

"The signs? You mean they just kept at it?"

"For three weeks straight," he said. "As far as I know, neither of them ever once mentioned it out loud to the other. After a while, I think they were just trying to prove who could be the most pigheaded."

We were a seven-minute walk from home by then. Up ahead, Elmhaven ran into Sycamore Drive, which would take us out of the southern hemisphere of Ponca Heights proper, up the hill, around the tree line, and back to Sycamore Court.

Tonight's patrol log: six beer cans, a few thousand mosquitoes, and one raccoon. A light shift. Normally, we'd have seen at least three or four raccoons. I liked watching them rise up on their hind legs when you caught them pawing through someone's trash, wearing their funny little masks.

"Anyway, it wasn't very long after that before Ben came home and told me he'd gotten this contract." Michael shrugged. "I didn't even know he'd been looking. Always wanted to live in the Pacific Northwest, he said. First I'd heard of that, too. But hey, you can't know everything about a person, right?"

I told him that I hadn't known that Sara wanted to be an associate dean at a Midwestern university until it came up.

"He asked me to go with him, but I wasn't about to leave Mom alone in that manor for six months," Michael said. "And the restaurant? I've worked my sweet ass off turning that kitchen into something. If I ever leave, I'm *leaving*. Not going away long enough for the whole thing to fall apart, just so I can come back to a pile of rubble. You know?"

"Sure."

"Supposedly, we're still operating on the theory that he's moving home at the end of the contract." Michael was quiet for half a block or so. Then he said, "But I think we both know that's not really going to happen."

"Oh?"

"We're just pretending something else for now."

"Michael," I said. "I'm sorry to hear that."

He smiled. "Nobody died."

"Still."

"Want to know what else? I think Roger was honestly sorry to see Ben go."

I thought about the battle of wills Michael had just described. After a minute, I said, "How do you feel about that?"

"About Roger being sorry?"

"About Ben going."

"I feel sad about it." Michael waved his hand. "But I never needed a law to say we were married. If he did, then we weren't." He clicked his flashlight absently—on, then off. "And if Mr. Ben's personal life plan only goes as far as getting his way or quitting, then we're probably better off with seventeen hundred miles between us."

I wasn't sure what to say, so I let it rest for a minute as we emerged from the lower subdivision and turned up Sycamore Drive. Ahead, I saw two green vests glowing in the moonlight. Pete and Barry, returning from Ponca Heights North.

One of them signaled with their flashlight: three short blinks, three long blinks, three more short blinks. SOS.

Had to be Pete. Maybe his mood had improved. Michael keyed his walkie-talkie. "Identify yourself or prepare to be destroyed."

The radio crackled, then Pete's voice came over the air. "Eat me."

"Please don't be screwing some bimbo," Michael muttered to the sky. He keyed the radio and said, "Copy that. We're heading your way."

As we walked up the hill to rejoin Pete and Barry, I said, "So how did the vote come out?"

"What vote is that?"

"The vote on Proposition 42."

"Ah." Michael chuckled. "Defeated in a landslide."

"I see."

"Shame, isn't it?"

"Well," I said. "If it makes you feel any better, we didn't win either."

"Who?"

"Pete and me," I said. "Yesterday. Roger and Barry ended up clipping us by a stroke on the last hole. We bought dinner."

Michael smiled. "That sounds like Roger."

Sara was sitting in bed reading a magazine when I finally got back to the house. I was sweaty and tired from walking, ready for a beer and a shower.

"How was it?"

"Highly dangerous," I said. "But Michael protected me."

"You and Michael tonight?"

"And Pete and Barry on the north side. Regular home team."

"That's nice."

"It was interesting," I said. "Listen to this."

While I took off my toy patrol gear and stripped out of my clothes, I told her the story of Ben Holland and Roger Mallory and the yard signs of Proposition 42.

"Really," she said.

"According to Michael. Back and forth with these signs. He'd keep putting them out, and Roger just kept taking them down."

"Poor Michael," she said. "I hope they can work it out."

She didn't appear to be listening very closely. Through all of this, she hadn't yet looked up from her magazine, which she didn't seem to be reading anyway, just flipping pages. Sara doesn't normally read magazines in the first place.

"All this good gossip I bring back? I thought you'd be proud of me."

At that point, she looked at me and smiled.

Two years ago, while soaping up in the shower, Sara found

a lump the size of a walnut in her right breast. It turned out to be benign, a fibroid mass that went away six months after she gave up coffee. But it was still a scare, and we'd spent a tense few days waiting for medical opinions and test results. She'd smiled this same smile after her shower that morning.

"What's the matter?"

"I'm bleeding," she said.

14.

AN ER NURSE at the university medical center took Sara's vitals and asked lots of questions. A different nurse drew a vial of blood from her arm, asked the same questions as the first nurse, and handed her a cup to pee into.

The attending physician reminded me a little bit of one of my grad students back at Dixson. He configured the gleaming steel stirrups on either side of the examination table and helped Sara in.

"You're still closed," he said when he'd finished, stripping off the latex glove and dropping it in the trash. "That's good."

A smile. A squirt of gel on Sara's belly.

An impossibly long minute or two, watching the doctor push the microphone-shaped probe around in the gel.

"How many weeks?" he asked, still smiling.

"Nine," Sara said.

Another squirt of gel. Had the doctor's smile faded slightly? I couldn't be sure.

All I knew for certain was that we hadn't yet heard the grainy, crackling *wow wow wow* sound we'd heard before—the day Sara's new doctor in Clark Falls had used the same kind of machine to let us hear, for the first time, this baby we'd been hearing about.

Wow.

We'd made that sound, I'd thought that day, holding Sara's hand the same way I held it now.

Wow.

We'd started a heartbeat.

Wow wow wow.

"It's an intangible," Dr. Finley told us the following afternoon.

We were sitting in his private office on the first floor of the Finley Pointer Clausen LLC building. Three chairs arranged in a loose triangle. Sara and I together, Finley on point.

Sara said, "But it's a possibility."

"Certainly we think that stress can be a factor," he said. "But we don't necessarily know how, or what kind of stress, or how much." He smiled kindly. "All I can say about that is, whatever you've found on the Internet that makes you think this is somehow your fault, Sara, you should regard that information as nonmedical bullshit. If you'll pardon my language."

"Of course," Sara said. But she didn't sound convinced.

Yesterday, while I'd been lounging off my hangover inside the air-conditioned house, she'd spent the afternoon outside, working in her flower garden in the suffocating August heat. I'd told her to come in and relax. She told Finley that she hadn't felt well once she finally did.

"Of course you didn't feel well," he said. "It was ninety-eight degrees yesterday. With a heat index of a hundred and twelve. You're probably lucky you didn't keel over in the marigolds." He shrugged. "But based on my experience, I'd be willing to bet a reasonable sum that working in your garden didn't terminate your pregnancy."

On the wall behind him, there hung a framed photograph of Finley with two teenage boys, whom I took to be his sons. All three of them were geared in helmets and bright yellow life jackets, paddling an inflatable raft through a whitewater run. While Dr. Finley talked, I found my eyes drawn to the photo.

"Not just yesterday," Sara said. "I've been feeling..."

"Yes?"

"Overwhelmed," she said. "For weeks. I know I haven't been taking the best—"

"Let's see," Finley said. "You've moved halfway across the country, away from your family and friends, to a new town where you didn't know a soul. Add the pregnancy. A challenging new job. For heaven's sake, Sara, add the fact that you were attacked just a few weeks ago." He shook his head, pantomiming amazement. "I feel overwhelmed just thinking about it."

"That's what I—"

Another gentle smile. "But in my opinion, the most likely culprit is simpler than all of that."

Sara sighed. "I know what you're going to say."

"Our statistics still suggest that an otherwise healthy woman's chances for miscarriage increase as she passes the age of thirty-five. That's all."

Finley was somewhere in his sixties himself. He'd been in the baby business more than half those years, and we'd felt comfortable with him almost immediately. Just then I felt strangely disappointed that we wouldn't need to come see him anymore.

"Even speaking as an economist," she said, "I can tell you that statistics don't seem like much comfort at the moment."

"Sara." Finley reached out and took her hand. He looked

at both of us. "There isn't a number in the world that tells anyone how to feel about something like this."

I put my hand on her back, completing the triangle. The look she gave me seemed apologetic. Almost ashamed.

"No," I said.

"I have more useful numbers to give you," Finley told us. "I know at least three people here in town whom I'd recommend to my own daughter, if you find that you'd like to talk to somebody. Either one of you."

Sara nodded. I copied her.

"And of course you can call me anytime."

"Thank you."

"Is there anything you'd like to ask now?"

"To be honest," she said, "I'm just wondering what happens next."

Finley took a moment to explain our options, the first being a procedure, which he would perform himself, here in the office. It was called a D & C, which stood for dilation and curettage.

"Or," he said, "you can wait to pass the tissue."

At first I thought he meant Kleenex. Being that it was a sad occasion. *Pass the tissue*. Then I realized what he meant.

"Nature will take its course," he assured us. "But it's really your decision, Sara."

"How long will it take?"

"The procedure? Normally it's a—"

"Nature."

Finley nodded. "Assuming everything proceeds normally, it could happen today. More likely sometime in the next day or two. I would generally expect you to complete inside the week, though these things are never entirely predictable."

"And I just wait?"

"If you choose," Finley said, "I can prescribe medication that may help nature along."

We sat there in silence for a few minutes. Sara nodded her head. It seemed almost an absent motion, as though she were listening to some advice I wished I could hear.

I looked back at the photo of Finley and his sons, manhandling Mother Nature. For the first time, it occurred to me to wonder: who had been operating the camera?

"Thank you," Sara said.

It was over by Thursday afternoon.

We stayed close to home and tried to stay busy. Early Wednesday evening, Sara went to bed with the chills. By Thursday morning, she'd started cramping, and by noon, regular contractions had set in.

A few months down the road, I'd have grabbed our bags and driven like hell for the hospital. Instead, I drove to the SaveMore on Belmont for more maxi pads. Michael Sprague came over to be with her while I was gone.

At a few minutes past five o'clock, Sara went to the bathroom one final time. She stayed there, behind the closed door, until almost five-thirty.

Eventually, from my spot on the couch in the living room, I heard the sound of the toilet flushing. The pipes rattled under the floor.

Sara came out, walked to the couch, and sat down beside me. I put my arm around her shoulders. She tucked up her feet and laid her head in my lap.

For the first time that week, she let herself cave in. We cried.

Two hours later, she told me, "I didn't know how much I'd wanted this until two hours ago."

I stroked her hair. "Me either."

We went on.

15.

I'M STALLING.

Douglas Bennett doesn't need to hear all of this. None of it is news to Sara. I played golf, Roger's a control freak, we're not going to be parents. Couldn't these points be summarized?

Of course they seem significant. To me.

And if I were one of my freshman composition students, and if this story were my term paper, I'd be slashing every page with a red pen.

Are these details necessary?

Condense.

Everybody has their tricks, and I know mine. How do we tell a convincing lie? By sticking as closely to the truth as we can. How do we make the truth compelling? By choosing our angles. Selecting which points to embellish or skim.

I'm trying to paint a realistic backdrop so that the preposterous, when I reach that point, will seem more believable. I'm attempting to establish a trustworthy narrative voice so that my own actions will seem easier to understand.

The truth is, Douglas Bennett doesn't need a realistic backdrop. He doesn't need every detail to get up to speed.

All Douglas Bennett really needs to know is that I'd quit the neighborhood patrol before the end of September. By October, my marriage was in trouble. In November, I made the worst mistake of my life. Afterward, Roger Mallory came to our house to inform me that he wanted me gone.

And that's what started all of this.

"Where is it that you think I'm going?" I'd asked Roger.

"That's up to you," he'd said.

"You're kidding."

"Don't think that I want this."

"Let me get this straight," I'd said. "You're banishing me. From the neighborhood."

"If that's the word you want to use."

"You mean, like in the Bible?"

"You can have until December sixteenth," Roger said. "That's the end of your semester."

I'd laughed in his face. "You're actually serious, aren't you?"

"Let's not keep asking that question."

"You honestly believe that we're going to pack up and move out? Because you *say* so?"

"I didn't create the situation, Paul." He spoke in a regretful tone. "And I haven't said anything about Sara."

"Ah. Right."

"We'll say the sixteenth, then."

"Or what, Roger?" I remember saying. "You'll tell on me?"

Cold Wars

16.

IN THE WEEKS FOLLOWING THE ATTACK, Sara developed a ritual. Each night before bed, she'd make a trip around the house, checking the locks on all the doors and windows. If I'd already set the alarm, Sara would punch in the standby code and rearm the system herself.

If observed, she'd laugh about it, like she realized this regimen was silly, though I'd never suggested that I thought so. Whenever that night came up in conversation, she'd speak freely about the subject, sometimes with a gallows chuckle over some small, unimportant detail that had grown to seem absurd with time. Generally, she gave little indication that the experience had created any lingering ill effects to speak of, and all our neighbors had expressed their admiration of her fortitude.

But in private, she still flinched sometimes when I touched her without warning.

One night in September, I sat in my chair with a book on my knee and watched Sara make her rounds. The next day, I cut my Friday afternoon class short, left campus, and drove to the county/city building downtown.

It had been a couple of weeks since I'd checked in with Detective Harmon. I didn't expect that he had any new information, but I wanted him to see my face again, just to remind him that we were still out there. A uniformed sergeant escorted me to Harmon's office in the Detectives Division on the second floor.

"Mr. Callaway, hello." Harmon stood and reached across his desk to shake my hand. That afternoon his shirtsleeves were rolled to the elbow, jacket and shoulder rig hanging on the back of his chair. He looked like he'd had a long day. "How are you?"

"I'm fine, thank you." I shook his hand and nodded to the other man sitting casually in one of the chairs in Harmon's office. "Sorry to interrupt, I should have called."

"Not at all." Harmon gestured to the man in the chair. "Paul, this is John Gardner. Old friend of mine. We were just catching up."

"By old friend, he means old boss." John Gardner grinned and shook my hand. He looked lanky and fit for a man I guessed to be in his sixties, completely bald-headed, with sharp features and smallish eyes that gave him a vaguely hawklike appearance. "And by catching up, he means bullshitting and wasting your tax dollars. Let me get the hell out of here."

Something in the way Gardner and Detective Harmon exchanged glances gave me the impression that I had, in fact, interrupted something more than a friendly visit. But before I could volunteer to leave and come back later, Gardner had risen from his chair, shrugged into a light jacket with a Ducks Unlimited patch on the sleeve, and headed for the door. "Fly low, Detective."

Harmon said, "Lieutenant. Love to Nancy."

Gardner waved a hand over his head and left us alone in the office.

"Paul, come on in." Detective Harmon sat and leaned back in his chair. He motioned me to the chair his old boss had just vacated. "Good to see you. How's Sara?"

"She's doing well enough, thanks. Keeping plenty busy."

"I know the feeling. How are you?"

"Me? Too much time on my hands, apparently." I wished I'd called ahead. "Listen, I know there's probably not much you can tell me, but I just wanted to check in and see if you'd come up with anything new. I don't mean to bother you."

"It's no bother," Detective Harmon said, sighing a little. "I just wish I had something new to give you."

"Nobody's come forward and confessed, I take it."

"And nothing's come in over the tip line." Harmon gave me the same look of empathy I remembered him giving us in our unassembled living room two months previously. "Fortunately for us, unfortunately for your particular case, our subject—so far as we know, anyway—hasn't tried his act again."

"I suppose that's a good thing," I said.

"Definitely a good thing." Harmon said. "But I understand your frustration."

"What about the golf club?" Somehow, my sand wedge had been lost in the shuffle between our house and the Property Unit here at the police department. "Did it ever turn up?"

Harmon pursed his lips as though this topic still chapped his hide. "Believe me, I chewed asses up and down the chain of custody. And I can tell you, we're in the middle of an internal procedure review, soup to nuts."

"I see."

"In all honesty, I don't believe we stand to gain much from the golf club that we weren't able to collect from elsewhere in the house," Harmon said. "But of course that's not the point. It was a royal screwup."

I didn't disagree.

"If you or Sara wanted to press the issue, you could probably hang somebody's job on your wall, and I wouldn't be able to say that I blamed you."

I'd thought about this more than once over the past few weeks, but in the end, it seemed that Harmon had a point. "Like you said," I told him. "We probably wouldn't stand to gain much."

We chatted awhile longer, Harmon did his best to reassure me that our case was still important to the Clark Falls Police Department, and I left with nothing more than I'd had when I arrived.

Outside, on my way back to my car, I felt a tingle at the back of my neck and glanced over my shoulder. John Gardner, Detective Harmon's old boss, stood smoking a cigarette in one of the building's exterior doorways, watching me. When I saw him there, he lifted his chin and held up a palm. I don't remember if I waved back or not.

Later that afternoon, Brit Seward returned a collection of short stories I'd given her, thinking it seemed like something she'd like. I asked her what she'd thought of the stories.

"I liked the main one," she said. "About the truck driver and his wife. It was sad."

"Something happier, then." I started browsing my shelves, looking for something funny but not too light. A challenge, but not too far beyond her. She was a tricky case. *Thirteen going on twenty-three,* Michael Sprague had said. He'd had it about right.

Brit said, "What about this?"

I took the book she'd pulled from the R's—a hardback copy of Russo's *Empire Falls*—and remembered her claim that she'd chosen to read Emily Brontë because *Wuthering Heights* reminded her of Ponca Heights. I liked that Brit liked titles and stories that reminded her of where she lived.

I nodded and handed the book back to her. "Happy parts," I said. "And sad parts."

"Sounds good."

"It's pretty good," I agreed. "What makes you pick this one?"

"My dad has the DVD."

"Yeah? Paul Newman?"

"I guess so. He's the old guy? Max?"

"Hey," I said. "Read the book before you watch the movie."

"Too late, but thanks for the advice."

"You're killing me."

Brit laughed. "Can I hang out here?"

I'd set up a reading nook for myself in the far alcove: a beat-up couch that had come from an early apartment of mine, with wide flat arms, where you could set a cup of coffee or a beer or a rocks glass or, in Brit's case, a plastic Diet Mountain Dew bottle; an unmatched footstool that stood at just the right height; and a floor lamp that had come from my grandmother's house in Cresskill, New Jersey, which seemed to make an ordinary lightbulb produce more pleasing light.

If allowed, Brit would spend all day up here. This had in fact become a habit of hers in recent weeks, but as long as Pete and Melody didn't mind, and I didn't have any work to do in the office, it didn't bother me.

"Fine by me," I said. "Your dad knows you're here?"

"I told Melody I was coming over."

"Fair enough."

"Like Melody's fair."

She liked to try and get me to take sides. "None of my business."

"I'm just saying." She hopped into the couch with the book and her soda and tucked her long legs up.

"That's a first edition," I said, heading for the stairs. "Don't spill on it."

"Yes, Mother."

"I'm just saying."

She stuck out her tongue. "Can I use your computer while I'm up here?"

"If you can figure out the password."

"What's the password?"

"The password is, 'You have your own computer.' "

"Yeah," she said, "but Dad has Net Nanny."

"Enjoy the book," I said.

That night, on patrol, Roger said, "I'd be careful."

"How do you mean?"

"Brit spends a lot of time at your place," he said. "You never know."

The whole conversation had caught me off guard. I said, "You never know what?"

"What people might be thinking."

We'd run a few kids out of the construction zone at the future site of Spoonbill Circle, and now we were heading back home. The hot weather had held on through Labor Day, and you could still feel summer in the air. But with nightfall came the first tangy threads of autumn.

I forced myself to wait before I spoke again. The problem with waiting was that it gave my annoyance more time to flare, which must have been apparent, because Roger said, "Don't take what I'm saying the wrong way."

"What *are* you saying?"

"I just notice that she's been spending a lot of time at your place. Sometimes when Sara's not home."

"You notice that, huh?"

"Easy, Doc." He chucked me on the shoulder. "I happened to notice today. That's all."

I'd grown tired of Roger chucking me on the shoulder and calling me Doc. "And?"

"Well, listen," he said. "I'm not saying it's fair, but in my experience, these are the types of situations where you can run into perception problems."

"Perception problems."

"I guess you probably know what I mean."

I knew what he meant. But now I was angry. "Are you telling me that there's a *perception* about Brit Seward coming over to our house?"

"I'm just—"

"I know Michael doesn't have a perception," I said. "If Pete and Melody have a perception, I haven't heard about it from them. Barry Firth wouldn't be able to keep a perception to himself if you locked him in a closet." I counted off the residents of Sycamore Court on one hand. By the time I was finished, only my index finger remained. I tilted that remaining finger toward Roger. "Who does that leave?"

He didn't seem perturbed by the gesture, which part of me already regretted as childish. Another part of me wanted to show him a different finger. As far as Roger seemed concerned, we might have been talking about the weather finally turning cooler.

"Don't forget Brit," he said. "She could have a perception."

"Not through any encouragement from me, she couldn't."

"Oh hell, Paul, I know that. Come on, now. That never crossed my mind."

It did cross your mind, I almost said. *It crossed your mind, and then you brought it up, and now we're talking about it.*

I became aware that I'd started walking faster. But Roger hadn't quickened his pace to keep up. He just kept moving along in his calm, steady stroll, which forced me to slow down or end up a block ahead, talking to myself in the dark. This annoyed me even more.

"Listen," he said. "I've known Brit since she was Sofie's size. If I had a perception I wanted you to be aware of, you'd be aware of it. Believe me."

I thought up half a dozen responses to that and stopped.

Maybe it was me. Sara had said that I'd begun to annoy easily, and that was probably true.

It annoyed me that the police hadn't managed to generate any leads on Sara's attacker in two months' time. It annoyed me that Barry Firth had blabbed about our pregnancy weeks ago, and that despite our intention to keep the result at least somewhat private, at least until we felt ready to share, everyone in the circle—based on Barry's inability to keep his trap shut,

Michael Sprague's unwavering dedication to the same task, and Sara's drinking margaritas at Pete and Melody's barbecue three weekends earlier—had been able to put two and two together.

On the subject of alcohol consumption, I didn't like the fact that Roger seemed to know how many beer and wine bottles went out in our recycling tub on garbage day. It annoyed me that he'd been able to spot the increase in number these past few weeks. It annoyed me that he'd found himself concerned enough to make a comment to Sara about it, which she'd conveyed to me.

Of course, everyone meant well. In offering their condolences. In expressing their concerns.

Maybe it all boiled down to the simple fact that Sara and I hadn't really *been* Sara and I lately. School had started, our schedules conflicted, and six weeks after losing the baby, we seemed to be operating on different frequencies. For the longest period in our marriage so far, we seemed to be struggling to tune in to each other.

And now this horseshit?

"Hell, forget all that," Roger said. "There's more you don't know, and that's not your fault."

"What don't I know?"

"Between you and me," he said, "turns out you're a pretty good alibi."

"What does that mean?"

While we worked our way back up Sycamore Drive, Roger proceeded to tell me about an instance he happened to be aware of, in which Brit had claimed to be at our place, but had in fact slipped away to Loess Lake in a Mustang convertible with her girlfriend Rachel, her banned bikini, and two seniors from Clark Falls High.

"That's the first I've heard about that," I said. "Pete and Melody haven't said a word."

"That's because Pete and Melody don't know about it," Roger said. "I was coming home from the hardware store, saw Brit get in the car down the hill there. Heard from Melody she'd gone to your place with an armload of books. I waited for the kid to come walking back up the hill four hours later. We had a little chat before she went in for supper."

He'd waited for her? For four hours? "No kidding."

"No kidding."

I chose my next words carefully. Actually, that's not true. I flat-out asked him what made having a chat with Brit Seward about her behavior *his* responsibility.

"Listen, Doc, it's not my place to be talking about it. But if you didn't know, Pete and Melody . . . well. They've been having a little rough patch here lately."

"Oh?" I thought of the night I'd overheard Roger talking to Pete, out on the deck at the country club. I didn't mention it. "That's too bad."

"Brit's a hell of a kid, but I'll tell you what. College prep smarts and that centerfold body and only thirteen years to know what to do with it all. That's a hell of a combination." He shook his head. "Point is, she's not making it any easier on 'em, all this running around. So we had a chat. One less thing for Pete and Mel to worry about."

We climbed the hill in silence. "Well," I finally said. "I guess it takes a village."

Roger stayed quiet for a moment. The moment passed. He flicked the ember from the end of his cigar, dropped the dead butt in his vest pocket, and said, "Careful, Doc."

We walked home without saying another word.

17.

EARLY THE NEXT MORNING, our front doorbell rang. When I answered, I found Roger standing on our stoop in a light jacket, khaki trousers, and hiking shoes.

Sara had gone for a run with Melody Seward. I'd just gotten a pot of coffee going. Roger had one hand in his jacket pocket, a steel thermal mug in the other.

"Morning," he said.

"Roger."

"Doc, I believe I owe you an apology."

After coming home the night before, I'd ranted to Sara for half an hour. She'd listened patiently, nodded along, and finally suggested that perhaps I was overreacting.

Maybe she'd been right. Either way, I didn't have the energy for a snit with a neighbor.

"Listen, forget it." I waved my hand. "I guess I'm a little touchy lately. Sara would tell you the same. No hard feelings."

"Well, I didn't like the way we left things. Wanted to come by and tell you that before the sun got too high."

"Come on in."

"Actually, I was just heading out for a walk," he said. "Thought I'd see if you'd mind keeping me company."

I was still in the sweatpants and T-shirt I'd slept in, and I didn't much feel like walking anywhere. On the other hand, I had a stack of student essays to grade before class on Monday, and I was already thinking of ways to avoid diving in. And Roger seemed to be hoping I'd agree.

So I threw on a pair of jeans, sneakers, and an old Dixson sweatshirt. On the way out of the house, I stopped in the kitchen long enough to fill a carry-along mug of my own.

Roger and I walked a short way down Sycamore Drive, chatting about the temperature. It was the first true fall morning so far. The air was crisp and misty, and the lawns all twinkled with dew. Halfway down the hill, Roger cut across a patch of empty ground. "Scenic route. Follow me." We crossed through a border of sumac and wildgrass and entered the nature preserve. Roger picked up a trampled deer path in the forest floor. "Here we go."

A hundred feet into the woods, the trees gathered in around us, and the temperature seemed to drop ten degrees. Occasional slivers of blue sky peeked in through the gaps in the whispering canopy high over our heads. The air smelled rich and musty; threads of steam leaked from our coffee mugs. The legs of my jeans were soaked from walking through the tall wet grass at the border, and I was glad I'd put on the sweatshirt. "When is tick season again?"

Roger chuckled. "It opens up here in a bit."

I ducked a branch and followed along.

"This was actually Omaha country back when," he said as we walked. "The Ponca were mostly on the other side of the river."

"No kidding. Omaha Heights, huh?"

"Guess somebody forgot to do their homework when they named the place." Roger winked and glanced over his shoulder, in the general direction of Ponca Heights behind us. "Or, hell. Maybe they just thought it sounded better. Big root sticking up here. Watch your step."

We walked in silence for a while, listening to the early-morning chatter of the birds, the creak and sigh of the treetops above, the sound of our feet crunching along through last year's leaf litter.

Though it was only September, I already missed fall back home. A New England autumn is like an explosion; by comparison, autumn in Clark Falls arrived quietly, in muted shades. If you didn't pay attention, you might not even notice the season changing in front of your eyes.

I began to wonder, the farther Roger and I walked into the woods, if the leaves would change before we made it home. The trail was narrow, too narrow to take side by side through the thicker timber. At some point I'd begun to notice that tree limbs had been pruned back in spots; the scarred ends of the branches had dried and gone brown. That was the first time I realized that we weren't on a deer path. I'd already started to suspect that we weren't on a casual morning walk, either.

Meanwhile, I'd worked up a sweat. My coffee was gone, and I was getting tired of carrying the empty mug. Though all the neighborhood patrolling had improved my fitness over the past few weeks, the hilly terrain inside the refuge had me breathing through the mouth.

"You okay back there, Doc?"

"Shipshape," I said. "How far does this go, anyway?"

"Not much farther. There's a good spot to turn around up ahead."

In a few minutes, we climbed a rise and emerged into a small clearing ringed with gnarly oaks and tall, slender birch trees, their white bark peeling like old paper.

"End of the line," he said.

"You might have to carry me back."

"We'll catch a breather here."

Ten or twelve feet away from where we stood, there grew a head-high stand of stalky, fernlike foliage, dotted with purple spots, scattered with clumps of small white flowers. Roger saw me looking and said, "Hemlock."

"What?"

"Same stuff they used on Socrates, if you believe the story."

"No kidding."

"Didn't used to grow here," Roger said. "Showed up one spring a few years ago. Gets thicker every year now."

He stood there with his coffee mug in one hand, the other in his jacket pocket, the same as he'd looked standing on our front stoop an hour earlier. Except for a little sweat-darkened area along the edges of his hairline, you'd never know we'd just trudged a mile and a half through heavy timber.

"Look there. Don't touch."

I saw where he pointed: woody vines growing close to the ground, winding in and out of the hemlock stand. Waxy green leaves, some tinged red at the tips.

"Know what that is?"

I smiled. "Afraid I wouldn't have made much of a Boy Scout."

"Poison ivy." He made a circular gesture around his head. "You can walk a mile in any direction without running into that stuff again. Just seems to grow right here for some reason. Funny."

His gaze seemed distant. I felt a tingle in my bowels. By then I thought I knew where we were standing. Standing here felt uncomfortable.

"Roger," I said.

"They found my boy there." He raised his mug to his lips, nodding toward the hemlock grove. "Ten years in April. He was a bookworm too. Not like Brit, but he did always like to read. The other day I thought, you know, he might have been in one of Doc's classes over there on campus now."

I didn't know what to say.

"The search came right through here," he said. "They figured, whoever took Brandon... they figured he must have still had him then. Had him somewhere. Figured he brought him here later. After."

"Roger," I said. "I don't—"

"One theory went that he might have made himself part of the search," Roger said. "He could have dropped Brandon's backpack in here on purpose. Gotten things started in a direction. Joined the volunteers so he'd know which areas had been cleared off the grid already. He could have doubled back later, used the search tracks to hide his own." He shrugged. "That was one theory. There were others. None of those ever checked out either."

Normally, I don't go in for capital-letter ideas like Good and Evil. As my students approach their critical essays on classroom reading assignments, I tell them that reliance on absolutes is—generally speaking—the wrong tool for the job.

This makes it difficult to describe what I felt standing next to Roger, gazing at the plot of overgrown soil that had once held the body of his murdered son. All I can say is that it was clear and sunny that day, but my memory of that clearing is black and overcast.

"They say if you leave it alone, it'll eventually take over the whole area." Roger took a sip of his coffee and nodded at the hemlock grove. "Gets thicker every year."

We didn't say much on the long walk back. After we'd finally left Roger's well-worn footpath to Brandon Mallory's original grave site—after we'd waded back through the boundary of sumac and wildgrass, and crossed the ground back to Sycamore Drive—Roger finally said, "I guess it probably seems like I stick my nose in where it doesn't belong sometimes," he said. "Maybe it's true."

"Listen, Roger—"

"The fact is, when it comes to our little circle, I don't much think in terms of 'neighbors.' " He opened his mug and tossed the last of his coffee onto the ground. "Pete and Melody, Barry and Trish, all the kids. Michael. Now you and Sara. This might come out sounding dramatic, Doc, but I think of you folks more as family."

I closed my mouth and said nothing.

"My son was taken in broad daylight." He hooked a pinky finger through the handle of his mug and walked along with his hands in his trouser pockets. The sun seemed to be turning the clock backward now, from autumn back to summer. "Middle of a school week, plenty of folks around. But nobody remembered seeing a thing.

"Hell, I know what it's like," he said. "You get tied up in your own life. Got your own job, your own bills, your own lawn to mow. You get a promotion. Build that nice house in Spoonbill Circle." He tipped his head back, gesturing down the hill. "Get the kids into the school district."

We walked.

"More people show up with the same idea. All of them living their lives. Neighborhood gets bigger, starts to spread out. Pretty soon you're nodding to the folks next door when you get the paper in the morning and you don't even know who lives across the street. Next thing you know, you're living in a great big maze. Turn left instead of right one day, you could end up lost in your own subdivision."

Don't, I thought. I saw where he was going. I didn't want him to go there. Not like this.

But Roger had something to say, and he'd been waiting all this time to say it. So I stayed quiet and let him.

"Maybe if we all mind each other's business a little, what happened to Brandon won't happen to Brit Seward," he said. "Or little Sofie, God forbid. Or Jordan or Jake. Maybe what happened to you and Sara at your place won't happen to anyone down the hill."

Was I being unfair?

"Maybe some of these other things you hear about happening other places... maybe they won't happen quite as often around here."

Wasn't there at least a small part of me that understood? Even agreed, to a point?

"Or maybe we can't change a thing," Roger said. "But it seems like we can sure as hell try."

Your own safety is at stake when your neighbor's house is ablaze. The ancient poet Horace was said to have written that line. I know because it's printed on the inside cover of the Ponca Heights Neighborhood Directory, which we kept in a drawer in the kitchen. It's also printed on the business card Roger had given us in case we ever needed to contact him at his Safer Places office. It was the organization's motto. The Safer Places version of *Always Be Prepared.*

I'd only been half-joking when I'd told Roger I wouldn't have made a very good Boy Scout.

"Well," he said as we reached the sidewalk in front of my house. "Thanks."

"For what?"

"For the company. Hell of a walk back up there."

A hell of a walk. Yes.

"I guess I just wanted to explain where I was coming from last night," Roger said. "Felt like we got onto some bad footing, and I'm sorry for that."

Over in the common, Trish Firth pushed the twins on the kiddie swings. She saw us and waved. We waved back. We'd been gone nearly two hours. I wondered if Sara was home yet.

"Roger," I said. "I'm so sorry about what happened to your family."

He nodded. "I know we haven't talked about it much. But you and Sara shouldn't feel like it's off-limits."

"I didn't know Brandon," I said. "And I didn't know Clair. But I can imagine how much you loved them." I meant every word of this. "I *can't* imagine what a thing like that does to a person."

"Well, I'd be a liar if I said you get over it. But everybody loses someone eventually." He shrugged and smiled a little, watching the Firth twins. "I guess we all learn how to move on."

"The place you showed me just now. What you shared with me up there?" I nodded as sincerely as I could. "I want you to know that I don't take it lightly."

"Meant a lot to have you there, Doc."

I said something cruel then. Part of me regretted saying it even as the words left my mouth. Part of me would say it again. "I also want you to know that I've never, in my entire life, felt as manipulated as I feel right now."

Roger's face seemed to jump. He looked at me as though I'd slapped him.

"Shame on you," I said.

Over in the common, the Firth twins giggled and kicked their legs, swinging back and forth in their bright blue safety harnesses. Trish smiled and tickled their feet as they came near, pushing them away again. If she could sense anything wrong between Roger and me, she didn't show it.

For a moment, Roger's expression seemed flat. Then his eyes went dark.

I realized that I'd never seen anger on Roger Mallory's face before that moment. If I had, maybe things would have happened differently. Or maybe not.

Either way, I left him standing there and went inside.

18.

THERE'S WEAR AND TEAR IN A MARRIAGE, my dad once told me. He was a lawn chair philosopher, Joe Callaway, with tavern-tested analogies for almost any occasion. For some reason, he seemed especially drawn to the topic of family relations, and by his retirement years, my father had accumulated more homespun marriage advice than Dr. Phil. *You drop it sometimes. Bang it around a little. It picks up tiny little cracks you can't even see.*

He told me that everyday moisture finds its way into those cracks over the years. Sweat, tears, plain old rain. If you don't stay on top of things, when the weather turns cold, the moisture expands. The cracks get wider.

That's how it happens, he said. *People think they're solid, then boom—one day the floor falls in.*

By late October, the weather in our house had cooled. It

wasn't any one thing. That summer and fall had been an exercise in displacement and exhaustion; first had come the discombobulating news of the pregnancy, followed by the move from Boston to Clark Falls, followed by the attack, and finally the miscarriage. This string of events had been like one cold shower after another, and Sara and I hadn't been physically intimate in months. Now, with school in session, we saw each other less. Argued more.

We'd been jarred out of alignment before, but for some reason, this time, the harder we tried to recalibrate, the more we seemed to tweak things out of shape. After a while, the constant need to wrestle the steering wheel became a frustration all its own.

As the semester wore on—as Sara's new job increased its demands on her time, and as my own step backward into what amounted to academic grunt work gradually wore my spirit down—it seemed almost as if we'd run out of gas.

I'd been looking forward to the last weekend in November. Sara had a conference in Albany, not far from Boston—a lovely afternoon's train ride through the Berkshire Mountains on the Lake Shore extension. I saw a chance for us to get back to the basics. A trip together back to our old stomping grounds. Find a B&B in Brookline or Cambridge. Spend the weekend. Come home remembering each other again.

Sara said, "You want to hang around an econ conference."

"Under no circumstances," I told her. "But the conference ends Thursday."

"What about your classes?"

"I can fly out Friday morning," I said. "Meet you at the train station. I'll be Cary Grant and you can be Eva Marie Saint."

She smiled. "It sounds nice."

"Doesn't it?"

Her smile faded slowly. After a minute, she sighed.

"To be honest," she said, "I'd been thinking I could use the time away."

"Exactly. It'll be perfect."

"For myself."

She looked at me like she wished she could think of a better way to say it. Her eyes said, *Don't be mad.* Her mouth said, "To recharge my batteries, I guess. I don't know. Empty out my head."

Class, do you see what I'm doing here?

Observe these techniques:

I begin with a brief anecdote about my father. As far as anyone knows, the anecedote might not even be true. But I've salted it with believable, blue-collar detail, and there's probably no way to judge its authenticity for sure.

It doesn't really matter what my father actually said or didn't say. My intent is to establish tone and perspective. My own reliability as narrator. The tone is meant to be down-to-earth; the perspective is meant to be that of a regular Joe. The kind of Joe who thinks of his father's advice. Did you notice that I named my father Joe?

Joe happens to be my father's name, but I could have named him anything. I have a PhD in English literature; I could just as easily have started with a passage from Shakespeare, or Faulkner, or even Gertrude Stein.

But then maybe I'd seem elevated when I want to seem relatable. Notice the way I describe my marriage as though it were a car. Most everybody has driven a car.

Sara's job is "demanding." We infer that perhaps she's been spending more time at work than at home. My job is described—no offense to you, Class—as a "step backward." An understandable disappointment for a once-tenured professor. Maybe even vaguely unfair.

No doubt my wife and I had any number of conversations between August and October. Maybe, at some point in time, one of these conversations hurt Sara's feelings. Maybe there was a time when I'd made her feel rejected? Like I cared more about my own feelings than I cared about hers?

We can't be sure. At my choosing, I've related only one

conversation. A conversation that left *me* feeling rejected. In this conversation, I'm the one who appears to be trying.

Do you see what I'm doing?

Time to get it over with.

The night I slept with Melody Seward:

She came over to talk to Sara, who was still in Albany. I was working my way through a bottle of overpriced Shiraz and feeling sorry for myself.

Melody was obviously upset, perhaps bordering on distraught. It was past nine o'clock on Friday night, and I asked her to come inside. She hesitated; we'd never gotten to know each other especially well, and we'd never been alone together. But she clearly needed to be somewhere other than home. Sofia was at Melody's mother's house; Brit was sleeping over at her girlfriend Rachel's.

And so she came in.

Pete was having an affair, she eventually told me. A woman Melody worked with at the bank. A loan officer, not one of the other tellers.

He'd claimed to have broken it off two months ago, but he hadn't been truthful. As a matter of fact, he was with the fucking bitch right now. Two glasses of wine, and her hands were still shaking.

I opened another bottle. If this is starting to sound like a horrible cliché, it's not over yet.

I don't spill the ups and downs of my marriage. Not to my dad, or even to Charlie Bernard. I've always been firm in thinking that my marriage is between Sara and me.

But Melody poured out her guts on our living room couch, and I commiserated with tales of my own. It only seemed fair. Humane, even. We finished the second bottle of wine, and I opened another.

After all of that wine, it happened just like it happens in the movies. One minute I was being a good listener; the next, she was returning the courtesy.

And then, somehow, we were all over each other. Music swells, clothing drops to the floor.

From there, it wasn't like the movies at all.

It was awkward. Mechanical. Even cold. No gasps or moans or breathless sighs. We grappled and struggled and stopped before either one of us had finished. After we'd dressed, we could barely look each other in the eye.

At four in the morning, Melody went home to 36 Sycamore Court like a disgraced bridesmaid sneaking back to her hotel room. Pete hadn't yet returned.

I collected our empty wine bottles, our stained glasses, and threw them all in the trash.

Twelve hours later—around four o'clock that Saturday afternoon—our front doorbell rang.

When I answered, I found Roger standing on the stoop. He looked at me like he'd heard a story that made him sad.

"This isn't working," he said.

Saturday, December 17—4:35 p.m.

19.

"HOLD THERE A MINUTE." Douglas Bennett leans forward. "Mallory actually stated a date. December sixteenth."

"A loose thread," I tell him. "That's what he said. He had this whole speech worked out about how a strong community was this tight-knit fabric, and if you pull on a loose thread, everything starts to unravel."

"He verbally directed you to move out of the neighborhood by sixteen December. Yesterday. I have that right?"

"He said that once a hole gets started, it only gets bigger. He said that there's no use patching the hole if you don't fix the snag. On Planet Roger, apparently, I'm the snag."

Bennett folds his hands. "Who else have you told about this?"

"Nobody."

"Not even what's-his-name. Michael?"

"Nobody," I say.

That statement, of course, includes my wife. I force myself to look at Sara. I'm cringing inside. Waiting.

She's staring at the floor. Her shoulders are rigid, hands limp in her lap.

Bennett glances at me and says, "Why don't I leave you two alone for a few minutes."

Before he can make a move, Sara draws herself together and stands up. Without looking at me, she walks around the table, collects her coat and purse, and leaves.

I sit like a block of wood and watch her go. What else can I do? It's pointless to run after her. I can't change anything. There's nothing I can say that won't sound absurd. I can't make myself disappear into this chair. Did I really think this moment wouldn't happen? How could I let it happen like this?

In a minute, I hear the glass doors rattle at the front of Bennett & Partners Trial Law. A minute after that, I hear the muffled sound of a car door slamming. An engine turning over. A distant bark of tires.

The silence settles.

Bennett finally sighs. "Tough day."

I nod.

"Listen," he says. "I know it doesn't mean much right now, but you've done the right thing. Now that I know the whole story, we can start looking at ways—"

"Oh, I'm not finished."

Bennett raises an eyebrow.

"There's more," I tell him.

"How much more?"

"I'm just getting started."

He settles back.

"I need you to meet somebody," I say.

20.

IT'S ALREADY DARK by the time we get on the road.

We take the Interstate forty minutes south, to a Flying J truck stop at the I-680 junction. Bennett drives us in a Mercedes instead of his personal BMW. The Mercedes is owned by the firm and parked in a secured lot behind the building.

By changing vehicles and using the rear exit, we manage to leave the Channel Five Clark Falls news van parked out front of Bennett & Partners. The Mercedes has heated leather seats and a speakerphone system, which Bennett can dial by voice. He talks on the phone half the trip, calling people at their homes, interrupting their weekends, explaining the basics of my situation one time after another.

He speaks to one of his interns back in Clark Falls. He speaks to a youth psychologist in Des Moines. He speaks to someone in Omaha who apparently knows everything about computers. He speaks to someone who apparently knows everything about photography in general, digital photography in particular.

Thirty miles out of town, Bennett leaves a voice-mail message at the county attorney's office, asking for a return call. Then he punches a button in the console by his hand.

"As long as we're exploring avenues," he says, "we should discuss Miss Seward."

"What else is there to discuss?"

"I'm sure this is something that you've considered," Bennett says, "but let's suppose that Mallory is right. She's developed an infatuation, or whatever you want to call it. A crush on you."

"I really don't think that's the case."

"Paul, if I've learned anything, I've learned that nobody—and I mean nobody—knows the teenage mind."

"She's barely a teenager."

"We live in troubling times." He checks his mirrors and merges into the passing lane. "For the sake of argument. She's got a crush."

"Okay."

"The girl finds out about you and Mom." He raises a finger. "*Step*mom. The woman I talked to on the phone just now, she'd tell you that can be a whole other can of worms."

Isn't he right? Isn't there a part of me that's already considered this? "I understand what you're saying. I just don't think—"

"I'm only telling you what our youth counselor might say." He passes a pickup truck pulling an empty livestock trailer and fades back into the cruising lane. "And what she might say is, this pattern of Brittany's—getting herself into trouble, getting herself grounded every five minutes—all of that could be her way of getting Daddy's attention. Maybe even her way of punishing him."

"Or she's bored."

"And maybe *this,*" Bennett says, gesturing between us, indicating our otherwise nonexistent relationship, "is her way of punishing *you.*"

My face hurts where Pete kicked me, and my head has been throbbing all afternoon. Despite my having gobbled a handful of Advils, the pain seems to be getting worse instead of better.

The oncoming headlights hurt my eyes. Even in the smooth-gliding Mercedes, the whine of tires on cold blacktop sounds like a drill in my ears. It occurs to me that maybe I should have seen a doctor after all. I could have a concussion or something.

"Maybe we're fixated on this deadline of Mallory's," he says, "instead of a more plausible explanation."

"Hell of a coincidence."

"Agreed."

"I know he's behind this."

"He's certainly involved. We know that much."

"He's got to be manipulating her somehow."

"Or maybe it's the other way around." Bennett glances over to gauge my reaction. "Can you be absolutely sure that Brittany Seward wasn't aware of this disagreement between you and Mallory? Even this eviction date you say he imposed on you?"

How can I be sure of anything? I see the bright lights of the Flying J a mile or so up ahead, illuminating the winter dark.

"In any case, you need to prepare yourself. This is going to get unpleasant for everybody."

"What does that mean?"

"It means that you've been accused of felony sexual misconduct," Bennett says. "And whether this girl is lying of her own accord or lying for Roger Mallory, she's your accuser. Which means we're going to need to beat her up a little."

"No it doesn't," I say. "I don't want—"

"It's not my idea of a good time either," Bennett assures me. "My niece is Brittany's age. But you're over a barrel. You need to understand that."

"I need to talk to Brit. This is ridiculous."

"Oh, no." He wags one gloved finger. "That's not going to be an option."

I say nothing. Our exit is coming up.

"Listen up, Professor. If I hear you went anywhere near that kid without me in the room, you won't have to fire me again. I'll drop your ass like it's radioactive. Let me know that you're hearing this."

"I'm hearing this."

"That's good." Bennett takes the off-ramp and falls in line behind a convoy of eighteen-wheelers, all following each other down the exit lane, around the curve of a service road, and up the hill toward shelter. "Now. When are you going to explain to me why the hell we've driven to a truck stop in the middle of nowhere?"

"There." I point to a neon sign around the corner of the main building. The diner. "He said to meet him there."

"You know, I've handled a number of noteworthy cases for a town this size." Bennett tilts his chin as though casting his mind back. "Five years ago, I defended a man who accidentally hired an undercover state trooper to murder his wife. Not a nice fellow. But a clear case of entrapment." He peels away from the caravan of trucks on their way to the bright halide glare of the fueling pavilion. "Nothing quite as cloak-and-dagger as this, however."

"I'm glad you're enjoying yourself."

"I was being sardonic."

There aren't any parking spots near the building. I see a few open spots in the middle rows. Bennett rolls slowly past each one, tires crunching over scattered road grit on the cracked surface of the parking lot. At last he pulls into an open space beneath a lamppost fifty yards away. We're perched on a treeless knob off the Interstate, miles of wide-open farmland all around us, and I can hear the wind howling outside the car. Bennett senses me looking at him.

"Door dents," he says of his parking job. "It's not my car."

With nightfall, the temperature has plummeted. The cutting wind catches us as we step outside the car, slapping our faces, pushing us around. We clutch our flapping coats and hustle across the lot, the pavement dry as old bone in the cold.

Inside, the diner is warm and boisterous, packed with truckers and travelers. The air smells like meat loaf and fried chicken; silverware clatters against plates. Through speakers in the ceiling, a twangy voice sings a country-western rendition of "Holly Jolly Christmas." Colored lights blink and twinkle all around the buffet.

Bennett nods at the garland-wrapped sign in the entry. "Apparently, we're to seat ourselves."

I'm already scanning the tables and booths. We're fifteen minutes late, and I'm wondering if we've blown it.

Then I see a head pop up. Last booth in the back, away from the windows.

It's no wonder I missed him. I doubt I'd have recognized Darius Calvin at all if it weren't apparent that he recognizes me.

"There he is." I start through the dining area. "Come on."

A middle-aged waitress with sinewy arms and a pot of coffee in each hand says, "Be with you boys in a minute."

"Last booth in the back," I tell her. Suddenly I'm starving. "Love some of that coffee."

"You got it, hon."

We make our way back. I slide into the booth without waiting for an invitation and say, "Guess you're working on a new look."

Darius Calvin says, "Guess you're late."

"Sorry." The difference in his appearance truly is startling. He's shaved his head bald, and a dense black beard covers his jaw. He looks a little bit like Isaac Hayes. I touch my own head. "Isn't it colder with no hair?"

"Man, that psycho cop been by twice since I seen you." He pushes back from his plate—a half-eaten pile of Salisbury steak and mashed potatoes, all smothered in brown gravy. Judging by the gelid dregs in the empty plate by his elbow, he's working on his second helping. He looks to his left, leans forward, drops his voice. "Tells me I see you come around again, I better be callin' him." Darius runs a hand over his bare scalp as if to remind himself of how different he looks.

I play dumb for Bennett's sake. "Which cop?"

"Man, you know which cop."

"Stockman?"

He spreads his fingers. *There you go*. Then he picks up his fork and his knife and saws off a bite of meat. "Saw you on the news."

"Oh?" I haven't seen the news yet.

"Guess you're in some trouble."

"It seems I am."

Darius Calvin points sideways with his fork, still chewing, eyes still on me. "Who's this?"

Bennett has remained standing there at the end of the table in his suede overcoat and gloves. He raises his eyebrows at me.

"This is my attorney, Douglas Bennett. Bennett, this is Darius Calvin. Tell him who you are, Darius."

"*You* called *me,* man."

He has a point. "Bennett, meet the man who attacked Sara."

Bennett says, "Excuse me?"

"Darius here broke into our house in July."

"Motherfucker hit me with a golf club," Darius says.

I nod. "It's true."

Now Douglas Bennett looks at me closely. He looks at our new friend Darius Calvin.

I say, "Remember when you said we didn't have to worry about how crazy anything was going to sound?"

Bennett stands there.

"I spoke prematurely," he finally says.

He takes off his coat and slides in beside me.

21.

I HIT THE BUFFET while Darius Calvin tells Bennett everything I already know. That he moved to Clark Falls ten months ago, from Ames, where he'd been out of work. That his cousin had gotten him a job at fifteen dollars an hour as a forklift operator in a medical supply warehouse on the south side of town.

According to Darius, he hadn't been aware of his cousin's side business until one Saturday night in June, when he was pulled over in a borrowed car, searched, and discovered to be carrying a loaded pistol, four glass pipes, and a spare tire lined with Baggies of methamphetamine.

"Told the cop that shit wasn't mine," he's saying as I return to the booth. "He's got his thumbs all in his belt, says yeah, he's never heard *that* one before. Look. I pay my bills, go to work, do my job, go home. Right? It ain't even my car."

My plate was still warm from the dishwasher when I

started down the buffet line. Now it's loaded with pot roast and mashed potatoes, two chicken drumsticks, and half a dozen deep-fried shrimp that caught my eye. I'm actually salivating.

"And this was Sergeant Stockman," Bennett says. "The officer who pulled you over?"

"How many times you want me to say it?"

"I'm sorry. Please, go on."

I start eating while Darius tells Bennett the rest. This food tastes incredible. I might have to go back for a second helping myself. When our waitress comes by with coffee, I want to hug her. She frowns at me. "Happened to your face, hon?"

"Long story."

"Always." She winks and fills my cup. Bennett and Darius fall silent while she goes around the table, topping off each of our mugs. She hardly stops pouring.

After she moves on, Bennett says, "I don't understand."

"He's telling me maybe he can do me a favor. Tells me if I do *him* a favor, maybe he cuts me loose on this stop. Says maybe he can call in an abandoned vehicle on State 175; that way, when it comes back on Tree, Tree just says somebody stole it."

"Tree?"

"My cousin." Darius shrugs. "He's six-ten."

"Ah."

"I wasn't gonna hurt your lady." Darius looks directly at me when he says this. "You know I wasn't."

I tell him that I believe him. I told him the same thing two weeks ago. The night I followed him home from the medical supply warehouse.

"Mr. Calvin," Bennett says. "Darius. I don't—"

"Dude told me it was all put on. Training volunteers or some shit. Tells me I'm supposed to walk in some house like a big black mofo and then scoot out the back when the people come home."

He makes quote marks in the air around *the people*. Listening to all of this, Bennett looks like he's just woken up in a strange room.

"Tells me some white folks got broke into last year, and he wants it to play like that. Shows me where to stand, what door to go in. Night he calls, tells me the car I'm looking for, tells me to wait 'til I see the headlights come up. White lady in bed when I go in, I figure it's all part of it. I'm just playin' along when this guy here comes in like Die Hard, starts whackin' on me with a golf club."

"Wait." Bennett actually pushes at the air with his hand, as if trying to make the words back up. "Sergeant Stockman took you to Paul and Sara's house? Before the night of the break-in?"

Darius shakes his newly bald head. Scratches his freshly grown beard. I'll bet his own mother wouldn't have recognized him at first glance. "The other one. Dude from the TV commercials, 'bout three one mornin'."

"Roger," I tell Bennett, growing impatient. Why isn't he getting this? "Roger staged the whole thing. He hired Darius to break into my house, scared the hell out of the whole neighborhood, earned thirty new volunteers for his goddamned neighborhood patrol, and told us not to thank him for the new alarm system." I tear off a piece of chicken with my teeth. "Roger Mallory hired this man to break into our house."

"Shit," Darius says. "He gave me a key."

Bennett looks at me.

He looks at Darius.

After a long minute, he says, "Please go on."

It's past nine o'clock by the time we get back on the road.

We ride most of the way home in silence. The lights of the Flying J slowly recede in the distance behind us, becoming a white glow on the horizon, slowly blending into the black. Ahead of us, the Interstate is dark and vacant.

We're halfway back to Clark Falls by the time Douglas Bennett finally speaks. "You found him how?"

"In our files."

"Your files?"

"The files I found in Roger's house."

"Ah."

For the first time all day, my headache is gone. My face doesn't seem to be throbbing anymore. I'm stuffed to the gills with food from a truck stop diner, the first I've eaten since that fried egg sandwich this morning in jail. It's hard to believe that was only this morning. It's hard to believe this morning was only earlier today.

I wonder if Sara is home. Is she asleep? Is she crying? Is she stuffing my clothes in the fireplace and dousing them with barbecue lighter fluid from the garage? I imagine her making her rounds, battening down the hatches before turning in for the day.

I lean my head against the passenger window. The glass is cold and feels good on my skin. The car's luxury glide seems to work like a lullaby; I doze for a few miles, wake up when my head falls forward. I can't get comfortable after that, so I sit up and watch the road.

Ten miles from Clark Falls, Douglas Bennett tilts his head and says, "And you've been keeping this to yourself why?"

"The victorious warrior wins first," I tell him. "And then goes to battle."

He looks at me. "What the hell does that mean?"

I'm starting to wonder.

22.

MY KITCHENETTE SUITE at the Residence Inn is clean, comfortable, and larger than my first apartment. There's a bedroom, a living room, and the advertised kitchenette, a spacious bathroom with a whirlpool tub, and a deck overlooking the river. Two televisions, two telephones, and free high-speed Internet access, if you have a computer. The Clark Falls Police Department has mine. Still, a person could live here comfortably.

I call my real house. Nobody answers. I call three more times before giving up.

The shower stings my swollen eye. When the hot water runs out, I dry off, put on sweats and a T-shirt, punch the button for Guest Services, and ask them to bring me a six-pack of anything.

While I'm waiting, I call my house again. Nobody answers.

There's a knock on the door, I sign for my beer. Good old-fashioned Budweiser in cans. My dad's beer. I wonder if Sara's gotten in touch with my folks.

Time passes. I want to sleep, but I can't seem to keep my eyes closed. I want to read, but I can't seem to concentrate. I crack a new beer and flip through television channels. There's not much on.

I end up watching a nature program about honeybees. Apparently, there's this virus, endemic to the American honeybee population, which causes some pupal bees to develop deformed wings. No flying. Early death. Very sad for the colony.

But according to the nature show, some Japanese scientists have managed to isolate a different virus, which is 99 percent the same as the deformed-wing virus, in the brains of aggressive guardian bees. According to the show, this 1 percent variation may be the difference between mangled wings and the instincts that serve to protect the colony.

This shit about bees amazes me. I finish another beer and pick up the telephone. It's one o'clock in the morning. Normal people are asleep.

"Hello?"

"You must be happy," I say.

Roger sighs in my ear. "Paul."

"You need help." I imagine him sitting alone in the dark. "Professionally. Do you even realize that?"

"It's late. Why don't you try and get some sleep."

"Why don't you tell me how you can do this?"

"I didn't create the situation."

I can't help laughing. Where have I heard that one? "You're a piece of work."

"I think we've established that you wouldn't be able to understand."

"Explain it to me again."

I crack open my last beer while I wait to hear what he'll say. Have I struck a nerve? Have I forced him to reconsider his actions? Or is he just wondering if I've got him on speakerphone?

During the long pause on Roger's end of the line, Roger also appears on the television. The effect is surreal. It's almost as though he's paused our conversation to stroll onto the screen in a pair of khakis and a denim shirt. In the background, guys in hard hats and safety glasses work on tying a rope to a tree limb.

Remember, TV Roger says. *Trees can provide second-story access to nimble intruders. And overgrown shrubs make good hiding places. Prune your low-hanging limbs and keep your hedges trimmed.*

This neighborhood safety message is brought to me by the Safer Places Organization.

Telephone Roger says, "Good-bye, Paul."

"There's a virus that infects the brains of honeybees," I tell him, but the line is already dead in my hand.

I meet Douglas Bennett at his office early in the morning. He's pulled in one of his interns from her Sunday off, an attractive young woman who doesn't seem to like me very much. At the moment, she's out getting coffee and bagels from some place down the street.

I'm sitting in Bennett's chair, behind his desk, in front of his computer, attempting to show him a few of the things I've discovered since finding Roger Mallory's neighborhood intelligence files.

"You've certainly been doing your homework," Bennett says.

"You sound impressed."

"Actually, I was just considering the fact that the police have confiscated *your* files."

"That's okay. I can work from memory."

"What occurs to me," he says, "is that the police could be forgiven for imagining that *you're* the one gathering intelligence on your neighbors."

I honestly haven't even considered this. But there's not much point in worrying about it now. "Roger started it."

"Of course."

"Here." I point to Bennett's computer screen, where I've pulled up the property information on 34 Sycamore Court from the county assessor's Web site. There's a link to the sales data for the house in which Sara and I now live. "This is everyone who's owned the place going back ten years."

"And you say you've contacted all of them?"

"That's right." There are three sets of names available, listed in order of most recent to oldest. I point to the last entry in the list, farthest down from ours: James and Myrna Webster. "I talked to Myrna. They lived here almost ten years. Husband walked out on her, she couldn't swing the mortgage alone, sold the place, and moved home to Sioux City with the kids."

I point to the next owner: Fallon, Brett M. "Wife's name is Tammy, they have five kids, bought a bigger house in the Himebaughs."

I move up to the most recent name on the list, just below Sara's and mine: Kennedy, Cynthia B. We'd purchased the house from Cynthia and her husband, Bill. "She's a finance manager, he's a computer programmer. Dual income, no kids, no plans for kids, moved to Denver for Bill's job."

"I feel like I know them already. Go on."

I run my finger back down to James and Myrna. "These folks knew Roger's whole family. If you ask Myrna Webster what the Mallorys were like as neighbors, you get nothing but warm fuzzies and sympathy." I continue up the list. "Brett and Tammy were in the house when Roger started Safer Places. Ask them, and they'll talk about Roger's mood swings."

Bennett listens quietly.

"Bill and Cynthia also belonged to the neighborhood association. Ask them, and they'll hem and haw and finally admit that Roger seemed nice enough but always made them feel a little uncomfortable. Especially Cynthia. She'll come right out. Not a Roger Mallory fan."

Bennett appears to be digesting what I'm telling him, but it's hard to gauge his reaction.

"And don't forget Ben Holland," I say.

"Who?

"Michael's partner."

"The one with the yard signs."

"That's right."

I'm attempting to illustrate the pattern as I see it. Three sets of neighbors in the house across the circle from Roger in ten years' time. Four including Sara and me. Our opinions of Roger deteriorate steadily.

Bennett understands what I'm getting at. "We can try talking to others in the community," he says, though I get the distinct impression that he's humoring me. "Maybe we can find a few other residents with complaints against the neighborhood patrol."

"I've got a list of names you can start with."

"So." Bennett kicks me out of his chair. "The character assassination portion of our defense package would appear to be under way."

"I was just thinking, maybe we don't have to beat up Brit. If we can discredit Roger first, show his personality changing over the years, maybe..."

"Maybe." Bennett waits for me to sit down on the other side of the desk, then folds his hands on his yellow notepad. "But we're getting ahead of ourselves. I have some news. Not the kind of news we'd like, I'm afraid." Bennett drums his fingers and leans back. I wait. "I've spoken with the prosecutor's office this morning," he says. "She called an hour ago to advise me that additional charges will be forthcoming."

My heart sinks. "What additional charges?"

"Additional counts, to be accurate. Based on the search of your personal computer."

I close my eyes.

"We've scheduled a disposition conference for Wednesday morning. We'll learn more then." He writes down a date and time on the back of a business card and slides it across the desk. "For the moment, let's set aside past neighbors, and Roger

Mallory's mood patterns, and put our heads together on the matter at hand. Namely, your computer."

"Okay."

"Besides you and Sara, who has access?"

"Nobody."

"Nobody?"

"I've got a password." The tech guy from the university made me give him one when he set me up to log on to the campus network from home.

"Do you keep your password written down anywhere? A sticky note, maybe? In a file somewhere?"

The fact is, I have two handfuls' worth of passwords. The university, various online accounts—bank, bills, assorted merchants, journals, LexisNexis—all with different requirements for how to make up a proper password. How can anybody be expected to remember them all?

I sigh. "Sticky note." Inside the middle drawer of my desk.

Bennett nods and repeats the original question. "Besides you and Sara, who has access to your computer?"

The only person I can think of who has regular access to my computer, other than the cleaning service that comes in twice a month, is Brit Seward.

Bennett already knows the answer. He decides not to press it for now. "Anything else on there?"

"Anything else like what?"

"Ever look at any porn? Featuring adults?"

"No."

"Not even a little?"

"No," I say.

"How about the house? Have you given a key to any of the other neighbors? Take care of the mail when you're out of town, that kind of thing?"

"Michael," I say. "But he's the only person with the new alarm code."

"You've changed your alarm code recently?" Bennett scribbles on his notepad. "When did you change it?"

"After the thing with Roger."

"You'll have to be more specific."

"After I found all the stuff on us in Roger's house. After I called the police and looked like a fool."

"Okay."

In the background, the front doors of Bennett & Partners rattle. I hear what sounds like muffled cursing. After a pause, I hear footsteps approaching Bennett's office. A moment later, Bennett's intern enters, carrying a paper bag in one hand, a cardboard coffee carrier in the other.

"There's a reporter outside," she informs us. "She tried to block me coming in. If my hands weren't full I'd have punched her in the nose."

With one notable exception, the news media seems content for now with yesterday's lopsided exhibition match between Pete and me at Sycamore Court. "That would be Maya Lamb," I tell her.

"I know who it is."

She really doesn't seem to like me very much. I wonder if I should take it as consolation that she doesn't seem to like Maya Lamb very much either. She brings in breakfast and leaves it on Bennett's desk.

Bennett says, "Thank you, Debbie."

"You're welcome." She works one of the tall paper cups free of the carrier and awaits further instructions.

"Paul, your alarm system," Bennett says. "Mallory told you that he knew the owner, got you a deal on the installation. Is that right?"

"That's right."

"And what's the name of the company?"

"Sentinel One Incorporated," I tell him.

"Debbie, will you log on to the business guide and pull up..."

"Whatever I can find on Sentinel One Incorporated." She turns and walks out the way she walked in.

"Thank you, Debbie."

I hear a mumbled reply, fading down the hall.

"I apologize." Bennett looks at me and shrugs. "Seems nobody likes to work on Sundays anymore."

The truth is, I don't even remember the last thing we were talking about. I stand up. "I need to see Sara. Can I meet you back here later?"

"Actually, Paul—"

"I'm sorry, but I haven't been able to get her to answer the phone." All at once, I don't have room in my head to think about additional charges and who might have tampered with my computer or who has the alarm code to our house. I have things to tell Sara, things I need to make right, and at the moment all I'm able to think about is how to get the hell out of here without little Maya Lamb following me home. "This is ridiculous. I need to see her."

"Paul, I've spoken with Sara."

"You talked to her? When?"

"Five minutes after I spoke with the county attorney. She called."

"She called here?"

"Yes."

"What did she say?"

"She left a telephone number where she could be reached," he tells me. "In case I needed to contact her in the next few days."

"What number?"

Bennett sits there a moment.

"What's the number, Bennett?"

He says, "I feel you should know that she asked me not to tell you, Paul."

I can't believe this. I square my shoulders and open my mouth, ready to lay into him, but before I can say anything, he recites a telephone number with a 215 area code. Her mother's house in Philly.

"She said that she'd booked a flight out of Omaha for later this morning."

I sit back down in my chair.

Bennett looks sympathetic. "I'm sure she just needs a little time. To absorb everything."

He doesn't know the half of it.

"And we've still got a lot of ground to cover here."

I look at him.

"So." Bennett glances at his notepad. "When you decide it's time to change your alarm code, what exactly does that process involve?"

It's fully dark outside by the time I finally leave Bennett's office. The temperature has dropped below zero; except for a few wisps of steam rising from the storm sewers, and a few tiny snowflakes swirling like gnats in the air, the streets are void of activity. Even Maya Lamb is gone, having given up her vigil in the parking lot of Bennett & Partners, presumably for warmer climes. Everything is quiet.

Douglas Bennett is back on retainer. We've gone over everything from five different angles. I have a regular pit bull for a lawyer, and he's getting that game plan together. First thing tomorrow, he assures me, gears will turn. Wheels will be put into motion. We're going to fix this.

I find myself struggling to maintain optimism. Darius Calvin's conscience may have taken him as far as a truck stop forty miles out of town, but will we really be able to change his mind about standing up and telling the truth in court? Will Bennett's experts be able to debunk any of this so-called evidence people keep finding on my computer? Will my wife ever be able to look at me again?

It's been a long day, and maybe I'm just tired, but I don't even notice the headlights in my rearview mirror until I'm halfway downtown. It wouldn't occur to me that I'm being followed if we weren't the only two cars on the street, now the only two cars turning in to the parking lot of my new home at the Residence Inn. It still wouldn't occur to me that I'm being followed if I didn't look over and recognize Pete's silver Lexus SUV pulling into the space immediately beside me.

I cut my headlights. Pete cuts his.

Perfect.

Too worn out to be scared, I get out of the car and try to look at the upside: if Pete pounds me to death right here in the parking lot, even considering funeral expenses, this whole mess will probably end up being a lot cheaper.

Nothing happens for a minute. The Lexus just sits there, silent except for the tick of the engine under the hood.

It's too cold to stand around waiting. I'm about to walk over and knock on his window when the driver's-side door opens. Melody gets out. She's bundled up in a short ski coat and earmuffs, a thick fuzzy scarf around her neck. She looks like she's been crying for days.

"Paul." Her breath is white in the air.

I could stand right here until we both freeze to death, listening to the *bing bing bing* of the seat belt alarm drifting from inside the SUV, and I still wouldn't know what to do.

She closes her door. The interior light goes dark, and the sound stops. "I need to talk to you."

23.

ONE OF THE FEW THINGS my suite lacks is a full-sized coffee-maker. The little hotel-sized machine in the kitchenette makes only four cups, and the mugs that go with it are slightly smaller than normal size. I feel like I've invited Melody Seward for a dollhouse tea party.

She's sitting at the small breakfast table, fiddling with her wedding ring. I set a full mug in front of her and stand at the counter. She hasn't spoken since we took off our coats, and neither have I. I haven't spoken to Melody alone, in person, since the night we decided to crash our lives into each other.

After a long silence, she finally says, "I've seen the pictures."

"They can't be real," I tell her. It's the first thing that comes to me. "I hope you know that. Computers, hell, anybody can—"

"They're real. Some of them . . ." She wraps her hands

around the mug and watches the steam curl up. "I have to keep reminding myself that she's thirteen years old."

I don't honestly believe her. It's not that I think she's lying, I just think that she must be wrong. Brit's a smart kid. Too smart for this. Anyone can see that. All I can think to say is, "I've never seen them."

"Be thankful."

"I didn't make them, either."

"I know." Melody sighs. "I walked in on her in the bathroom while she was undressing for the shower one night. It was an accident. I knocked, but she had her iPod on."

I stand there with my coffee, wishing I could listen faster.

"I would have thought it was one of those stick-ons if she hadn't covered up so fast. Right here." She leans one hip forward and reaches around her back, pointing to her tailbone, a couple inches below the waist of her jeans. "A butterfly."

"Are you talking about a tattoo?"

"Somehow she and Rachel managed to get their hands on a pair of phony IDs. They went together, came out with matching ones. Butterflies. I swear, those two..."

I know the name Rachel, Brit's best friend and cohort. "What does—"

"Paul, this was in June." She looks at me. "A month before you and Sara moved in."

My fingers are tingling.

"I never told Pete. My God, his head would have exploded."

"This tattoo..."

"We had a long talk. Brit and I. We kept it between us girls. World's greatest stepmom, that's me." She smiles bitterly and shakes her head, as though recalling a foolish thought. "You can't see her tattoo in the pictures."

I feel myself starting to breathe faster. What is she telling me?

"It's just not there. In one of them, she's looking back at the camera, over her shoulder, and you can see..." She puts a hand over her eyes. "Christ, she's thirteen."

I never told Pete.

Is it possible that this is something Roger also doesn't know? Is it still theoretically possible that something might be permitted to occur within our cozy, well-monitored fiefdom without Roger Mallory's knowledge?

I honestly don't know whether to feel elated or heartbroken by this news. Melody is handing me a piece of information that can disprove any charges that I created the photographs I'm said to possess. She's also telling me that she believes the photographs are authentic, which means that *somebody* made them.

"I don't know what to do anymore," she says. "I'm just so goddamned worried about her."

My legs feel rubbery. I pull the other chair and sit down at the other side of the table. I'm not sure how to talk about this, how to phrase things. "Did Brit tell you anything? About... who it might be?"

"I sat down with her this afternoon. Pete and Sofie were asleep on the couch, and I went into her room and rubbed her back and told her that we loved her." She wipes her eyes. "I told her that if there was anything she needed to tell somebody, that I was there for her. She gave me a hug and broke down sobbing and didn't say a word."

What did she say when you told her about the tattoo? Did you tell her that you knew it couldn't be me? I can't seem to find a way to ask these things.

"We've had our ups and downs, Paul. She hasn't hugged me in... I don't even know when." Melody takes a ragged breath. "It's been harder as she's gotten older. Her mother doesn't even call on her birthday anymore. But I've never seen her like this."

I don't know what to say. I think about everything Douglas Bennett said about stepdaughters and stepmothers, but I'm out of my element.

"I want to shake her by the neck, but I'm afraid she'll crack in a million pieces." Melody rubs her eyes with a knuckle.

"God, what is she hiding?" She looks at the wall, the ceiling. "Why on earth would she go to *Roger*?"

I reach over and grab a box of tissues from the nearby lamp table. She thanks me. I wait until she's finished blowing her nose and dabbing her eyes. When the tears are dry, I ask, "What did Pete say?"

"I haven't told him yet. I haven't told anyone yet. I thought...I thought you should know first."

I reach out and touch her fingers.

"It's going to kill him when he finds out." She pulls her hand away and takes another tissue. "I'm so sorry about yesterday. Pete's always liked you. I hope you know that."

"Let me talk to her."

She rolls her eyes. *Sure.*

"I'm serious, Melody. Let me talk to her. Just the two of us. If she knows that I'm not mad at her...if she knows that I'm still her friend, that I'm on her side...I just don't believe that she could look me in the face and—"

"No, Paul. It's bad enough as it is. And if anybody finds out, you'll go to jail."

"Let me worry about that."

"No." She stands up. "I have to go. I'll call your lawyer in the morning, and I'll tell him what I just told you. I wanted you to know first."

She leaves her coffee untouched. I stare into mine, trying to decide how much of my side of this story I should be telling her. She deserves to know something. Then again, she's got her own set of problems. Does she really need more to think about right at this moment?

She's halfway into her coat by the time I cross the room. "Melody."

"Yes."

"Thank you."

We stand there a minute. I move my arms, intending a shrug, and Melody walks straight into me. It's like holding a Melody-sized pillow, all bundled up in her winter coat. We stand there for two or three seconds, and then she steps away. "I'll call your lawyer in the morning."

"Melody, I..." What do I say? "Sara knows what happened. With us, I mean. She's flown to her mother's."

She wipes her eyes, looks away.

"Pete?"

She shakes her head. No. Pete doesn't know yet.

There's a whole world of things that Pete doesn't know yet, isn't there? *Pete, I've got good news and bad news. The good news is, I didn't sleep with your daughter.*

"I'll call your lawyer in the morning," Melody says, grabbing her scarf on the way out the door.

24.

I'M IN THE MIDDLE OF DIALING Douglas Bennett at his home when I hear a knock. I hang up the phone, grab the earmuffs and wool mittens Melody forgot on the breakfast table, and hand her things forward as I open the door. "Here they are."

Roger Mallory looks at my hand, then looks up at me. He says, "I don't think they're my size."

The surprise of seeing him sets me back. I hold the door and take a deep breath. I gather myself.

Roger says, "I can deliver them if you want."

"What the hell are you doing here?"

"I thought we could talk."

"Oh, yeah?"

"Yes."

"You should be careful," I tell him. Why don't I close the

door? Why am I standing here, literally giving him an opening? "You could run into perception problems."

Roger smirks at that.

"What do you want, Roger?"

Without any apparent trace of irony, he looks me in the eye and says, "A truce."

Roger stands inside the door, holding his gloves in one hand, as if waiting for an invitation to sit.

I don't extend one. I go get my coffee from where I left it on the counter and sit down on the couch by myself. The coffee is lukewarm by now, but it tastes fine. I don't look at Roger. "A truce, huh?"

"That's what I said."

"It's a little late for peace talks, wouldn't you say?"

"If I thought so, I wouldn't be here."

I grab the remote control from the side table by my shoulder and make Roger wait while I flip through channels. I see there's another show playing on the nature channel. Sharks tonight. The topic seems so sublimely appropriate that I leave it there for the sake of metaphor.

Though I'm doing my best to be insulting, Roger doesn't seem perturbed. He walks in and sits on the arm of the chair a few feet away, where I can see him. He hasn't taken off his coat.

"Suppose I was able to encourage Brittany to tell the truth about how these photographs really got started."

"You mean she hasn't been truthful?"

"We'll save time if we can talk like adults."

On the television, a salty old fisherman with only one arm talks to the documentary crew. While he's telling his story, the screen cuts to a grainy photograph of some type of shark or other—a toothy 12-footer, gutted and bloody around the gills, hanging upside down on a hook. Men stand around the carcass.

"If Brit were encourged to tell the truth," I ask him, "what would she say?"

Roger sighs a little. *Kids these days.* "She'd come clean and admit that she and her best girlfriend cooked all this up."

Best girlfriend? I try to remember the names I've heard Brit use. "You mean Rachel?"

Roger doesn't exactly brighten with recognition, but he nods and waves his hand anyway. He says, "She'd tell the folks who matter that she and little miss Rachel got bored one summer day, used Pete's employee number at the cable company to order some free adult channels, just for giggles. And then they ended up taking a bunch of racy pictures of each other, just for more giggles."

I do my best to appear indifferent to the story he's telling me. But Roger now has my full attention, and he knows it. Nothing about this situation is beyond his grasp. It never has been.

"What else would she say?"

"She'd say that summer ended, and school started again, and along the way, the two of them wound up getting into a spat over some boy." He nods sadly. *True story.* "She'd say that it turned out her best girlfriend Rachel hadn't deleted those pictures the way she'd said." He leans forward, elbows on his knees. "She'd admit that, around November, her best girlfriend Rachel threatened to e-mail a few of those pictures to the eighth-grade football team, including the boy they were fighting over in the first place."

"How do you know all this, Roger?"

"Brit told me."

"She told you."

He leans back again. "Not sure if the poor kid was more afraid of the pictures getting out or the thought of the school calling her folks." A shrug. "So she came to someone she knew she could count on."

"And that would be you?"

"That would be me," he says. "And I took care of it."

"How do you mean, you took care of it?"

"That's not important."

Of course it isn't. Silly me. None of this sounds believable to me. How would it sound believable to anyone else? "And Brit's lying about all of this now because..."

"Because I told her to, Paul. I think you know that I had my reasons. When I tell her it's time to tell the truth, that's just what she'll do."

"Hang on a sec. Let me go get my tape recorder."

Roger smirks like he just can't help but like me, despite our differences. "All kidding aside, I don't want to see you go to prison. You can believe that or not, but I don't. I don't want it for you, don't want it for Sara."

"That's sweet of you."

"But I still can't have you in the circle. Not anymore."

I nod along. "Loose threads and whatnot. Communities unravel, society crumbles. The terrorists win."

"Make fun all you like. I'm still here."

"Offering a truce. Right."

"I'm offering you a chance to walk away from all this."

"What about Brit?"

He raises his eyebrows.

"What chance does she get to walk away from this?"

"Brit's a tough kid. Maybe she'll even learn a little something. A few years down the road, this will all be behind her."

It's amazing, really. Looking at Roger, having a casual conversation in some other context, you'd never imagine the worms twisting around inside his head. "You mean like how to trust the people in her life she thinks she can count on? Something like that?"

"Paul, there are things—"

"Wait, don't tell me. There are things I don't know."

"Did you know that Melody found marijuana in Brit's dresser drawer a couple weeks ago?"

"Nope." I write it down in an imaginary notepad. "Things Paul doesn't know. Item one."

"Did you know that Pete caught her with a—"

"You're right," I say. "I guess I don't watch what my neighbors are up to quite as closely as you do."

"I can tell you one thing I've watched." He takes a grave tone. "When I was on the force, I watched kids no older than Brit end up in court, in rehab, pregnant, in car wrecks, couple of 'em even in caskets. I could tell you—"

"That's not necessary," I say. "You obviously have the girl's best interests at heart. She's lucky to have someone like you in her life."

"The fact is, Brittany made me a promise not very long ago. So far, it's a promise she hasn't been doing a very good job of keeping." Roger straightens his spine. "At this point, maybe a good kick in the ass is the best thing for her."

I've reached my limit. There's no arguing this.

I think about what Roger has told me. This story of a hormone-drenched feud between two teenage girls. It makes a prime-time-news kind of sense, and I honestly feel relief for Brittany. These photos were just a dumb gag.

And then again, it doesn't make any sense at all. According to Roger, Brit was so scared at the thought of the photos floating around that she went to him for help. And now she's turned the same photos over to the police? Instead of being embarrassed at school, she's put herself in the lead story at six and ten?

And what about Roger? *This* is his idea of promoting neighborhood stability?

Your own safety is at stake when your neighbor's house is ablaze. Unless you burn it down yourself.

He looks at me. "What?"

I hadn't realized I'd spoken aloud. "Never mind."

On the television, there's a leathery, sun-bleached, middle-aged surfer showing the documentary crew a jagged half-moon scar on his ribs. The scar goes from nipple to hip and connects to a matching crescent on his back. A giant bite mark. How the hell is this guy walking around? I grab the remote and turn the volume up a notch.

"Well." Roger stands. "Call me when you're ready to talk about this."

As he moves toward the door, I say, "Can I ask one question?"

"Sure."

"How come I'm the one getting kicked out of the neighborhood? Why not Melody?"

"She has seniority."

"Ah."

"And the children."

"The children. Right." I nod. "Sara and I don't have any of those."

"I'm sorry to say it like that. But it is what it is."

I turn on the couch to face him directly. "Sara knows about what happened between me and Melody. Pete's going to find out soon enough. You don't think that's going to create any hard feelings across the old backyard fence?"

"I imagine it will," he says. "But Sara's told me how she's been feeling lately."

"Oh? How has she been feeling?"

"Well. I know the new job isn't quite what she'd imagined." Roger shrugs. "And I know she misses Boston."

Sara hasn't mentioned any of this to me. Rationally, I know that I can't be sure she's actually confided anything in Roger, either. But hearing him say it still heats up my blood.

"Hell," he says. "A little time, a change of scenery, I figure you two will find a way to patch things up. You've got a good thing there. I can see that."

I want to leap up and declare war. I want to see his face when I tell him that I know all about Darius Calvin, and Brit has a tattoo, and I've been talking to his old neighbors. My attorney will be conducting interviews. He's picked the wrong guy.

I want to rattle his cage. Send him away with something to think about.

I sit there frozen, staring at the television.

On the program, they're talking about the main attraction

now. The shark to beat all sharks. The most fearsome creature in all the deep. According to the program, a great white rolls its eyes back when it strikes, protecting its only vulnerable spot, but making itself blind at the moment of attack. I wonder if we get this channel with the cable package Pete hooked up for us at the house.

Roger opens the door to leave.

"Hey, Roger."

"Yes?"

"Imagine if Sara and I went back to Boston and lived happily ever after."

"I'd be happy to hear that."

"And Pete and Melody fell apart anyway." I look at him. "Wouldn't that be something?"

He stops as though he needs to think about that. But I know it's an act. Of course he's already thought about it.

"They may have their troubles," he says. "But my guess is, after this business is finished, all of that's going to seem like small potatoes."

What does he think? That making this truce will somehow return order to his world? Is it possible that he really imagines this to be true?

Has it honestly not occurred to Roger that I'm onto him?

"What doesn't kill us makes us stronger." I'm quoting the middle-aged surfer, who just said the same thing on television. "Right?"

"That's the way it was explained to me."

Roger zips his coat and puts on his gloves.

"Think it over. I'll be at home."

25.

MAYBE I SHOULD FORGET academia and look into a second career in broadcast journalism. Apparently, if you're a television news reporter, you get lots of time to hang out in parking lots and hotel lobbies, catching up on your reading.

Monday morning, I spot Maya Lamb as soon as I step off the elevator. She's parked in an armchair near the big Christmas tree in the lobby of the Residence Inn, dressed in jeans and a turtleneck sweater, her coat and bag on the floor by her feet. She glances up to check the elevators and sees me approaching.

"Miss Lamb," I say.

"Professor." She marks her page and closes her book. "Good morning."

I glance down and see that she's reading *Lolita* by Vladimir Nabokov. I can't help chuckling.

"It's pretty good," she says. "I had no idea."

"No? I got the impression you'd read it before."

Thanks to Douglas Bennett's office TiVo machine I've now seen myself on the news. Both reporters in town managed to make use of the obvious reference to Nabokov's best-known story. Of the two, Maya Lamb's approach is my favorite. She actually worked a subtle quote from the opening passage of the book into her sign-off: *We'll continue to look at this tangle of thorns as it develops.*

"I'm cramming," she says. "What can I say?"

"You know, I went to grad school with a guy who teaches at Cornell now," I tell her. "He has Nabokov's old office in the English building there. He told me people come by all the time, just to stand in the space. His students, other professors, people he's never even seen before. He told me that a woman once came in, said nothing, sat down on his couch, and cried."

"No kidding?"

"That's what he tells me."

"That's quite a story," she says.

"Actually, I'm lying. I read that somewhere. Never met the guy."

She raises her chin, still smiling. "You're not a very good liar, if you don't mind me saying."

"Tell me something." I make a show of looking around the lobby. "How come you're the only reporter following me around?"

"Uncommonly keen story sense?"

"Network job didn't pan out, huh?"

"I'm working on it."

Forty feet away, I notice the concierge talking with the girl behind the check-in counter. They're both looking at me. When they see me looking back, they drop their eyes and go about their business.

"Theoretically," I ask her, "what would you say if I told you I was completely innocent and I can prove it?"

"Are you, and can you?"

"I'm working on it."

"In that case, I guess I'd ask if you'd like to go get some coffee."

I shake my head. "Not a good time, but I have a proposition. Want to hear it?"

"Absolutely."

"Your story is about to get good. I can tell you how and why. There's nothing you'll be able to report yet, but I'll tell you everything there is."

"Yeah? How good?"

"Pretty good. It's got lies, adultery, subterfuge, police corruption, you name it. I'm prepared to offer complete preemptive access to the wrongly accused."

"Who would be you?"

"And I'll talk to you exclusively. If"—I raise a finger dramatically—"you promise to quit stalking me."

Maya Lamb leans forward and slips her book into the outside pocket of her bag. She brushes a lock of dark hair from her eyes. "I've been stalking you for three days. Why are you suddenly so eager to talk to me now?"

"Because I want you to quit following me. And because maybe we can help each other."

"How do you think we might be able to do that?"

"Do you want the deal or not?"

She taps her fingertips on the arms of the chair and narrows her eyes. "I'd need a down payment."

"Do you have one in mind?"

"Well, in the five minutes we've been talking, you've already admitted to telling me one tall tale."

"Yes, but I admitted it. That shows credibility."

"How about something that shows me what kind of a tale we're talking about this time?"

"Sure," I say. "But bear in mind, I could be fibbing again, so if you report this before it's confirmed by some other source, you could look foolish."

"With all due respect, Professor, based on this exchange, I'm willing to bet that I'm a better journalist than you are a fibber."

"All right. Try this and tell me if I'm fibbing."

Without naming my source, I tell her about the mystery tattoo that doesn't appear in the photographs of Brit Seward.

"A butterfly," Maya Lamb says.

"That's what I'm told. I've never seen it myself."

Her smile gets bigger.

"That's just an appetizer," I say.

"When do we eat?"

"Does that mean you agree to the terms?"

"If you agree to meet with me exclusively before the day is over, then yes. We have a deal."

"Done." I reach into my pocket and take out the cell phone Douglas Bennett gave me so that we'll be able to keep in touch at all times. "What's your mobile number?"

I punch in the numbers as she speaks them. In a moment, her bag begins to play muffled music, and I recognize the tune she's using as a ring tone. It's an old hit from the seventies. Blondie. "One Way or Another."

She digs the phone out, flips it open, and says, "Hello?"

"Nice ringer."

"I like it." She smiles and closes her phone against her cheek.

"So now I've got your number," I say. "You have mine. We'll stay in touch and meet up later."

"Before the end of the day. That's our deal, right?"

"That's our deal."

As I turn and head for the doors, she says, "So where are you off to? You're not dressed for lawyers."

I hold an imaginary cell phone to my ear—*We'll stay in touch*—and push out into the morning cold.

At the 7-Eleven on Belmont, I fill up and buy coffee. There's a woman in line in front of me on her way to work reading meters for the gas company. The guy behind the register says, "Can you make 'em go backward? My heat bill's through the roof."

She laughs and tells him they should swap each other. "I've got eighty bucks until payday, and I just put forty in the tank."

Listening to this, I'm seized by an idea that I know is silly. But this morning I seem to have woken up with an overpowering urge to throw good sense to the wind.

I step out of line and offer the woman two twenty-dollar bills to take my phone, dial Sara's mother's house in Philly, and pretend to be the dean of Western Iowa University.

She gives me the kind of look I'd expect. Then she glances at the bills in my hand and screws up her mouth. One hand on the door handle, she says, "Do what?"

I tell her the truth: I need to apologize to someone, but I can't get an audience. "All you have to do is ask for Sara. I promise, I'm mostly harmless."

She shrugs and takes the money. I hand her the phone. A minute later, she hands it back to me and says, "She's coming."

"I can't tell you how much I appreciate this."

"Ho ho ho," the woman says, saluting with my two folded twenties on her way out the door.

Frigid air streams in and swirls around me. I walk to an empty spot over by the slushie machines, hold the phone to my ear, and wait. In a few moments, Sara's voice comes onto the line.

"Dean Palmer, hello. I intended to call you myself this morning and—"

"Sara, it's me. Don't hang up. Please."

Silence.

"I just needed to hear your voice."

More silence. Colder than the air outside.

"Tell me what you want me to do," I say. "Whatever it is, I'll do it."

"I want you to go back in time and decide not to hump our next-door neighbor," Sara says. "Will you do that?"

"If I could, I would."

"Our *neighbor.* My jogging partner. Goddamn you both."

"Sara, I can't erase it, and I don't know how to make it up to you, but I'll kill myself trying."

"You'll be able to do that from prison?"

I realize now that in our years together, Sara has never spoken a truly cruel word to me. This is what it feels like.

"Wow." It's all I can come up with.

"I'm sorry." She breathes an angry sigh in my ear. "That was rotten."

"Sara..."

"If you really want to do something for me, don't call here. Because I can't do this yet."

She pauses, as though she's about to say something else. Then she hangs up instead.

The sound of the dial tone in my ear might as well be the sound of a heart monitor going flatline. I woke up two hours ago ready to take on the world, or at least Iowa. Now I want to go back to my room and pull the drapes and order scotch for breakfast.

I head for the doors. Just as I push the handle, a voice behind me says, "Sir?"

The guy behind the register is looking at me cynically. I say, "Yes?"

"You planning on paying for that coffee?" He nods toward the windows. "And the thirty bucks in gas you pumped on three?"

Oh. "I'm sorry. Of course."

I work out my wallet with my free hand as I walk back to the counter. I pretend to ignore the fidgets and sighs and eye-rolls from the people waiting in line, the slow nod from the guy behind the register. *Nice try, buddy.*

I'm halfway to Ponca Heights when the cell phone rings.

"Melody just called," Bennett says.

I feel a quick shot of disappointment that it isn't Sara.

Then relief creeps in. *Melody just called.*

I hadn't doubted her, but the relief is still there. She called first thing in the morning, just like she said she would; she's slept on this, and she hasn't changed her mind. "When will you talk to her?"

"She's coming in this morning," Bennett says. "How soon can you be here?"

"Actually, I'm a little tied up at the moment."

"Sorry to complicate your busy schedule. Tied up how?"

"Isn't it better if I'm not there anyway? So she can speak freely or whatever?"

There's a pause, then Bennett says, "What are you up to?"

"Just errands," I tell him. "I need a toothbrush. And a razor. Maybe a new tie for the thing on Wednesday."

"Hey, as long as you're running around, do me a favor, would you?"

"Sure."

"Save the bullshit for the reporters."

I don't have a response for that.

"Let me tell you something, Paul, if you're thinking about trying to go talk to Brittany Seward while her dad's at work and Melody's here—"

"Give me some credit," I say. "I'm not stupid."

"That's good."

"Look, if you think I should be there, I'll come in."

For a moment, Bennett doesn't say anything. Even his silence sounds frustrated with me.

Finally, he says, "Subtle pattern."

"Sorry?"

"The tie you're buying for Wednesday. Best to go with a subtle pattern. Nothing flashy."

"Oh." Does this mean I'm off the hook? "Thanks for the tip."

"Make sure you keep the phone with you."

"It's practically an extension of my hand."

Bennett hangs up just as I'm turning left off Belmont. I drop the phone into the console and follow Wildwood into the subdivision. I've never actually entered Ponca Heights from this direction; even after patrolling the area on foot, the meandering network of streets and roundabouts and cul-de-sacs plays with my sense of direction.

Around me, smoke trails from the chimneys of the homes of Ponca Heights South. Rooftops and windowpanes shimmer with frost. It's mid-morning and sunny—18 degrees, according to the sign at the bank downtown—and of course I haven't been entirely truthful with Douglas Bennett.

I might well be stupid. I'm also forbidden from contacting Brittany Seward. That much I've come to accept.

But nobody's ever said anything about me talking with her friend Rachel.

The McNallys live on a corner lot in one of the newer sections. My plan is simple: find a place along the curb, park, walk to the front door, and ring the bell.

It's Monday morning, and the Clark Falls public schools have released early, due to storm predictions, for the holidays. Best case, I get lucky, Rachel is home alone, and I'm somehow able to convince her not to slam the door in my face and call the police. But even in the probable case—that this goes nowhere—I'm confident of one thing:

It will get back to Roger that I came here and rang the doorbell. I'd like Roger to know that. I want him to know that we have no truce, and if it puts him at ease to think that ringing Rachel McNally's doorbell is the best defense maneuver I can come up with, so much the better.

The minivan backing out of the McNally driveway makes all of this strategy a moot point. Rachel's mother is behind the wheel. At a glimpse, I take the girl in the passenger seat to be Rachel's older sister. Through the minivan's tinted back windows, I can just make out a third head of hair.

I pull to the curb and watch my rearview mirror. From the corner of my eye, I become aware of the irony of my position:

I'm sitting directly beneath one of our curbside Safer Places coalition signs. *This neighborhood is monitored by the Ponca Heights Neighborhood Patrol.*

The minivan turns onto Walnut and heads away down the hill.

I doubt that Douglas Bennett would advise me to turn around in the nearest driveway and follow.

26.

THE PARKING LOT of the Loess Point Shopping Mall is aswarm. Holiday shoppers stream from their cars onto the sidewalks, making lines toward all visible entrances. The Salvation Army is out in force, standing by their red buckets, scarves over their mouths. The peal of handbells fills the air.

The McNally family minivan pulls to a stop in front of the main atrium and sits there, circled in exhaust. I luck into a parking space and watch my mirrors.

After a few minutes, the minivan's passenger side opens up. Rachel and her sister emerge onto the sidewalk and heave their doors shut.

Bye, Mom.

• • •

What I'm doing may not be well-advised, but it's disturbingly easy.

A hundred feet inside the main entrance to the mall, in front of the towering, ribboned Norway spruce rising up to the domed skylights three stories overhead, Rachel and her older sister stand bickering for a minute. The sister finally makes a zipping motion across her mouth, stabs a finger at her cell phone, and heads off in the other direction.

I watch as big sis meets up with a group of friends and disappears into the crowd. I watch as Rachel takes off her stocking hat and heads glumly toward the escalators alone.

And this is what I can't help thinking, as I shadow a thirteen-year-old girl through a busy shopping mall, a crowd of oblivious faces circulating around us:

It isn't difficult. If I were the kind of person I'm accused of being, it wouldn't be difficult to get close to this kid. I could be even worse than the kind of person I'm accused of being.

Keeping a margin between us, I follow Rachel McNally up the escalators and around the second level. She stops at a few windows but doesn't go into the stores. She spends a few minutes looking at cheap earrings at a jewelry pagoda.

She ducks into a music store and buys a CD, paying at the register with two crumpled bills she pulls from her purse. She counts her change—a couple bucks and a few coins—and tucks what's left in the front pocket of her jeans.

We spend close to an hour at the big computer store at the far end of the mall. Rachel spends the whole time at the same counter, fiddling wistfully with the iPods.

At last she looks at her watch and pulls herself away. She leaves the computer store and heads for the food court. She uses the money in her front pocket to buy a smoothie at the Jamba Juice.

I watch her pick out a table by the railing and give her a few minutes to get settled.

Then I walk over. "Rachel," I say, smiling. "Hi there."

Her first expression is a smile in return. She's been trained to be polite.

But she recognizes me almost immediately. Her smile falters and melts away. By the time I sit down, she's staring straight ahead, eyes wide, holding her smoothie in both hands, sucking purposefully on her straw.

"Don't be scared." I speak softly, partly to seem as unthreatening as possible, partly to avoid being heard by the people sitting at nearby tables. It's almost lunchtime. Pretty soon, the food court will be packed. "I'm a friend. I promise."

"Go away."

"I just want to talk to you for a minute."

"Go *away.*"

I do my best to appear relaxed and familiar. Like maybe I'm her father. A father having a tangle with his difficult teenager.

Rachel McNally looks the way it seems to me a thirteen-year-old ought to look. Skinny. Freckles. Braces on her teeth. I imagine that it must be hard for her sometimes, being best friends with Brit Seward. Especially in the boys' department.

It's funny, but based on the stories I've heard from Melody and Pete, I'd always sort of assumed that Rachel must have been the instigator of most of her and Brittany's unapproved adventures together. Now I wonder. What kind of jerk accepts a fake ID from this kid?

"Listen," I say. "I know you're in a bind."

She scrunches up her eyes.

"I'm in a bind too. I think we can help each other."

"You're a creep. Leave me alone."

"Rachel—"

"I'm calling my sister."

"You know I'm not a creep."

"She'll bring a security guard." She's put down her smoothie and she's digging in her purse.

"Listen, Rachel, I know all about the pictures. I know you and Brit were just goofing around. It's okay."

Her eyes are slits now. "What?"

"I'm telling you, it's okay. I'm not here to get you in trouble. I just need to talk to you a minute. Please?"

"Get me in what trouble? What's your *deal*?"

"I know about the pictures, kiddo."

Her cheeks flush pink, and she looks away, over the railing. Below us, on the lower level of the atrium, a bunch of little kids stand in line with their moms and dads in an aisle made of giant candy canes, waiting to get their picture taken with Santa Claus.

Rachel's face clouds over. "Bet you got off on 'em, too. Creep."

"Don't worry. I've never seen them. Any of them."

"Whatev."

"Rachel, I know that you took those pictures of Brit. I know she took some of you. Hell, when I was your age I know I did some—"

"What are you *talking* about?" Her whole face seems to crunch toward a central point between her eyes. "That is so gross."

"You don't have to prete—"

"Brit totally wants to die. I hope you know that."

"Rachel."

"She totally trusted you."

"Brit knows I had nothing to do with this. So do you."

"What*ever*," she says. "You stole 'em out of that guy's house. Everybody knows."

The table seems to tilt slightly. *That guy's house?* She's obviously talking about Roger, and something sinks in my stomach. All this time, I've been trusting my assumption that he's somehow manipulated Brit into playing infantry in his lunatic aggression against me. But it's never occurred to me that he's actually turned Brit against me.

But of course he has. She wouldn't tell these lies otherwise. I hadn't realized that it would be possible to feel worse about all of this.

"Brit really thinks I e-mailed her those pictures?"

Silence.

"But that's not true."

"She totally trusted you." Rachel stands up. "And you're the same as Mr. B."

Mr. B?

What are you talking about?

That is so gross.

"Rachel."

"I'm outta here."

"What are you telling me?"

"Dude, shut up."

"No." I stand up with her. I try not to tower, but I can't help it. I'm a grown man, and she's only thirteen. "Please talk to me."

Maybe she really does want to talk to me. Or maybe it's that I'm an adult and she's been brought up to respect us. Or maybe she's just terrified.

"Please," I say. "I need your help."

She casts her gaze over the food court as if looking for help herself.

"Tell me who took those pictures, Rachel. I need to know."

A few people are starting to look back at us.

I'm in a bind.

"Listen," I say. "I have an idea."

She doesn't want to listen, but she's listening.

What do I do?

I take a breath and do exactly what I imagine I'd do if I were the kind of person I'm accused of being.

We end up walking all the way back to the computer store on the far side of the mall together. Not unlike a father and his teenage daughter.

I buy her the most expensive iPod they sell, and she tells me even more than I wanted to know.

27.

"IT'S BEEN A PRODUCTIVE MORNING," Douglas Bennett informs me.

"How did she seem?"

"Melody? Like she'd spent the night in hell."

I take a right on Van Dorn, which cuts through town on a diagonal. In doing so, I accidentally pull in front of another car in the oncoming lane and receive an angry horn blast for my mistake. I wonder if Bennett has one of those little hands-free earpieces I could borrow. This talking and driving is dangerous as hell.

"But she's committed," he tells me. "Obviously, what she has to say won't help us with the possession and distributing charges, but it's one hell of a step in the right direction."

"So what happens now?"

"What happens now," he says, "is that you point your car toward my office. Meanwhile, I reschedule your PDC on Wednesday to be combined with Monday's hearing instead. I'll tell them that we need the week to get our ducks in a row. Then, Monday morning, I'll hit them with initial discovery and move for dismissal of the producing charges at the same time. From there, our position improves considerably."

I'm not entirely following this barrage of new strategy, but it all sounds promising.

Bennett says, "When can you be here?"

"I have another appointment."

"Very funny."

"I'm heading there now. I just need to stop at the hotel first and use the printer in the business center."

After a pause, Bennett says, "Professor, you're beginning to piss me off."

"Listen." Traffic slows to a crawl. There's some kind of fender bender up ahead. "Have one of your interns do all the research they can on a guy named Timothy Brand. Last name spelled B, R—"

"Who's Timothy Brand?"

"He *was* a history teacher at Bluffs View Middle School. Also Brit Seward's seventh-grade volleyball coach." I pause to pay attention while a patrol cop diverts traffic around the crash—a red pickup truck and a van from the Clark Falls Public Power District, hoods crumpled, glass everywhere. "I don't know what he is now."

Bennett says nothing.

"She got mixed up with a teacher at her school," I tell him. "He's the one who took the photos."

"How do you know this?"

"I'll fill you in after my meeting."

"I want you to fill me in right—"

"Look, Bennett, I just want to get started finding this guy, okay? I called the school, but they wouldn't give me any forwarding—"

"Stop. For your own sake, stop what you're doing. Right now."

"I just need to—"

"Are you listening? Get your ass to your attorney's office where you can't do any more damage. I swear to God, I'll have Debbie track you down by scent. What meeting?"

I'm afraid he might accidentally hurt himself if I tell him.

"I'll call you after," I say.

The Firehouse is a brewpub not far from my hotel, housed in a historic downtown building that used to be a fire station before it was converted into a brewpub.

The interior is warm and dark, with old plank floors, modern finishes, brick walls hung with antiquated gear once used to battle blazes but now used as decoration. It's two in the afternoon when I get there, and patrons are sparse. A few late lunchers. A few people at the main bar, watching a basketball game on a plasma screen.

I spot Maya Lamb right away, sitting alone in a booth in a small alcove in back. Apparently, this is her regular spot; when I called her two hours ago, she told me that she uses this booth as an office on her days off. The afternoon regulars are used to seeing her, and the staff knows to leave her alone.

The fact that being on television makes Maya Lamb a celebrity in a town the size of Clark Falls is only one of the reasons why I want to do this.

Here in Clark Falls, Roger Mallory is a well-known face people trust. Maybe I can get a well-known face people trust on *my* side. She sees me coming, lays down her *Lolita,* and motions to the guy behind the taps.

"Miss Lamb," I say.

"Professor Callaway." She smiles. "Call me Maya, and I'll call you Paul. What do you say?"

"Maya, I feel like we're practically old friends by now."

"In that case, how was your day, buddy?"

"Illuminating." I take off my coat and gloves. "Yours?"

"Anticipatory."

As I slide into the booth across from her, she strips the menu card from its clip between the salt and pepper shakers and hands it to me. "Best beer in the Falls."

According to the card, there's nothing stingy about the Ebenezer Stout. When our waitress comes over, that's what I order. Maya orders the Backdraft Bock and studies me while we wait for our beers to arrive.

"So," she finally says. "How do we start helping each other?"

It's a good question. Sitting here, I find myself with the same narrative problem I encountered sitting across the square in my jail cell three nights ago: starting.

"I have a story for you."

"I'm counting on it."

"It's a long one."

"I love long stories."

I think I've learned how to tell this one now. It starts the same place it always started. This time, my job is easier. Maya Lamb already knows the beginning.

So I start at joining the Ponca Heights Neighborhood Patrol. I summarize the progression of my relationship with Roger Mallory, from becoming friendly to falling out. When our beers arrive, we toast the new year and raise our glasses.

After an impressive swig, Maya Lamb wipes her mouth and says, "Proximity is perhaps the strongest predictor of friendship."

"Oh?" I have no idea what she means by this.

"Of course, proximity also provides opportunities for assaults, rapes, and murders. Myers. *Exploring Psychology.*"

"Who?"

"Textbook I had in college. For some reason I always remembered that line."

"College," I say. I can't help smiling. "That was what, last year?"

"Thanks for the compliment. I'm twenty-nine."

I decide to see her quotation and raise her with Roger's favorite: *Your own safety is at stake when your neighbor's house is ablaze.* Doing so, I'm struck pleasantly by the thematic aptness of our surroundings: a defunct firehouse.

"You should work that into your story," I tell her. "People like irony."

"Oh, I don't know. I'm still feeling the Lolita angle."

"I suppose clichés are nice, too."

"Besides, in your situation, the jury's still out on irony, don't you think?"

"How do you mean?"

"You could be found guilty," Maya Lamb says. "As far as I know, you could actually *be* guilty."

"I suppose that's true."

"And I know we've got plenty of viewers out there who would say that Roger Mallory's organization has more than proven its worth."

"I'm sure you have plenty of viewers out there who would say all kinds of things."

"Look at the numbers." She slides her beer to one side and leans forward. "In the seven years since Mallory organized the neighborhood associations and watch groups under the Safer Places banner, crime rates in nearly all the so-called residential categories—"

"Oh," I say. "Those numbers."

She ticks off the categories on her fingers anyway, continuing as though she hasn't been interrupted. "Destruction of property. Car theft. Burglaries. Trespassing, window-peeking, animal control. Hell, even noise violations." She sweeps her hand as if erasing them all. "Over the past seven years, all categories have trended down."

"Sounds just like one of Roger's press releases."

"Give me some credit. I've validated the organization's literature against official CFPD statistics." She tilts her head. "Did you know that, as of the department's latest Comstat report, domestic dispute calls across every coalition neighborhood zone are at an all-time low?"

I can't say that I knew that.

"Meanwhile, real estate markets are approaching all-time highs." Her eyes seem defiant. *Look it up if you don't believe me.* "Especially new construction. This, bear in mind, at a time when interest rates are high, statewide income per capita is stagnant, and housing markets in comparable cities are flat to declining."

I take a long pull from my beer, lick the droopy foam mustache from my top lip, and wonder if I'm stupid after all. For the first time, it occurs to me that perhaps there's more going on here than cub reporter ambition.

Why *is* Maya Lamb the only reporter following me around?

Maybe Roger got to her first? Maybe he had this idea long before I did. Maybe he's found, in Maya Lamb, his own personal media mouthpiece for Safer Places. Or maybe Safer Places just pays her station a bundle for its public service announcements.

"So you can see," Maya says, "how comparing Safer Places to a decommissioned fire station would probably seem, to some viewers, more like sarcasm." She sips her beer and looks at me. "As opposed to irony."

Douglas Bennett's words are crackling like static in my head: *Get your ass to your attorney's office where you can't do any more damage.* He practically begged me, but I wouldn't listen.

"What *I'd* like to know," Maya says, "is the reason you filed a privacy complaint against Roger Mallory three weeks ago."

"Right." I drink my beer. "I'll bet he told you all about that, didn't he?"

"Nobody told me anything."

"Then how do you know about it?"

"I know about it because I've been checking the police department's shift records every couple of weeks since mid-July. For any reports involving your address."

I must look surprised. Maya Lamb bounces her eyebrows at me.

"Why would you do that?"

"I told you. Uncommonly keen story sense."

"No, wait a minute. Seriously."

"Come on, Paul." She's smirking now. "This morning? You might as well have asked me why I'm the only reporter in Clark Falls who thought that break-in at your house was a little bit tough to swallow."

"What?"

"Listen, I covered the so-called Moving Day Burglaries last year; hell, I'm the one who named 'em. I don't care what the Comstat reports say, the neighborhood patrols shut that operation down, not the police department."

"I'm not following."

"Fourteen months later, out of the blue, these burglaries suddenly start up again? For one night only? In the middle of what my aunt Jamie would tell you is the real estate market's slowest sales month?" She rolls her eyes. "Right across the street from the head of the neighborhood safety coalition? That's a little cute, don't you think?"

Listening to her, I almost wonder why it took *me* so long to figure all this out. When Maya says it, it all sounds so obvious. And she's not even finished.

"Did you know that, according to records on file at the Safer Places administrative office, last July marked the lowest number of active neighborhood association volunteers on roster at any time in the previous three-year period?"

I can't say that I knew that, either.

"It's a fact. How's your beer?"

I look at my glass. "Not bad."

She says, "I think I'll order that one next."

"That's funny. I was looking at yours and thinking the same thing."

"I guess we think alike." She smiles. "You were telling me a story about Roger Mallory?"

Suburbetrators

28.

I COULD HAVE BLAMED THE DOG.

Wes had been in a bad way since mid-September. Even before things went sour between Roger and me, I'd noticed that the dog's gait had twisted and gone crooked, finally deteriorating to the point that he no longer accompanied Roger on his morning walks back into the woods.

Still, on more than one morning, I'd seen Wes follow Roger outside to get the newspaper, dragging his haunches as though his hind legs had quit on him. He'd lost control of his bowels by then, earning himself a bed and a space heater out in Roger's garage. His bark had gone silent, and he'd begun losing teeth. By the time the leaves started falling, the neighborhood squirrels, rabbits, opossums, and raccoons had come to enjoy free passage where Tyrannosaurus Wes had once stood guard.

I've always heard that old dogs can sense when the end is

near. My own childhood pooch, a sweet-tempered mutt named Bruce Banner, had lived sixteen years before limping off one evening into the New Jersey woods, never to return.

But old Wes hadn't given up yet. As the weather turned cool, he'd developed the habit of dragging himself after Roger's Yukon whenever Roger backed out of the garage.

I'd wondered about that. Was the broken-down shepherd clinging to the same blood-bred instincts that made an untrained young herd dog prone to chase cars? Did the old dog recognize, in the sound of the truck's engine, that his owner would be roaming farther afield than he could on foot? Or was the roar of the motor just too loud inside the garage?

No matter the reason, the result was the same nearly every time Roger left the house on wheels.

Step 1: Back out of the garage.

Step 2: Here comes Wes.

Step 3: Dog trips the invisible safety beam, causing the garage door to stop, change directions, and roll back up again.

Step 4: Stop truck, get Wes. Take him back in.

Step 5: Close the garage door from the inside.

Step 6: Reexit house through the front door.

Maybe two times out of every ten, Wes either failed to make the garage door before it closed to the ground, or he failed to rouse himself, period. Those occasions of respite left Roger free to go about his business without interruption.

I'd wondered about that, too.

Why not find some way of penning the dog in? Surely it wouldn't take much. Did the 20 percent chance that Wes wouldn't come scrabbling out of the darkness really make it worth going through the entire process the rest of the time?

Or was Roger clinging to the 80 percent? Maybe it encouraged him to see Wes hanging tough. Maybe Roger reserved, for the dog, the same optimism he apparently couldn't spare his neighbors. Or maybe he just couldn't bring himself to tether the old boy.

How did I know so much about Roger's comings and goings, and whether Wes followed him or didn't?

I guess I must have been watching.

On a gray afternoon in November, Roger left the house in a hurry. I assumed that he must have been preoccupied, because he didn't stop to wait for Wes, and it turned out to be one of the dog's good days.

By the time Roger turned out of the circle and sped away down Sycamore Drive, Wes had dragged himself to the end of the driveway, gathered his hind legs beneath him, and begun hobbling down the street in pursuit.

It was an empty weekday in Sycamore Court. Sara was still on campus. The Sewards and the Firths were at work. The Firth twins were at day care, Brit was in school, and I'd seen Michael leaving for the restaurant when I'd returned from my last class of the day twenty minutes earlier.

So it was me and Wes against the world.

And my quarrel with Roger certainly didn't extend to the dog. I grabbed my jacket, went to the kitchen, and got a few cubes of stew meat from the package I'd picked up at the butcher counter on my way home. Poor Wes had made it almost to the stone pillars at the mouth of the circle by the time I caught up with him. He'd collapsed onto his side and had laid his head on the ground.

"Hey there, buddy." I gave him a scratch and stroked his dull coat. He thumped the sidewalk with his tail. "That's a boy." I stooped down and gathered him up in my arms. "Here we go."

He was shockingly light for such a big guy. I could feel his knobby bones through his skin. I straightened and carried the dog back up the sidewalk. In Roger's garage, I settled Wes in his bed and held out my hand. He couldn't chew the stew meat, but I held it for him while he licked my palm and fingers.

A foul smell rose up, half sweet, half rancid. I looked down and noticed a glistening brown puddle on the sleeve of my jacket.

Wes had leaked. As soon as I noticed the mess—now feeling the warmth on my arm—the smell became overpowering. I had to look away to keep from gagging.

Wes stared up at me with sad, tired eyes, as if in apology. *This is what it comes down to,* he seemed to be saying. *One damned indignity after another.*

I left the cubes of meat on the concrete floor where he could reach them. After a short search, I found a roll of black plastic garbage bags, tore one free, and slipped out of my reeking jacket as deftly as I could. I dropped the jacket in the bag and tied the top shut.

"Okay, buddy." I gave the dog one last scratch between the ears. "You take it easy."

Wes whined a little. Thumped his tail.

I ran the garage door down and went inside.

If you were to stand outside—by the swing set in the common, say—and compare our house with Roger's, you'd probably see more differences than similarities.

Other than being made out of bricks, they don't seem much alike to the eye. Roger expanded his second story at some point, and he's built two or three additions onto the main level over the years. His chimney faces north, ours faces south. His windows have shutters, and his roof is shingled. Our windows are bare, and we have wood shakes.

But I'd noticed early on that our two houses must have been built around the same time, most likely by the same builder. If you look closely at Roger's place, you can see, in the midst of his modified sprawl, that the basic architecture is actually the same as mine.

Our houses started out as mirror images of each other. The truth is, if you take away sixty-odd years of development, our houses aren't much different from the new homes going up in South Ponca, all of them starting out on bare lots, all seemingly cut from the same two or three plans.

I'd never actually been *inside* Roger's house before that afternoon.

My intention hadn't been to snoop. It started on my way to the front door, as I passed a shelf of wedding pictures. I stopped to ponder a much younger Roger: handsome, athletic, ready for anything the world had to dish out. Clair Mallory—formerly Clair Stockman, according to the framed invitation standing nearby—had been a pretty bride. Her eyes seemed full of sparkle. Her hair framed her face in glossy black spirals.

Before I knew it, I was moving around the living room, browsing photographs. A few faces from the wedding party could be found in snapshots of Roger posing with fellow officers from the force. I spotted his best man, assorted groomsmen, the father of the bride—all tuxedoed in one set of photos, uniformed in the other.

It felt uncomfortable to be wandering around in Roger's house, and not just because I hadn't been invited. The whole atmosphere reminded me of my grandmother's old house in Cresskill, after my grandfather died: outdated, too quiet, too neat, not a throw pillow out of place.

But who *was* this guy? Roger Mallory. Who was he really?

There were no lingering smells from recent meals in Roger's kitchen. The living room had a curious, unlived-in quality. Even the air in the place felt trapped and stale, or at least it seemed that way to me.

I found myself lingering in one corner, at a built-in bookcase filled with family snapshots. There were photos showing Roger and Clair in a hospital room, holding their new baby boy. Photos of the boy toddling around in a diaper and a cowboy hat. Growing into a dimple-cheeked kid.

There were photos of holidays, vacations, first days of school. Christmas presents unwrapped very near the spot where I stood. One photo showed Brandon Mallory at six or seven years of age; he had a birthday hat on his shaggy mop head and a German shepherd puppy squirming in his arms. In the photo, Brandon Mallory is beaming at the camera. Puppy Wes is licking his face. Clair Mallory is laughing, caught half in and half out of the frame, one hand on her hip, the other touching her mouth.

My feud with Roger seemed profoundly silly just then. Of course it was unreasonable for Roger to think that he could dictate who lived in his circle. But then, by some measures, it was probably unreasonable to continue wasting food on an old dying dog.

Thinking back to that moment—remembering how I felt, looking at a single faded snapshot of everything Roger Mallory had lost—I know that I would have made an effort to change things between us if Wes hadn't started barking.

I never blamed the dog.

29.

AT FIRST, the barking confused me. It wasn't much of a bark, more a series of whines, but it came from upstairs, not from the garage.

I went out and checked on Wes. He was asleep with his mouth open, dry tongue lolling. He pawed feebly at the air with one foreleg; I imagined him chasing the neighborhood rabbits and raccoons in his sleep. While I watched him, a thin whine gathered in his bony chest, releasing in a quick yip. I heard the sound in front of me and behind me at the same time.

I closed the door, went back into the house, and followed the sound upstairs to the second floor. The first door off the staircase was closed. On the door hung a faded Iowa Hawkeye football poster. I could tell by the crusty old adhesive marks that the poster had once been taped at the corners. It must have fallen down eventually and been tacked back up with pushpins.

I looked at the dark blue *Property of CFPD* sticker pasted to the door above the poster, right about chin level. *Brandon.*

The door was locked. The game schedule printed on the Hawkeye poster was from eleven seasons ago.

Across the hall, the next door had the same dark blue property sticker, marked with the same young handwriting: *Mom and Dad.* Also locked.

I heard Wes growl once, then fall silent. I walked down the hall to a third door, pushed it open, and poked my head into the room.

Roger's office. Bookshelves, file cabinets, stacks of papers. A cluttered bulletin board. Even a trash can with trash in it. So far, it was the only room in the house other than Wes's corner of the garage that looked lived in.

Beneath the eastern slope of the roof sat a big old Leopold office desk. On the desk sat a computer, a stapler, a tape dispenser, a gooseneck lamp.

And a Graco brand baby monitor, obviously receiving transmissions from the garage.

I had to smile. One story below, Wes yipped again; on the monitor, the red signal lights ramped up and fell away.

I looked around. Beneath the western slope of the roof, there was a couch and a coffee table, a small television. It wasn't unlike the reading nook I'd set up in my own office, except that Roger's couch had a bedsheet draped over it, a pillow against one arm, an old patchwork quilt thrown over the back.

In the wrinkled bedding I could see that this wasn't just Roger's office. He slept in here.

I scanned the walls. There were diplomas from high school, college, the police academy. There was a shadow box displaying Roger's badge and sergeant's stripes on dark blue velvet. I saw a variety of civic service awards for the Safer Places Organization. A framed letter of commendation, signed by the governor. There were group photos of the classes that had graduated from the Citizens' Academy Roger taught through the police department. Photos of Roger in a suit, shaking hands with people who looked important.

And now I felt like a legitimate intruder.

I really had no right to be up here, and it was past time to go. Still feeling moved by the photographs I'd seen downstairs, I went over to Roger's desk and sat down in his chair. I'd intended to leave him a short note: *Wes got out. Heard the monitor, came up to make sure all was well. Can we talk? Paul.*

While looking for a piece of scrap paper to write on, I found my own credit card statement beneath the tape dispenser. For a minute, I couldn't quite decide what I was looking at. I could see my name and address printed at the top. I could see that it was the statement I'd just paid.

The same one I'd torn up and added to the load for the recycling truck the night before.

Little by little, my spirit darkened. I looked at the careful job Roger had done, piecing the torn statement back together. My face felt hot.

A sudden growl of an engine and a grinding of metal startled me half out of my skin. Red lights danced on the baby monitor.

Shit.

Roger was home.

30.

OPTIONS:

I could run downstairs, slip out the front door, hope Roger didn't see me. I could walk downstairs, meet Roger in the garage, and shove my credit card statement in his face. I could hide up here under the desk.

Meanwhile, the engine growl grew louder, shifted to a lower pitch. I heard what sounded like a screech of steel on steel. What sounded like a chain rattling.

What the hell was he doing down there, ramming the house? I went to the window, peeled back the curtain.

Down below, on the street, I saw a big green truck from Deffenbaugh Waste & Recycling making its way around the circle. Two guys in orange vests hopped off the back of the truck, hauled the garbage cans and the recycling tub from the curb in front of Pete and Melody's house. I heard the sound of glass, clattering and shattering. I could actually hear voices; the guys in the orange vests were talking to each other.

It sounded almost as though the voices were coming from inside the walls. I realized that I wasn't hearing this over the baby monitor.

On this side of Roger's desk, the east wall of the office made a right angle into an open alcove. I looked around the corner and noticed, for the first time, another door.

This door didn't match the others on the upper floor. It had been drilled and outfitted with hardware, but never painted. Along the edge, I saw combination keypads for not one, not two, but three separate dead bolts.

The door itself stood slightly ajar.

Roger really had left in a hurry.

I suppose you could write a paper on the occurrence of magic doors in literature—portals through which a character passes into another world, leaving the familiar one behind.

On the other side of Roger's door, I found attic space that had been walled off into a sort of secret garret. Maybe ten feet long by five feet deep, the slope of the roof disappearing just overhead. The space smelled like insulation and lumber.

There was another chair in here, parked in front of a built-in ledge with a laptop computer connected to an array of external hard drives. The sound of the garbage truck continued to bang and clank from a small speaker box mounted on a wall stud.

Sitting in the chair, I could watch the sanitation crew outside on the bank of video monitors Roger had installed in here. He had nine screens in all, mounted in a configuration that approximated the layout of Sycamore Court.

The largest screen dominated the center, displaying the playground in full color. Around this screen, there were smaller black-and-white monitors mounted in pairs. Each set of monitors displayed the front of a house on top, a backyard beneath.

Looking at the arrangement of screens like a clock, I could see my own house at eight. Pete and Melody at ten. Trish and Barry at noon, Michael at two.

The grumbling growl of the city garbage truck grew louder over the speaker as the truck pulled into the top screen of the last pair of monitors. The truck was right outside, in front of Roger's house, the four o'clock position in the circle of screens.

The speaker clanked and hissed.

Almost without thinking, I touched the pad of the laptop. The screen flared to life. It didn't occur to me then, but thinking back, it seems ironic that there was no password required. Who needed a password with three combination dead bolts on the door?

There were open file directories for each house in the circle. Each directory contained video files named by date, sorted by month. It looked as though Roger had been working on archiving the past few weeks' worth of surveillance footage.

I rolled the chair forward and accidentally kicked a heavy object beneath the ledge. The object turned out to be a banker's box. I got down on my knees and pulled the box out. It had a white label on the lid: *36 Sycamore Court.* Printed on the label beneath the address was the name *Seward1.* I pulled out the box next to it. *Seward2.*

The space beneath the ledge turned out to be lined with boxes, each labeled—same as the file directories on the laptop—according to address.

At last I reached the box with our name on it. I felt like I'd stepped into some absurdist dimension, maybe ten feet long by five feet deep, located somewhere behind the north wall of reality.

Screech, clank, growl. The garbage truck pulled away from the curb, out of the frame of the security monitor. The growl slowly faded, and the small black speaker fell silent. The sudden stillness clanged in my ears.

Faintly, on the other side of the wall, Wes yipped in his sleep.

I opened the box labeled *Callaway* and followed my own rabbit down into its hole.

31.

"HUH," the first cop said.

I said, "Do you see?"

The other cop looked at the tree and scratched his head. "Huh," he agreed.

They both looked to be in their late forties, early fifties. The first cop was tall and thin, the other short and round. I imagined them riding the midday shift until their pensions kicked in.

The three of us stood at the split rail fence separating the back line of our property from the nature preserve. Ten minutes in Roger's attic was all I could stomach before calling the police and making a trespassing complaint. Setting aside a misplaced golf club, our break-in that July had left me more or less impressed with the local law. Even my last meeting with Detective Harmon, while frustrating in its outcome, reinforced my general perception of competence and professionalism.

Not so much that afternoon. It was as if the Clark Falls Police Department had resurrected Abbott and Costello, dressed them in guns and uniforms, and sent them over to my house.

"They're all the way around the circle." I made a revolving motion around my head.

"I see," said Officer Tall.

Officer Short nodded. "Okay."

While the trees stood nearly bare of leaves, it still had taken me nearly thirty minutes of searching before I'd finally found what I now showed the cops: a small wireless camera, about the size of a deck of playing cards, mounted in the crook of a hackberry tree just outside the fence. The mounting bracket and the camera itself were both colored in a forest camouflage pattern. From the yard, the device was difficult to see even after you knew where to look.

I looked at the two cops. "Well?"

They looked at each other. *Any ideas?*

Officer Tall said, "Is it even on?"

"I don't see a light," Officer Short said. "Seems like there'd be a light."

"It's on," I said. I'd told them an edited version of my experience inside Roger's house: dog, note, open door, video monitors. "I'm telling you, if Roger were home right now, he'd be able to watch us standing here."

Officer Tall looked at Officer Short. "Is that illegal?"

Short thought long and hard. He finally said, "I guess it's state property, technically."

"The camera?"

"The tree."

"Guys, come on." I couldn't believe what I was hearing. It was as if the three of us weren't speaking the same language. "Surely there's some kind of law. Invasion of privacy or . . . hell, *something*. Right?"

Tall seemed to understand my distress. "You'd think so."

"Playground and the sidewalks are public areas," Officer Short said. "I don't think anything says you can't point a camera at a public area."

"This isn't a public area," I said. "This is my backyard."

Officer Short squinted at the camera, then turned to look at the house. Seemingly to no one in particular, he said, "Can it see in through the windows?"

"If you'd found the camera *inside* the house," Officer Tall said, "then we'd definitely have something."

Either these guys were screwing with me, or I really had stumped them with my camera-in-a-tree problem. Either way, I'd given up on them. "Is there somebody else you could call?"

"Call?"

"To look in the statutes or something. You can't go around planting cameras on your neighbors, can you?"

"Well, sir, it's like I said—"

"Put yourself in my place. You guys have homes, right? Families?" I pointed at the camera. "How would *you* feel?"

Officer Short looked at the tree one more time. He looked at the house again. He glanced toward Pete and Melody's backyard, where I'd showed them the exact same sort of camera mounted in the lower branches of a big Dutch elm.

"Seems a little creepy," he finally said. "I'll give you that."

Officer Tall said, "Have you discussed the issue with any of the neighbors?"

"I will, believe me. But I just found the things. Everybody's at work."

"And are you employed yourself?"

"What the hell does that have to do with anything?"

"Nothing," Officer Short said. He gave Officer Tall a sideways look.

"I teach at the university," I told them. I hadn't intended to lose my patience. "Do you need to see my vita before you can help me?"

"No offense intended, Mr. Callaway. My partner's just establishing a framework."

Officer Tall said, "What's a vita?"

I was finished. "What kind of framework do you need? I'm telling you that Roger Mallory put *that* camera"—I pointed at the camera, then the tree—"in *that* tree. Without my permission and without my knowledge. Without my wife's knowledge."

Officer Short nodded along. He understood. He was here to help me. He said, "Any ideas as to why Mr. Mallory might do something like that? If you had to speculate?"

"He's filming a reality show. He's romantically obsessed with my wife. He's had a psychotic break and thinks he's Generalissimo Francisco Franco." I threw up my hands. "How should I know why Roger put a camera up a tree?"

"Mr. Callaway—"

"If I had to speculate, I guess I'd say he did it so that he could watch what we're doing without our knowledge." I touched my chin. *Hmm.* "I think it's the camouflage on the camera. You know, the way it's all hidden there in the tree and everything?"

Officer Short straightened his posture.

Officer Tall seemed to be scrutinizing me a bit more closely now.

I sighed. *Piss off the cops you called yourself. Good plan.* "Guys, I'm sorry. I'm just a little bit wound up about this. I don't mean to be difficult."

"Sure," Officer Tall said.

Officer Short nodded. "It's an unusual situation."

"Bottom line, I guess all I really want is for that camera to come down. The one pointed at the front of our house, too, wherever that one is."

Of course, I wanted more than that, but I needed to be careful. I couldn't just fly at these cops with everything I'd found while snooping inside Roger's house. For one thing, I'd been snooping inside Roger's house. And I was already starting to sound like a lunatic.

But I could point to this little camouflaged spy camera I'd found in this tree behind my house, and both of these cops could see it with their own two eyes. It was a start.

"We can certainly understand," Officer Short said.

"Just for our knowledge," Officer Tall said, "have you asked Mr. Mallory to remove the cameras?"

"Like I told you. I just found it."

"Well. We'll certainly talk to Mr. Mallory."

Even as he spoke, I could hear a car approaching. In a moment, I saw the side of Roger's GMC flashing between the bare trees along Sycamore Drive.

"Speak of the devil," I said.

It turned out that Roger had been called away from home unexpectedly. One of the elderly residents down the hill had taken a nasty fall on her back steps, and instead of dialing 911, she'd crawled to the nearest phone and called Roger.

Sure. Why not?

Officer Tall, it turned out further, was named Bill. Officer Short answered to Stump.

What the hell had I been thinking? Of course they'd all be on a first-name basis with Roger. He'd been on the force. Three cops, plus a little old lady who had broken her ankle and had nobody to help her.

And then there was me.

"Paul," Roger said, as though I'd hurt his feelings. "What's this all about?"

"That's what I'd like to know." I tried to make my eyes say, *Go ahead. Tell Bill and Stump here what this is all about.*

"But you signed the service contract." Roger glanced over his shoulder. "I have it on file in the house."

Officer Bill said, "Service contract?"

"Roger." I shook my head. "Come on."

Roger seemed genuinely pained by my antagonism. "I don't know what to say."

"This service contract," Officer Bill said. "Do you remember signing anything like that?"

I said, "I have no idea what he's talking about."

"Rodge, sorry," Officer Stump said. "Maybe you can—"

"I didn't sign up for a camera in a tree, or anywhere else, I can assure you."

Officer Bill held a hand up to me. Officer Stump followed with a warning glance. To Roger, he said, "Maybe you can explain?"

I could hardly fault these two cops. They were just doing their jobs. And Roger had an answer for everything.

He began by explaining that each home in the circle was secured by an alarm system from Sentinel One, Incorporated. "John Gardner's outfit. Either of you guys know Johnny Gardner before he retired?"

John Gardner. I thought of the bald, hawk-faced man I'd met in Detective Harmon's office several weeks earlier. So *that* was Roger's old friend from the force? I thought of the way he'd watched me in the parking lot that day.

"Lieutenant Gardner," Officer Bill said. "Sure."

"Well, he's on my board of directors," Roger said. "And I do a little consulting for Sentinel One. Don't tell any of John's other customers, but he runs a little value-add for us over here."

"How's that?"

"Whole circle's wired for video," Roger said. "Sentinel provides the equipment, I maintain the feeds, do the backups there in the house."

"So the other neighbors are aware of the cameras, then?"

"Aware of them?" Roger chuckled. "Hell, they pay for 'em."

Both cops looked at me. My head felt numb. I said, "Nobody told me anything about video cameras."

"Paul, I just don't know what to say."

Roger was putting on a hell of a show. I looked at him.

"I figured you knew what you were signing." He sighed. "I'm truly sorry. If you and Sara want your cameras down, we'll get them right down."

"Oh, I'll bet."

Just then, Melody Seward turned in to the circle in her Acura, on her way home from her shift at the bank. Her eyes widened as she drove around, passing me and two cops standing in Big Brother Mallory's driveway. I thought back to one of the video files I'd scanned on his laptop. A Saturday night, only three weeks ago. On fast forward, it looked like Melody jogging over to our house, staying for an hour, then sprinting back to her house.

"I was even sorrier Heartland Realty wouldn't let me get a feed up while your place was on the market," Roger said. He gave Officers Bill and Stump the quick rundown of our break-in, then explained that the previous owners hadn't wanted an alarm system from Sentinel, despite the neighborhood discount. "We'd had the cameras running that night, maybe we'd have caught the son of a bitch." He looked at me as though daring me to keep going. *Anything else you want to add?*

"This is incredible." I turned to the cops, unable to stop myself. "He's been going through our garbage, too."

"Sir?"

"I found my credit card statement on his desk." My voice seemed to be climbing in spite of my efforts to seem like the reasonable party here. "I tore it up last night, and he taped it back together again."

The conversation went downhill from there. According to Roger, the raccoons had gotten into our trash. It had been windy overnight, and the litter had blown into his yard.

"I guess I probably stepped over the line a bit." He put on a sheepish look. "I'll admit that."

The cops nodded along supportively, waiting to hear more.

"Paul," Roger said, speaking to me, but framing his words for Officers Bill and Stump, "I was going to give that thing back to you and Sara next time I saw you. Figured maybe I could talk you folks into getting yourselves a paper shredder." He sighed. "I just wanted to show you how easy it would be for a person to piece together all kinds of personal information if they wanted. You just never know what somebody out there might do."

"Not these days," Officer Bill said.

"Bought my wife one of those things," Officer Stump conceded. "Paper shredder, I mean. You can get 'em pretty cheap."

At that point, watching Officers Bill and Stump swallow Roger's ridiculous explanation hook, line, and sinker, I realized that these two ham hocks were taking every word he said as gospel.

Ask him to explain why he's got personal files on all his neighbors, I wanted to tell them. *Ask where he got our Social Security numbers. Ask him to explain why he's got a copy of my doctoral thesis from the NYU library. While you're at it, ask him to tell you about some guy named Darius Calvin. Because he's got all kinds of information about some guy named Darius Calvin. I'm anxious to hear more about that one myself.*

But it was three against one. I was outnumbered and outgunned. The victorious warrior wins first.

I said, "You guys aren't going to do anything about this, are you?"

Officer Stump turned to me. "Sir, I'll be honest. At this point, I'm not clear on what exactly you'd like us to do."

"As far as I can see," Officer Bill added, "the trespassing complaint here isn't yours."

They both looked at Roger.

Roger shook his head. "No, guys. There's no complaint here."

"You sure about that, Rodge?"

"I think all we have here is a misunderstanding." Roger shook his head again for emphasis. "As far as I'm concerned, Paul did me a favor."

"Oh?"

"No telling where Wessie might have ended up." Roger looked at the officers. Then he looked at me. He was still looking at me when he said, "I'm just glad somebody was paying attention."

32.

AN HOUR AFTER THE POLICE HAD GONE, Sara returned home from campus to find me in our driveway, in full view of Roger's house, demolishing a wireless security camera with a hammer from the garage. She watched awhile, then said, "Bad day?"

"Hi, honey." I gave her a kiss. "There's a stew on in the house." Then I went back to work on the camera.

Everyone in the circle knew they had these damned things pointed at their houses? And they'd actually signed up for it? My first instinct was disbelief, but logic suggested strongly that Roger wouldn't have claimed such an easily verifiable fact if it weren't true. I just couldn't believe that during all the nights I'd spent walking the neighborhood with Pete, or Michael, or even Barry Firth, not once had anybody expressed any qualms or concerns regarding this neighborhood surveillance feed. Was I the only one who found such a thing intolerable?

As I thought about it, I decided it wasn't surprising that I hadn't received any complaints from Barry, who clearly hungered for Roger's approval. It seemed that Pete Seward had withdrawn a bit since that first day we'd spent on the golf course, when I'd overheard his conversation with Roger on the clubhouse deck. But Pete had his own reasons for that. The truth was, ever since that night I still wished I could unspend with Melody, I'd withdrawn more than a little myself.

I decided I'd go over to Michael's after he got home from the restaurant. If I was overreacting to any or all of this, I could count on Michael to tell me so.

Meanwhile, I hadn't finished reacting yet. While I took a certain amount of satisfaction in mangling the camera, this was ultimately kid stuff, and the feeling didn't last for very long after I was through.

I considered walking over and leaving the camera shrapnel on Roger's doorstep. Then I got a better idea, went inside, and looked up the street address for Sentinel One, Incorporated. I kissed Sara again on my way out, told her I'd be back for dinner, and drove to Sentinel One's office building on Dewberry Street.

"I'm sorry, sir," the receptionist told me. She had a wide mouth and lank brown hair, and I believe there was something about my demeanor that scared her a little. "Mr. Gardner is gone for the day."

"Is that what he told you?" I nodded at her phone, which she'd just hung up. "Call back and tell him it's Paul Callaway. One of Roger's neighbors."

"I told him your name, sir."

I smiled. "I thought you said he'd left for the day?"

The receptionist blanched. Her eyes darted to one side, then the other. There was nobody else in the reception area. It was only her and me.

"All right," I said. Even with my temper up, I felt a little sorry for her. She was only doing her job. I raised the plastic SaveMore bag, which contained the remains of our backyard camera. "Tell Mr. Gardner that we'll be discontinuing the special service at 34 Sycamore Court."

The receptionist recoiled slightly when I dropped the sack on the desk in front of her with a clatter. She blinked at me. She looked at the sack. She took up a pen and began scribbling on a memo pad. I turned and walked out the door I'd come in.

The days had grown shorter. It was already dusk outside, fading by the minute. On my way through the customer parking lot behind the Sentinel One office building, I felt a familiar tingle at the back of my neck and glanced over my shoulder.

In a lighted window, behind open blinds, I saw a figure watching me. I could discern the shape of a bald head from where I stood. Almost as soon as I turned, the light in the window went dark. The glass turned flat, reflecting the indigo sky.

Gone for the day, my ass.

Sara sighed when I finished describing the events of the afternoon. "Paul," she said.

"Me? What me?" I pointed over my shoulder, generally indicating the neighborhood beyond our door, specifically meaning Roger's house on the other side of the circle. *"Him."*

She shook her head, poured us each a glass of wine. "I just don't know."

On the table between us sat our Sentinel One service contract, which I'd found upstairs. Sara picked up the contract, folded the pages back, and reread the video security clause. We'd found the provision together, along with my initials, right where Roger had claimed they would be.

Gently, she said, "Weren't you here with the installers that day?"

Of course I'd been here. I'd gotten the hell out of the way, tried to ignore the racket, and when the guys from Sentinel One were finished, I'd signed where the guy told me, thanked him for all the work, and closed the door behind him. Which was all, as far as I was concerned, completely beside the point.

"Cameras or no cameras." I flicked the contract with the back of my finger. "Nothing in here changes the fact that Roger's got a filing box full of *our* personal information hidden away over there." I drank half my wine in a gulp. "The son of a bitch probably knows more about us than *I* do off the top of my head."

She frowned. "What was his explanation?"

"Who, Roger?"

"What did he say when you talked to him?"

"I wasn't interested in Roger's explanation," I told her. "There *is* no explanation."

Sara tilted her wineglass back and forth on its base. She chewed her lip the way she did when she was thinking hard about what to say next.

I waited as long as I could, then finally said, "What?"

"Nothing," she said. Then she shrugged. "I was just thinking of Larry Anders for some reason."

I couldn't help rolling my eyes. Larry Anders had been our next-door neighbor back in Newton. "This isn't even remotely the—"

"Remember the time he came over and recommended that lawn service?" She seemed vaguely nostalgic, as though watching the memory replay in her wineglass. "He gave you their business card. And a coupon, as I recall."

"Sara..."

"You told him to get bent," she reminded me. "In so many words. And then you let the yard go for the rest of the summer."

"Larry Anders was a jackass," I reminded her. "You never liked him either."

"True," she said. "But I didn't make him my personal sworn nemesis." As soon as I opened my mouth to argue, she waved the comment away. *Withdrawn, Your Honor.* "What did the police say?"

"I told you, they just stood there agreeing with everything Roger—"

"Not about the cameras," she said. "I mean this box of stuff you found."

"I didn't tell them about any of that."

She looked at me. "Should I even bother to ask why not?"

"What was I supposed to say? Officers, I was poking around in Roger's attic and I found *this*?" I knocked back the rest of my wine. "Believe me, they were already pretty sure that *I* was the problem."

I caught Sara glancing toward the service contract on the table, a seemingly accidental gesture, which she covered quickly. She said nothing.

Little by little, I began to recognize how unconvincing my reasoning must have sounded to Sara—in part because I hadn't told her the full scope of my feud with Roger. And now I was forced to stop and consider my position.

I couldn't tell Sara everything. Not without telling her everything.

And in telling Sara only part of the truth, I knew that I was telling her a lie. Just as surely as I'd been lying to her for weeks now: by pretending that what had happened between me and Melody Seward, that one irredeemably rotten-headed night, hadn't really happened at all.

The same way I was lying to myself: by telling myself that one thing had nothing to do with the other. By telling myself that I was, in some way, protecting our marriage by pretending as if I hadn't betrayed it.

"I haven't told you everything," I said.

She smiled a little. "You mean there's more?"

I felt as though I were flying low with a full payload. I nodded at her wineglass. "You'd better have some of that."

She gave me a stern look.

So I told her about the paperwork I'd found. Employment history records, duplicate copies of photo ID cards, even a copy of birth certificate, all filed neatly away in Roger's box labeled *34 Sycamore Court.* All about a man named Darius Calvin. Our wolf.

I watched Sara's face as this piece of heavy ordnance drifted toward her, suspended on my carefully constructed parachute of narrative. By the time I'd stopped talking, she wasn't looking at me anymore.

"Four months," I said, reaching across the table. "Four months, and the cops don't even pretend to have any leads."

Her hand felt stiff in mine.

"How is it," I said, "that Roger Mallory has a whole damned *dossier* on this guy, whom the cops can't seem to find, in a box with our name on it?"

Sara looked down at her wine. While I'd finished mine, she still hadn't taken the first sip of hers.

I waited.

After a long minute of silence, she pulled her hand away casually and said, "Paul, I don't know what you saw over there."

"I'm telling you what I saw."

"What you're telling me doesn't make any sense."

"That's exactly my point."

More silence. I couldn't read the expression on her face. I said, "Say something."

She swirled her wine carefully in her glass. At last, she met my eye.

I held her gaze. "What?"

"You said it yourself." She sighed. "It happened months ago."

"And?"

"And we were both out of our wits. And it all happened so fast."

I saw where this was going. It felt like something wilting in my chest.

Sara said, "Can you be sure you'd even recognize him? If you saw him now?"

Without pausing to check myself, I said, "Would you?"

Her expression hardened. She straightened her spine, placed her wineglass on the table. Folded her hands in front of her.

"I'm sorry," I said. "But I think we both remember that night pretty clearly."

"I don't know what you saw over there," she said. Unlike me, she appeared to be measuring her words carefully. "I wasn't with you. I didn't see it for myself."

"But you think that I don't—"

"I think that this isn't about Roger," she said. "And it's not about the cameras. Or a box. Or the neighborhood patrol, or any of it."

"No?" My voice had acquired a peevish tone that even I didn't like. "Then what do you think this is about? I mean, tell me. Because I can't—"

"I know you're not happy here," she said, and now I did recognize her expression. Sadness. "I know that you resent me a little bit for taking this job, even if you've done a good job hiding it."

I think it was the look on her face, more than her words, that set me back on my heels. But the words still landed like a blind punch. When had Sara formulated this theory? I hadn't seen it coming. I had no defense.

I said, "What?"

"I can't even say that I blame you," she said. "I certainly can't blame you for being frustrated. Neither of us have been ourselves since we left home. Especially since the baby."

"Sara."

"You've been distant," she said. "*I've* been distant. I'm not blaming either one of us."

"Just stop a minute."

She held up a hand, stopping *me* instead. "I don't know what's going on with you and Roger. You never gave me a straight answer about why you dropped out of the neighborhood watch, and for now that's fine. I don't know what he did to make you his enemy, and that's fine for now too." She took a long sip of her wine. "I don't know what you found over there."

I tried to take her hand again. She moved beyond my reach. "Sara, please."

"All I know," she said, "is that we need help."

I pulled my hand back and looked at her.

She looked at her wine.

"You've got finals," she finally said. "I've got a million things. We've got the party to plan." She took another sip, then placed her wineglass down on the table. "But once this god-awful semester is finally over and done with, I want us to find a good marriage counselor."

How had this conversation brought us here?

"Maybe sometime after that," Sara said, "we can worry about Roger."

I was out of words.

She was too.

We sat and looked at each other.

Later that night, I received an e-mail from Roger. I'd never given him my e-mail address, but there it was:

Paul,

You left your jacket here. Sorry about Wes, and thank you again. I sent the jacket to the cleaners and will pick up the bill. They say it will be ready December 16.

RM

I sat upstairs at my computer for a long time, imagining Roger across the circle, sitting at his.

I finally bent over the keyboard and carefully drafted several good, subtle counterthreats regarding my soiled jacket, particularly with regard to its December 16 availability. I sat awhile longer, trying to decide which reply I liked best. I finally scrapped them all and typed:

Roger,

Get bent.

Paul

Still later—long after Sara had double-checked all the doors and windows and collapsed into bed, after I was sure she'd fallen asleep—I went back upstairs and printed an Internet map. I went downstairs and found my old duffel bag under the stairs in the basement.

Then I went out to the garage, got in my car, and drove to a medical supply warehouse on the south side of town.

33.

ACCORDING TO THE RECORDS I'd found in Roger's files, Darius Calvin worked swing shift on the shipping and receiving dock at Missouri Valley Medical Shipping & Warehousing Incorporated.

From my spot across the service road, in the dark lot of an abandoned auto parts store, I could see the entire loading bay and most of the employee parking area.

I dug around in the glove box, found my penlight, and read a book while I waited. I'd just picked up the latest paperback in the series about the ass-kicking drifter; it seemed like just the inspiration I needed. I pretended it was a self-help book.

By the time the 5–2 shift at the warehouse ended, the hero in the novel was on his way to a gunfight at the countryside enclave of the underground militia group, who ran a giant meth lab to generate funding for their various domestic terrorism projects. I cornered the page and started the car. Waited.

Darius Calvin eventually stepped out onto the well-lighted loading dock with a thermos in one hand, a canvas work coat in the other. I'd only seen him once before, and under duress at that. But even at a hundred yards, I recognized the man who'd attacked Sara in our bedroom.

He rolled his shoulders and cracked his neck. He seemed to look right at me for a moment, though I knew there was no way he could see me in the dark. Was there?

Then he nodded to some guys and headed in the other direction, toward a rusted Ford Tempo in the employee parking lot.

I followed him to a peeling, sagging little one-story house near the railroad tracks. It wasn't a Safer Places neighborhood.

Darius Calvin didn't have an alarm system from Sentinel One Incorporated. He didn't have an alarm system from anybody. He didn't even have curtains on his windows.

He was asleep on a moth-eaten couch, in front of an old *Barney Miller* repeat on the rabbit-eared television, when I kicked his foot. He jerked awake—still in his work clothes—to find some crazy white intruder standing over him with an aluminum softball bat.

"What the fuck?" he said.

"You don't lock your front door?" It was actually exhilarating, in a dry-heave sort of way. Being there. Having the upper hand. I tried to talk like the hero from the novel I'd been reading. "That doesn't seem very safe."

Calvin rubbed his eyes, looked at me closely. Recognition seeped into his eyes. He said, "Aw, hell no."

"So you do remember me? I wasn't sure if you would."

He started to sit up on the couch. At his first flinch, I drew the bat back, slugger style. My heart was pounding in my throat. I felt a little dizzy. The bat hadn't been out of my duffel bag since the Dixson English department softball team broke up.

I pulled myself together and said, “Fair warning. I was a better softball player than I am a golfer.”

Darius Calvin closed his eyes and sighed like a punctured tire.

34.

HE TOLD ME EVERYTHING. About his run-in with a cop named Stockman. About his arrangement with Roger Mallory. About $1,000 in cash, which Roger apparently had paid him later as hush money.

Looking back, I could see all the ways our tender new roots in Clark Falls had been fertilized by this single harrowing experience: the night I'd found Darius Calvin in our bedroom, covering Sara's mouth with his hand. But of all the things Darius Calvin told me that night, one thing stuck in the front of my mind:

I could tell they were beefin'.

"Beefing?" I'd put away my softball bat by then. "What does that mean? Beefing?"

"Like maybe they weren't exactly on the same page," he'd said. "The cop and what's-his-name."

"Roger?"

"That's the dude from TV?"

"Yes."

"Yeah, well." Darius shrugged. "It was him runnin' the show, not the cop. Matter of fact, that cop seemed nervous to be there, you ask me."

"Beefing," I'd said, and then asked him, "What were they saying to each other?"

"Man, I stayed outta that shit."

The next morning, I spent a half hour on the Internet, then an hour in the microfiche room at the *Clark Falls Telegram*. In that time I'd pieced together an engagement notice and a wedding announcement for Roger Mallory and Clair Stockman. I found obituaries for Brandon and Clair Mallory. I found enough news coverage of the Brandon Mallory abduction to identify the overlaps between Darius Calvin's story, Roger's family photographs, and the Clark Falls Police Department. I was certain that the cop Darius had known only as "Stockman" was a patrol sergeant named Van Stockman. Brandon's uncle, Clair's brother. Roger's best man.

Why had Van and Roger been "beefing" over Darius Calvin? My thoughts ran back to my father's take on marriage. Those little cracks you couldn't see until they opened up. Had cracks formed between Roger and his old partner?

Was there a way to slip into one? Pry it open a little?

All I knew was that I couldn't take on Roger Mallory alone. I needed volunteers for the resistance, and it would be one hell of a coup if Van Stockman turned out to be my first recruit.

I canceled my classes for the day and drove to Stockman's yellow brick duplex near Expedition Park. I parked beneath a hanging willow, walked up the stone path, and knocked on the door marked with Stockman's address.

A middle-aged woman in a sweatshirt and jeans answered. "Can I help you?"

"Hi," I said. "Mrs. Stockman?"

She dried her chapped hands on a dish towel and eyed me. "I'm Valerie Stockman. What can I do for you?"

"Actually, I'm here to see Van." I'd planned my lie on the way over. A variation on a page from the Maya Lamb playbook. "I'm with the *Des Moines Register.* We're doing a feature story on the Safer Places Organization?"

"Oh, sure," she said. She smiled. "Of course."

"I'm sorry to barge in like this. I should have called ahead."

"No, not at all."

"Is your husband at home?"

She looked confused.

"Mr. Stockman," I said. "I know he works nights, thought it might be best to try him during the afternoon."

"You're talking about Van, right?"

"I'm sorry," I said. "I should call and schedule a—"

Valerie laughed and opened the door. "You really do need help with your story."

"I do?"

"Van's my brother," she said. "He lives on the other side. Come on in."

"Oh." I pretended to look embarrassed, but honestly, I didn't need to pretend very hard. Apparently I hadn't done my homework so well after all. "Sorry again. I can go across."

"Never mind, we connect in the middle. I'll go on over and tell him you're here." She led me through the entry into a small living room, where an old man sat in a recliner, dressed in pajamas, watching a game show on the television. "Can I get you anything? Coffee?"

"Oh, thanks, no. I'm fine."

"Well, make yourself comfortable. I'll get Van. Dad, this is . . . What was your name?"

I threw out the first name that popped into my head. "Ben Holland."

"Ben Holland, Dad. He's doing a story on Roger."

The old man grimaced, never lifting his gaze from the television screen. Valerie rolled her eyes, swiped a hand at him, and gave me an apologetic look. *He's stubborn.* "I'll be right back."

"Thanks," I said. "I'll be fine."

She disappeared around a corner and down the adjoining hall. In her absence, awkward silence slowly enveloped the living room. The old man—Clair Mallory's father, I presumed—appeared to be swimming in his pajamas. He had a clear tube taped under his nose. The tubing trailed across his afghan to an oxygen tank on the floor beside the chair. The table next to him was crowded with medicine bottles and used tissues.

On another table, I saw a portable nebulizer machine similar to the one I'd had as a kid, right up until I'd outgrown my asthma at the age of twelve. I saw a blue bulb syringe like I'd seen Trish Firth use on the twins' noses when they had colds.

There were other items I couldn't name. They all looked medical. The room had the sour, musty smell of age and illness.

"Afternoon, sir." I nodded politely. "How are you?"

He coughed. It was a horrid, gurgling sound deep in his chest. It seemed to start slowly, gathering momentum until finally seizing him in a fit. By the end he'd nearly doubled over in the chair. As the afghan shifted, I saw blue veins and pale white ankles and what looked like a Foley bag propped on the leg rest of the recliner between his slippered feet. He spat into a tissue, looked at the result, scowled, and tossed the tissue onto the table with the others.

"Dying," he said, without looking at me. "How the hell are you?"

I stood mute.

"Take a picture," he said. "You can look at it later."

I looked away quickly, embarrassed, moving my gaze around the room. Curio cabinet in the corner. Pendulum clock above the television. A replica of a familiar painting over the couch: Jesus praying in the Garden of Gethsemane, face turned up toward a beam from the heavens, disciples asleep in the background. My parents had a smaller version of the same portrait in their guest bedroom.

Somewhere in the house, I heard voices, followed by footfalls that sounded heavier coming back than Valerie Stockman's had sounded going away.

In a moment, she reappeared in the living room. "Ben," she said. "This is my brother, Van."

A man filled the doorway behind her. He was built like a pile of sandbags, somewhere in his late forties, with a full mustache, razored salt-and-pepper hair, and dark, watchful eyes. Dressed in a nylon flight jacket, he looked very much like an off-duty cop, or possibly the defensive line coach for the university football program. Seeing him, I had the distinct feeling that I'd met him before, though I couldn't think where or why.

"Sergeant Stockman," I said, already anxious to dispense with this reporter ruse. I didn't know how Maya Lamb managed to do this for a living. "I'm sorry to bother you. I was just in town doing a—"

"Sure, Val filled me in." He smiled, crossing the floor in three strides and offering his hand. "No bother at all, Ben. Roger's family, happy to help."

"You look like you're on your way somewhere."

"Work," he said. "But I got ten or fifteen I can spare. Nice little coffee shop down the street. Care to follow?"

"That sounds great," I said.

He stepped over to the recliner, bent down, and kissed the old man on top of his head. "Take it easy, Pop."

Without looking away from the television, the old man reached out with one tremor-stricken hand and patted his son on the wrist.

"And stop giving Val so much shit. Take your goddamned meds when she says. Hear?"

The old man grunted.

Van Stockman rolled his eyes in much the same way his sister had a few moments earlier. "Follow me."

I turned to Valerie Stockman. "Thanks for your help."

"My pleasure," she said.

I followed her brother out the door, down the steps, and

across the yard to a big, gleaming Dodge Ram pickup sitting in the driveway on the other side of the duplex. He was chuckling to himself by the time we got there.

"Listen," I said.

"Des Moines." He turned to look at me, shaking his head. "You're not all that fuckin' smart for a college professor, are you?"

I don't remember how I responded to that. I suppose I stood there looking not all that smart.

"Don't remember me, do you?" He had a cold smile.

I was certainly trying.

Van Stockman went on shaking his head. But something changed in his eyes. I thought back to another thing Darius Calvin had told me. *Dude gave me this look, shrank my nuts.* In that moment, looking at Van Stockman, I believed that I understood what Darius had been talking about.

"Watch your step," Stockman said. "Professor."

With that, he walked around the tailgate, got into his truck, and left me standing there.

Later that night, I sat up in bed. Sara stirred beside me. Voice thick with sleep, she said, "What's the matter?"

"A mustache."

"What?"

"He has a mustache."

She yawned, patted me on the leg, turned over. "You're dreaming. Go back to sleep."

I knew I couldn't be dreaming, because I hadn't been to sleep yet. My alarm clock read 3 a.m.; it had taken me that long to realize why Sergeant Van Stockman had seemed so familiar to me earlier that afternoon.

It wasn't because I'd seen his face in Roger's family photos, or in the newspaper articles I'd retrieved from the *Telegram*. I'd seen him in person before. Right here in our house. The night we moved in.

In the darkness of our bedroom, I pictured the burly cop who'd carried my golf club out the front door. He'd nodded to us as he left. I'd only seen him for a moment, but now that I'd placed him, I found that I could call his image up from memory—as it seemed I could so many details regarding that night—with high clarity.

Middle-aged. Clean-shaven. Same thick face, same pocked cheeks, same watchful eyes.

In my mind, I transferred his face to a sketch pad and scribbled a mustache on him.

Safer Places one, resistance zip.

Monday, December 19—3:45 p.m.

35.

WHILE I'VE BEEN TALKING, The Firehouse has filled up with people. Maya Lamb and I have finished our beers and ordered a second round.

I'm kicking myself under the table, knowing I've gone too far. I only intended to warm her up with Roger's video cameras and my adventures this morning at the Loess Point Mall. I didn't mean to bring up Van Stockman, and I definitely didn't mean to get into the whole concept of Darius Calvin. At least not yet. But I got caught up in my own story, and now here we are.

"You're kidding," she says. "Right?"

I shrug. "Wish I were."

When she drops her eyes, I realize that she doesn't believe a word of this. I'm not sure that I would if I were sitting on her side of the table.

Then she looks up and says, "We need to bushwhack this dirtball schoolteacher before the lawyers get to him." She produces a notepad and a pen as if from the air. "Brand, you said. Timothy? That's his name?"

"Hold on," I say, holding up my hands, surprised at her response. "Wait a minute. We had a deal. Remember?"

Maya does her best to pantomime the appearance of patience. But she's practically vibrating in place on her side of the booth. She says, "Paul, listen. Let me tell you what's going to happen."

"I help you, and you help me," I say. "Right? You gave me your word."

"Exactly. That's exactly what I'm—"

"How does 'bushwhacking' Timothy Brand help me, exactly?"

"That's what I'm trying to—"

"I'll be lucky if my attorney doesn't quit when he hears I've been talking to you in the first place."

"Just listen to me for a minute. Will you hear me out?"

I stop talking. Drink my beer.

"Actually," she says, "answer me something first. You say that Roger Mallory told you he wanted you to move out of the neighborhood. Right?"

"Right."

"How did you respond?"

"I laughed at him."

"Right. Now take this teacher, Brand. Mr. B, the McNally girl called him?" She opens her hands for comparison: me on the one hand, Mr. B on the other. "Brittany gets in over her head with some scumbag schoolteacher who likes to take pictures. She's scared to tell her folks, so she goes to Roger Mallory for help. Roger Mallory decides to protect her from shame and scandal, spare her the scarlet letter."

I toast her ongoing facility with the lit references. I'll bet she was that one kid who always showed up for class early and sat in front.

"So Mallory pays the schoolteacher the same kind of visit he paid you. How do you guess that went?"

"I don't know, I wasn't there."

"And Timothy Brand, apparently, is no longer a history teacher at Bluffs View Middle. Me?" She sips her beer. "I'd guess that Mallory must have put the fear of God into him."

"I'm still not following your argument."

"It's a no-brainer," she says. "Timothy Brand suddenly quits his job and leaves town? If that's the deal he made with Roger Mallory to keep himself out of trouble, why would he come clean now?"

"I assume he'll be subpoenaed."

"What makes you think he'll tell anyone the truth?"

"He'll have to. According to Rachel McNally—"

"You mean the girl who told you a story because you bought her a four-hundred-dollar iPod? That Rachel McNally?"

"Wait a minute..."

"Do you have anything that backs up her little story? Any corroborating sources?" She raises her eyebrows. She shakes her head. *I didn't think so.* "What you've got are the statements of a thirteen-year-old girl whom you bribed to talk to you. And then you've got *another* thirteen-year-old girl who's already named *you* as the photographer."

For all I know, she's absolutely right about all of this. But I still feel like I've put my foot in a bucket of trouble.

"Anyway," Maya says, "you don't even need the schoolteacher for your case anymore. Brit Seward's tattoo clears you on that front. You couldn't have taken the pictures if you weren't here."

"Obviously."

"So your attorney?" She points at my chest. "I promise you, he's only thinking about what was actually found on your computer at this point. The schoolteacher has nothing to do with that. So what do you care?"

"If Mr. B's got no reason to tell the truth, he's certainly not going to talk to a reporter."

"You'd be surprised how far you can get with people," she tells me, "if you can trip them up on camera."

"If you say so."

"I got *you* talking on camera, didn't I?"

I suppose I can't argue that.

Maya senses my frustration and eases up on the full-court press. "Look, I gave you my word. Believe it or not, I'm one of those strange little people who still thinks that counts for something." She fiddles with her sodden beer coaster a moment. "How about this? Let's make it a bet."

"How do you mean?"

"Call your lawyer. See if he's found Timothy Brand yet."

"First tell me—"

"Just call him."

What the hell. I pull out the cell phone Douglas Bennett gave me. The Firehouse has gotten busier since I first arrived; all around us, people are talking and laughing and toasting the holidays. I slide out of the booth, walk to a quieter spot, and dial Bennett's direct line.

"Paul," he says. "Where are you?"

"Any word on Timothy Brand?"

"Debbie's working on it," he says. "I just got off the phone with the county attorney. What the hell is this I hear about you buying Rachel McNally an iPod?"

I hang up and walk back to the booth.

Maya Lamb says, "Well?"

"They're all over it."

"Okay, then. Are you game?"

"Tell me the bet first."

"If your attorney's office finds Timothy Brand before I can, I'll back off. Otherwise, first come, first served."

I think about the terms. Debbie the Intern has almost a five-hour head start. She's been working on this all afternoon. Anyway, Maya Lamb is right. At this point, Mr. B isn't my stay-out-of-jail card.

"Fine," I tell her. "If it makes you happy, call it a bet. I'm going to the bathroom."

I go. When I return to our booth in the alcove, Maya Lamb is talking on her cell phone. Her laptop computer is sitting on the table in front of her. She sees me coming, finishes her conversation, and snaps the phone shut. Then she closes her laptop, puts it back into her bag, and climbs out of the booth.

"Got him," she says.

"You gotta be kidding."

Maya Lamb grins. "Want to come along and supervise?"

36.

SOMEHOW, within one hour's time, Maya Lamb has managed to locate Timothy Brand, determine that he's answering his home telephone, and finagle from her news station a Ford Explorer, a set of long-range Motorola walkie-talkies, and a cameraman named Josh. It's a little bit fascinating to observe her at work.

"Timothy Brand," she says over the walkie-talkie. I can hear Blondie blaring in the background. "Gonna getcha getcha getcha."

I'm following the Explorer in my car. I key my radio. It's almost like being back on the old neighborhood patrol. "You realize it'll be midnight before we get there."

Beep. Crackle. Maya says, "My boy Josh drives fast. Better keep up."

Monday afternoon rush-hour traffic thins quickly on the edge of town. Forty minutes south, we approach the Flying J truck stop where Douglas Bennett and I met Darius Calvin just two nights ago. This time, instead of taking the off-ramp, I follow Maya and Josh through the interchange, onto I-80, heading east.

Maya's research blitz has tracked Timothy Brand to a rental house in Iowa City, on the opposite side of the state. It's a five-hour drive—more or less the same drive Sara and I made five months ago, traveling the other direction. We'd stayed the night at a Holiday Inn off the Interstate. Our last stop on our way to Clark Falls.

Maya Lamb, Josh the camera guy, and I manage to make the whole trip without stopping or being pulled over by the state patrol. It's half past ten by the time we arrive in town. My back feels stiff, kidneys crunched. I'd probably be asleep at the wheel if I didn't need a bathroom so badly.

Maya's voice comes over the radio. "Josh needs to pee. There's a Kwik Star up ahead."

I key the button. "Right behind you."

Beep. Crackle. "Emphasis on Kwik."

10:45 p.m.

We pull to the curb on a quiet residential street on the east side of town. Timothy Brand's house is conspicuous by virtue of being the only house on the block not outlined in holiday lights.

It's cold, but not brutal. A few snowflakes drift in the air, floating gently toward the bare ground. The weatherpeople say it looks to be a white Christmas.

"Hey." Josh nods toward my hybrid as he pulls his camera gear from the back of the Explorer. "How many miles you get on that, anyway?"

"I've never kept track," I tell him. "You?"

"Put seventy bucks in the tank back there."

"Long drive."

"The station pays for the gas," Maya says. "Now shut up, you guys. It's work time."

We move up the sidewalk, toward Timothy Brand's undecorated rental house. The blue glow of a television bleeds through one of the curtains upstairs.

"Watch but don't talk," Maya tells me. "Okay?"

"You're the professional."

"Hey, Josh, throw the hood over the camera."

Josh looks at the sky. "Just flurries."

"I don't care about the snow, I want you to cover our call sign. And turn your hat backward, huh?"

Josh shrugs, turns his Channel Five cap backward, and pulls a black canvas shroud from the bag on his shoulder.

We head up the steps, onto the front porch. Maya signals with her hand, and Josh veers to her left, stepping lightly, settling his camera on his shoulder as he moves. We could be a small liberal arts and communications SWAT team getting ready to smash down the door. I decide to move back down the steps and wait at the bottom.

"Here we go," Maya says. "Ready?" Josh gives a thumbs-up and nestles his eye against the viewfinder. Maya rings the doorbell.

Nothing happens. We stand around.

Maya rings the bell again and a dog barks somewhere in the house. In a moment, the porch light comes on, sudden and blinding. Curtains move. For at least a minute, nothing else happens.

Then comes the sound of locks tumbling.

Everyone seems to pause at the sight of the guy who opens the front door. Josh actually moves his eye away from the viewfinder. It's the first time I've ever seen Maya Lamb hesitate. There's a brief hiccup in her rhythm while she finds her smile and puts it on. "Mr. Brand?"

"Yes?"

Maybe I expected some greasy-haired bogeyman. Brit's

seventh-grade volleyball coach appears to be about my age. He appears to have been a handsome, athletic guy.

He also appears as though he may be recovering from an airplane crash. He holds the door with one hand, which is encased in some kind of orthopedic brace; his other hand supports his weight on the handle of a four-legged cane. A medium-sized mutt stands guard by his ankle, watching us.

But it's his face we're all looking at. Timothy Brand is a mess, bitten all over by what look like relatively fresh scars. The area beneath one of his eyes has a buckled appearance, the cheekbone dented in like a soda can. The eye itself seems to wander independently. In one spot, matching scars on his top and bottom lips make one side of his mouth appear sewn together, as though cinched by heavy thread.

"Can I help you?"

Maya finally finds a voice to go with the smile. "We're sorry to bother you so late. I'm with Channel Nine Iowa City, and we're covering reports of a—"

"Hey, don't I recognize you?" He looks closer, moving stiffly. His bathrobe hangs open, showing an old T-shirt, faded gym shorts, bony legs, and house slippers. I see thick, wormy surgical scars on both knees. "You're Maya Lamb, aren't you?"

"That's right," she says. "I'm flattered. You must be a regular viewer."

"I usually watch Eleven." Brand smiles. "But I used to see you all the time in Clark Falls. Channel Five, right? How long have you been here?"

"Actually, this is my very first story," she says.

"Wow. I guess I'm the one who's flattered."

What the hell kind of bushwhack is this? I expected an overpowering barrage of questions. After a five-hour drive, I figured we'd be going Mike Wallace on this guy. Shocking and awing. Getting the goods. Maya Lamb seems off her game.

But she keeps right on smiling. "You lived in Clark Falls?"

"I taught school there," he says. "Until this past June."

Something about Brand's smile seems off to me. His front

three or four teeth seem whiter than the others. A little too square. In the porch light, I catch a glint of metal in the corner of his mouth and figure out the oddity: he's wearing a partial denture. I try and imagine him without it. In my imagination, his smile has a wide ragged hole in the middle.

Brand shifts his weight to his other leg. As he props himself against the open door, the stretched neck of his T-shirt sags to reveal another pink scar in the pit of his throat. A horizontal line with a pucker in the middle.

I've seen this kind of scar before. One of the poets back at Dixson acquired one after a dicey bout with viral meningitis, and my first wife's grandmother had one for some reason I'd never learned. This kind of scar means that at some point in fairly recent history, Timothy Brand was connected to a breathing machine.

The dog barks once, from his throat, as though reminding his owner it's late to be having visitors, then disappears into the house.

"I'm sorry," Brand says. "What's your story, again?"

"Reports of vandalism in the neighborhood," Maya repeats. She sounds distracted.

"I haven't heard anything about—"

"Listen, Mr. Brand, as long as I'm here, would you mind if I asked you something completely off the subject?"

Honestly, she sounds like an amateur. And Timothy Brand is beginning to seem suspicious.

"I'm working on a new feature series," she tells him, obviously making this up as she goes along. It's almost embarrassing. "Survivor stories. For the Living segment. Forgive me for being opportunistic, but I can't help noticing that you've been through something quite serious yourself."

"I was involved in a car accident," he explains, by rote, as though he can't get through the line at the grocery store without answering this question. "Shortly after I moved here."

"I'm so sorry," Maya says. "Would you mind if I asked—"

"It was a hit-and-run, I spent three weeks in the hospital, I still have physical therapy six days a week, and no, I don't think I'm interested in being the subject of a survivor story."

"My gosh," Maya says.

I catch movement in the curtains from the corner of my eye. In the front window, the dog now stands with its front paws on the back of a sofa, watching us.

Bark bark.

Each time the dog sounds off, Timothy Brand's guard seems to rise. "Why is he still filming me?"

"Did they catch the guy who ran you down?"

Brand's smile is gone, and his eyes have gone wary. "How do you know my name? I haven't heard about any vandalism in the neighborhood. Why do you know my name?"

I'm getting cold standing here. Timothy Brand has told this hit-and-run lie so many times that it fits like an old pair of jeans. Of course, there's no evidence to back up what I know, in my gut, really happened to this guy.

"We have reports," I say.

"Who are *you*?"

Maya glares at me.

As I climb the steps, she tries to call me off with her eyes. When she sees me reaching into the inside pocket of my coat, she gives her head a very small, very hard shake.

"We have reports that this man has been defacing property in the neighborhood." *Defacing property.* A good line, if I do say so. "Ever seen him around?"

I hand him the portrait I'd printed from the Clark Falls PD Web site on my way to meet Maya Lamb at the brewpub earlier this afternoon. The laser printer in the business suite of the Residence Inn was low on toner, so the photo fades out toward the bottom, and you can't see the badge. But Van Stockman's face is perfectly legible.

It didn't have nearly the impact on Maya Lamb when I showed it to her that it seems to have on Timothy Brand. It's as if I've handed him a coiled and deadly snake. His eyes go wide. His whole body seems to tense. When he looks at me over the top edge of the paper, I see the printout trembling at the corners.

I nod. "Guess you have. How'd you sell that hit-and-run story to the doctors, anyway? He beat you with a car bumper or something?"

I'm starting to become familiar with the look I'm seeing in Brand's eyes. It's the same one I saw in Darius Calvin's eyes, when he woke on his own couch, after a long shift at work, to find a softball bat aimed at his head. It's a version of the same thing I remember seeing in Sara's eyes, the night Darius Calvin covered her mouth with his hand.

Timothy Brand is scared shitless. One look at a copy of a computer scan of an outdated portrait of a cop named Van Stockman is all it takes.

"I almost forgot," I tell him. "Roger Mallory says Merry Christmas."

"Please go away." He hobbles back and closes the door.

The dog disappears from the window.

The porch light goes dark.

I turn to Josh. "Did you get that?"

Something sharp slams into the meaty part of my arm. It's Maya Lamb's fist. Her eyes are blazing. "What the *hell*?"

"You said supervise."

She punches me again. Same place. It hurts more the second time. "Watch and don't talk. How hard is that?"

"Come on, he was onto us. I had to do something."

"You can be a real asshole," she says.

We regroup in the warmth of an all-night diner off Dubuque Street. There's hot coffee and six kinds of pie, Chet Baker doing "Winter Wonderland" on the jukebox, and a few other late-nighters scattered about.

As a man with costly training in American fiction I'm aware of my immediate geography here in Iowa City, gravid as it is with academic significance. As it happens, many notable Americans have concocted stories in this little university burg over the last century or so. O'Connor, Irving, Roth, Vonnegut, Timothy Brand—the list is long and interesting.

"I am so pissed off at you right now," Maya Lamb says. She scowls at her cell phone. "Midnight, and we're eating goddamned pie."

I wonder if Raymond Carver ever tried the pie at this place. For a moment, I think Maya is going to reach across the table and punch me again.

She drops her fork and says, "I forged my assignment editor's signature to get the car. Do you realize that? And I'm on the air tomorrow. No, wait." She consults her phone. "I'm on the air today."

"I thought this was a mistake in the first place," I remind her.

"Oh, it was definitely a mistake. Letting you come along was definitely a mistake."

As far as I'm concerned, our bet has paid out both ways. I know everything I need to know about Timothy Brand. Everything else is Douglas Bennett's job. Maya Lamb still has reams of information that no other reporter has yet. Her job hasn't changed.

She spits out a laugh. "Know what I find interesting?"

"I don't."

"Here you are, claiming you've been set up. Claiming you've been falsely accused of diddling some thirteen-year-old girl."

" 'Diddling,' Maya?" I pause with my fork halfway to my mouth. " 'Claiming'?"

"Ever stop and think that this guy Brand is in the same situation you are?"

"Come on."

"What? Where's *your* evidence against *him*? A thirteen-year-old girl told you a story?" She smirks. "Different girl, different story. That's all."

"You saw his face when I showed him Stockman's photo."

"That's not the point."

"And you know what's going on here. Same as I do." I finish my last bite and drink my coffee. I might get another piece of this pie. "You were right all along, Maya. Roger put the fear of God into him, all right. And then he sent his one-man goon patrol to make sure it stuck."

"You don't have any idea what I'm talking about, do you?"

"Roger might have wanted to protect Brittany from shame and scandal, but he couldn't just let some 'diddler' off the hook, could he? That wouldn't be making the world a safer place."

"Forget it." Maya climbs out of the booth. "I'm going to check my messages."

Once she's gone, I look at Josh. He's leaning over his empty plate, eyes bleary. "Long drive back," I say.

He sighs. Rubs his eyes with his knuckles.

"Think you guys will get in trouble?"

"Fired, probably," he says. "If it was anybody else."

"Anybody else?"

"That girl can talk her ass out of anything." Josh shrugs. "Me, I just go where I'm told."

As long as Maya Lamb is checking her messages, I dig in the pocket of my coat and pull out the phone Douglas Bennett gave me. I turned the ringer off hours ago, tired of hearing it. I've missed a long list of calls, mostly from Bennett & Partners.

At the very top of the list, there are a few out-of-town numbers. No caller IDs attached, but I recognize them all.

Sara called from her mother's an hour ago. Twice. Apparently, she's passed this number along to my folks; they called from New Jersey around the same time Sara did. In their time zone, it's past one o'clock in the morning.

There's even a Boston number on the list, also around the same time. The number belongs to my friend Charlie Bernard.

What's so important?

That's what I'm wondering when Maya Lamb returns to

the table. Her demeanor has changed. Either she's not mad at me anymore, or she's in bigger trouble than she expected.

I finish my coffee. "What's wrong?"

She looks at me with an expression I can't quite interpret.

"Come on," she says to Josh. "We need to get back."

"Now?"

"Right now."

She's already put on her coat by the time I stand up. I sense that her purpose has been renewed. But it's not the same sort of energy I felt on the sidewalk in front of Timothy Brand's house. A bad feeling settles in my stomach.

"What's going on?"

She opens her mouth to say something, and then she does the last thing I expect. She touches my arm, near the spot where she punched me earlier.

Then she leaves me with the bill for the coffee and pie, grabs her bag, grabs Josh, and heads for the door.

37.

BY THE TIME I LEAVE THE DINER, I've checked my voicemail messages.

Neither Maya nor Josh responds when I key the walkie-talkie, which I still have in the glove compartment of my car. I scan the Interstate ahead of me for a Channel Five Ford Explorer, but I never quite manage to catch up with them.

Fifteen miles north of Clark Falls, the Decatur toll bridge takes Highway 175 across the Missouri River.

Dawn is still two hours away when I get there. I don't get closer than the state police barricades a quarter-mile away. Beyond a cordon of road flares, the bridge is crawling with people. Police and emergency vehicles crowd the scene. The skeletal crisscross of beams and girders casts long strobing shadows in the swirl of red and blue lights.

From the side of the highway, I can see news trucks from

Clark Falls and Sioux City. In the middle of the bridge, I can see a familiar silver Lexus SUV parked askew, doors open.

A helicopter circles overhead, scanning the swift dark water with a blinding column of light. Flashlight beams move along the banks downstream.

No, I keep thinking, but that doesn't change anything.

Tuesday, December 20—7:15 a.m.

38.

THEY FIND HER a little over twelve miles downriver, just north of the Loess Hills Observatory.

Divers finally pull Brit Seward's unclothed body from the frigid water just after daybreak. It's said to be a stroke of luck for the rescue operation that she snagged on an underwater deadfall just off the main channel. Given the strength of the current, the temperature of the water, and reports of heavy snow on the way, they say there's no telling whether they'd have found her at all.

Maya Lamb is on the scene, bundled in a North Face parka and earmuffs, strands of dark hair blowing wild in the dawn breeze off the river. You'd never know she's been up all night. Behind her, in the distance, rescue workers load a white plastic body bag onto a bright yellow stretcher.

It doesn't seem real, watching this on television. Two hours ago, I was at the same river that I see on the screen. Standing beside my car, on the side of the highway, I could smell the water, hear the *whop-whop-whop* of the rescue chopper, feel the heavy sense of disaster in the air. Now I'm sitting up in bed drinking bourbon, and all of it seems like anything else you'd watch on the news.

These facts are known, according to Maya Lamb's ongoing field report:

On December 19, Clark Falls residents Peter and Melody Seward had reported their daughter, Brittany Lynn, age thirteen, missing.

The family had spent most of the day at the office of a Clark Falls attorney. Late in the afternoon, Brittany had excused herself to the restroom. After a noticeable amount of time had passed without her return, Melody Seward had gone to check on her. Mrs. Seward had found the restroom empty, her car keys missing from her purse, and the family vehicle gone from the parking lot.

At approximately 5:30 p.m., the Clark Falls Police Department issued a lookout bulletin for a silver Lexus RX 350. Approximately five hours later, a motorist called the state patrol's emergency number to report an abandoned vehicle and a pile of winter clothing on the Decatur toll bridge.

By approximately 10:45 p.m., the responding trooper had matched the license plate on the vehicle to the bulletin out of Clark Falls.

Ice floes made search conditions treacherous. Teams had worked through the night.

I like the funny ones, she told me once. *But the sad ones seem more real.*

Read the funny ones, I'd advised her. *You've got plenty of time for the sad ones.*

Which book had she taken from my library that day?

It doesn't really matter. I just wish I could remember.

• • •

"I'm sending Debbie to pick you up." Douglas Bennett is gentle but firm. "The room is under our account, so if you don't answer your door, she'll just get the management to open it for her."

"Maybe I won't be here," I tell him.

"It sounds to me like you'll be there."

"If I am, then I'll answer the door."

Silence.

"It's a bad day," Bennett finally says. "But it isn't your fault, Paul."

I drop the phone on the night table by the bed. I top off my glass, but then let it sit.

Remember, TV Roger tells me. On-screen, he's wearing a sweater and blue jeans, standing on a patch of green lawn in front of a swing set. *Simple precautions, awareness, and common sense can help make your neighborhood a safer place.*

Back to Maya Lamb, standing on a patch of frozen mud in front of a swollen river. The camera cuts away, following the county sheriff and a brace of deputies as they escort a grim, haggard couple up a steep slope. The faces of the man and woman are so bereft that I honestly don't recognize them as Pete and Melody until a caption labels them, with all the sensitivity of a rib spreader, *Parents of Teen Bridge-Jumper.*

I jump at the buzz of the cell phone beside me. The phone glides across the table on its own vibration, stopping against my glass. Each ring causes the bourbon in the glass to ripple. I think of helicopter blades rippling water.

I pick up the phone. "I'm not going anywhere, Bennett. Send her already."

A pause. "It's me."

The surprise of Sara's voice in my ear is almost more than I can take. It's as if the last of my will runs out of my body through my fingertips.

"Paul?" Another pause. "Are you there?"

I clear my throat, sit up. I can hear noise in the background. "Where are you?"

"I'm at PHL."

I picture Sara at Philly International, her roll-around suitcase beside her, cell phone to her ear. "Are you coming home?"

"Trying."

"When will you be here?"

"I don't know. There are snowstorms in Chicago and Minneapolis. I've already been canceled twice. I just got on standby through Dallas, but everything's jammed."

I picture her looking around the terminal, sighing at the long lines. I wish she'd keep talking. I'd listen to her read the departures board if that's all she had to say.

Neither of us says anything for a minute. The silence doesn't feel hostile. Just awful.

"How are you?" I'm only flailing at the silence between us now.

"I'm stuck in an airport." She lets out a ragged sigh. "Mom is trying to ring in, I'm stuck in an airport, and my heart is breaking for a woman I really need to be able to hate right now."

I don't know what to say to all that.

"God, Paul." Her voice catches. "Poor Brit."

There's a sharp knock on the door.

"Sweetie, hang on." I switch the phone to my other ear, walk out of the bedroom, through the front. The knock comes again before I'm halfway to the door, louder this time. I check the peephole.

Debbie the Intern drives fast.

There's a small conference room tucked away in the crannies of Bennett & Partners Trial Law. Debbie deposits her bag in a chair at the far end of the long table. I see boxes of file folders, stacks of paper, index cards laid out in a grid.

"Mr. Bennett is on a call," she says. "He asked me to have you wait in here. Will that be all right?"

"I'll be fine."

Debbie the Intern seems to dislike me somewhat less this morning. "Can I get you anything?"

I haven't slept in the past thirty hours. It's Tuesday, and all I've had to eat since Saturday night is a piece of pie on the other side of Iowa. It's eight-thirty in the morning and I'm half in the bag. "I don't think so," I tell her. "But thank you."

She glances toward a coffeepot on the credenza in the corner. "Help yourself, if you feel like it. Mr. Bennett should be ready soon."

Once Debbie leaves, I realize that the coffee smells pretty good after all. I take off my coat and pour myself a cup. While I wait for Bennett, I sit down and glance over the stuff fanned out on the table.

When it comes to tracking down an address, Bennett's intern may not be quite as quick on the draw as Maya Lamb, but I have to give credit where credit is due: she's accumulated and notated an impressive amount of material in the space of a single business day.

Just like Maya, she's obtained copies of police reports involving our address, beginning with my complaint call against Roger three weeks ago, going back to our break-in, dated 12 July.

But I see that Debbie has gone back even further. There's a third report, this one dated eight years ago.

The reporting party named in this older document is Webster, Myrna, 34 Sycamore Court. I sit forward in the chair.

I've spoken with Myrna Webster. I called her on the phone not two weeks ago to ply her for information about Roger. Myrna and her husband, James, now separated, are listed as previous owners of 34 Sycamore Court. Their names are listed in the county assessor's online database I showed Douglas Bennett on the computer in his office.

I scan the summary section of the report.

M. Webster (age 37) reports James Webster (husband, age 39) as absent from the home since 2 June. M. Webster states her belief that husband effectuated threats to leave the marriage in order to pursue a long-standing affair with a coworker.

R. Mallory (Sgt, ret, CFPD, 40 Sycamore Court) urged M. Webster to pursue child support for two children, aged 12 and 10 years.

M. Webster reports no contact with J. Webster and no knowledge re: current location.

Debbie has highlighted Roger's name in bright yellow. In bright green, she's highlighted the signature of the cop who took the report: *Ofc. T. Harmon.* It's the same signature she's highlighted, in the same color green, on our own burglary/assault record: *Det. Lt. T. Harmon.*

I feel a quick tingle of association at the sight of Detective Harmon's matching signatures. Only the rank is different. He was Officer Harmon eight years ago, when he filed Myrna Webster's report. He was Detective Lieutenant Harmon by the time he filed ours.

Debbie's system is simple but effective. She's color-coded her research so that I can find overlaps at a glance. Specific names each get their own color—for example, yellow for Roger, green for Detective Harmon, and so on. Each color corresponds to index cards Debbie has scribbled with notes.

In the supplemental reports attached to Myrna Webster's case, the presiding officer's signature is highlighted in sky blue: *Det. Lt. J. Gardner.*

I cross-reference blue with blue, finding my way to a hard-copy printout from *The Clark Falls Business Guide.* The print-out is a business profile for Sentinel One Incorporated, our security alarm company. The company owner's name is high-lighted: *John G. Gardner.* My eye jumps to a thin slash of yel-low halfway down the page. Topping a short list of Sentinel One's consulting business partners: *Roger M. Mallory.*

I can almost hear Roger speaking to Officer Bill and Officer Stump that day in his driveway, two weeks ago: *Either of you guys know Johnny Gardner before he retired?* I can almost see John Gardner standing at his office window, watching me through the blinds.

I go back to the material attached to Myrna Webster's police report and start reading. According to the report, a three-week investigation declared James Webster a "Voluntary Missing Adult," and the case was turned over to the Iowa Department of Human Services for child support collection. The commanding officer's signature is highlighted in purple: *Cpt. Gaylon Stockman.*

My pulse kicks up a notch. I know from my own research that Gaylon Stockman was Clair Mallory's father. I flash on the image of an old man in a recliner, a Foley bag between his ankles, a death rattle in his chest. I find the index card with the purple dot in the corner, same as the color highlighting Captain Stockman's name. There's only one note jotted on the card: *Rm 242, CF Mercy General.*

A hand falls on my shoulder. I jump in my chair, jostling my mug, sloshing coffee onto one of the index cards. A few lines of Debbie's careful notes run together in the spill.

"Careful," Douglas Bennett says. "Debbie'll have your ass."

I look up at him.

He smiles. "Sorry. Didn't mean to startle you."

I look back at the index cards on the table. Bennett joins me for a moment, and says, "When you lay them all out side by side like that, it starts to look a little clubby, doesn't it?"

My thoughts are swirling like Debbie's handwriting in the puddle of coffee from my cup. Detective Thomas Harmon. Retired detective John Gardner. Retired captain Gaylon Stockman. Active sergeant Van Stockman.

Retired sergeant Roger Mallory.

34 Sycamore Court.

I look at Bennett. "What is all this?"

"I'm sure I wouldn't be able to say." Bennett moves a card

with his finger, tilts his head to look at it. He shrugs. "We're just trying to connect all the dots for now. It's probably all coincidental. Smallish town, Clark Falls." He doesn't say this as though he really believes it. "Anyway, it's good practice for Debbie."

My mouth feels dry. I take a sip of coffee.

"And we have more important things to focus on at the moment." Bennett sits down. "How are you doing?"

"Do you want an honest answer? Or do you want to hear me say that I'm doing fine?"

"It's a tough day." He looks off for a minute, shakes his head. "And not a very merry Christmas for Pete and Melody Seward."

It occurs to me that every Christmas from now on will bring them a white body bag. "Not very."

"It's not my field," Bennett says, "but if there's anything you feel like talking about, we've got a little time."

What could we possibly say? "It is what it is."

"I suppose it is."

I sit back in my chair. Pull my eyes away from all the stuff on the table in front of me. "So what happens now?"

This question brings us back into Bennett's area, where I think we both feel more comfortable. "The police want to speak with you."

"Why do they want to speak with me?"

"It's pretty clear what's happened, but they'll need to make an official ruling. Given the circumstances, your whereabouts yesterday will need to be verified."

The circumstances. "You mean I'll be questioned." This truly hasn't occurred to me before now. "Like a suspect?"

"Just procedure, Paul. I've arranged a voluntary interview at Central Station for ten-thirty this morning."

I look at my watch. It's 8:45.

"In the meantime, why don't you start with buying Rachel McNally an iPod. We can go from there."

39.

A DETECTIVE BRINGS IN LUNCH from Petrow's. Cheeseburgers and fries for everyone.

Douglas Bennett and I eat our meals in the interview room, which is carpeted and has a plant in one corner, along with the one-way glass window I've seen in the movies. Otherwise, it's not an uncomfortable spot for lunch. I wonder if Detective Bell is eating his cheeseburger on the other side of the glass.

The last time I saw Detective Bell before today, he was arresting me. Except for the warrant and the overcoat and the Taser-toting officers on either hip, he looks the same as I remember him. We're just finishing our food when he returns to the interview room and sits down on the other side of the table. Bell reviews his notes a moment, then says, "Yesterday afternoon. What time did you say you left Clark Falls?"

We go on like this for nearly two more hours. Following

Douglas Bennett's counsel, I confine my comments strictly to my "unanticipated" run-in with Rachel McNally at the mall, and my subsequent trip to visit Timothy Brand. I mention nothing related to Sergeant Van Stockman. I don't get into my position on Roger Mallory. By all means, I steer entirely clear of the topic of Darius Calvin.

I account for myself between the hours of 5 and 10 p.m. yesterday: the approximate time the police bulletin on the Seward Lexus went out, up until the approximate time at which they found the car abandoned on the Decatur toll bridge. I tell them that Maya Lamb of Channel Five Clark Falls will be able to corroborate my statements. And that's all.

Bell asks questions, and I answer them. Occasionally he asks the same questions, and I answer them again.

We determine that because I've crossed no state lines, I haven't violated the conditions of my bail agreement by traveling to Iowa City. We determine that I haven't violated my court order, which specified contact with Brit, by approaching Rachel McNally in a public area. I could be reading too much into the conversation, but Bell seems disappointed on both counts.

At some point, the same detective who brought in lunch brings in a laptop computer. My online bank records threaten to corroborate at least part of my story, placing my ATM card at a Kwik Star gas pump in Iowa City at 10:30 p.m. last night. Even I know that the computer can't prove the card was in my hand at the time of the transaction, but this information seems to hold Detective Bell, at least for the moment, on the question of my whereabouts during the time frame in question.

Every so often, we break. Detective Bell leaves and comes back. He comes up with more questions, then asks some of the old ones again, just in case I have different answers this time. I don't.

Finally, a few minutes after two o'clock, Bell expresses his appreciation for my cooperation, and advises us to expect a follow-up.

"My client will be available," Bennett says.

"With the story he's telling," Detective Bell says, "he'll certainly need to be."

Whoever schedules press conferences has scheduled one for four o'clock this afternoon. From a closet in his office, Bennett selects a necktie with a subtle pattern and puts it on skillfully, by feel alone.

"We'll tie up the media for an hour, if nothing else," he says. He scribbles something on a notepad and tears off the sheet. He hands me the slip of paper, along with a set of keys. "Congratulations. You're free to move about the city."

"What's this?"

"Eric comes home in three weeks. My son."

I nod to indicate that I remember what he's told me of Eric. I think about Van Stockman's not-so-subtle threat against Bennett and his family. I want to ask him how he's going to protect his son after he comes home. But I don't.

"We've been getting the guesthouse ready for him. Those are the keys." Bennett nods toward the slip of paper. "That's the address, and the alarm code for the gate. I've told Cheryl to expect you."

"Guesthouse?"

"You and Sara are welcome to stay." Bennett puts on a suit coat, opens a cabinet door, finally checks himself in a mirror. It isn't necessary; he looks like he's been groomed by a team of professionals. "It's not a palace, but it's not the Residence Inn. And I think we can promise fewer reporters over these next few days."

"This is very nice of you."

"Call it case management."

He doesn't want me running around loose, I realize. I suppose I can understand his perspective. As I look at the keys to Bennett's guesthouse, it occurs to me that my court order mandates only that I stay away from Brit Seward. But Brit doesn't live in Sycamore Court anymore. Technically, I could go home now.

For the first time all day, I feel something other than numbness and exhaustion.

Anger.

"Go get your things, take them over to the house," Bennett says. "Get a bite to eat. Try and get some rest. Have you heard from Sara?"

"She has a three-thirty flight." I look at my watch. "Couple hours in Dallas. She should be here tonight."

"That's good." Bennett makes a point of catching my eye and adds, in a way that seems meant to convey extra meaning, "You could use a night in."

I pack my bags and take my leave of the Residence Inn. I can feel the glares from various staff members as I walk out through the front lobby. They've seen me on the news.

Getting a bite to eat would be a good idea. Getting some rest would be a good idea. Almost anything would be a better idea than driving to see Darius Calvin.

But I can't seem to make myself sit still. Every time I stop moving for more than a minute, I think of a frozen riverbank. A white body bag on a yellow stretcher. I see Brit Seward curled up on my reading couch, poking her tongue out at me. All I can feel is a burning in my stomach.

I need something to make this burn go away, and it isn't food. I want Sara back. I want my life back. But whatever else happens, right now, on this drive to Darius Calvin's tattered clapboard house on the ass end of town, I only need to destroy Roger Mallory.

I park in front, climb the rotting porch, and knock on the flimsy door. I plan what I'm going to say, how I'm going to convince Darius Calvin to join the resistance. When no one answers, I take off my glove and rap harder.

Calvin works nights. His shift doesn't start for an hour. He's asleep, or he's in the shower. The doorbell is two rusty wires where a doorbell used to be.

I knock again. I end up pounding the door for ten seconds straight before I remember that he doesn't lock his door in the first place.

The little house is cold inside.

The closets are empty.

There's a note to the landlord on the kitchen table, along with five twenty-dollar bills and a set of keys. Calvin is gone.

Can I honestly blame him?

"Mrs. Webster?"

"Yes?"

"This is Ben Holland. I spoke with you last week?"

Myrna Webster's voice brightens with recognition. "Well, hello, Ben." I hear pans rattling in the background. "How's your story coming?"

I tell her it's coming along. As far as Myrna Webster knows, I'm a reporter doing a story on Roger Mallory and the Safer Places Organization; it's the same simple ruse that failed so miserably the day I approached Van Stockman at his home, but it's served its purpose since. At least none of the previous owners of 34 Sycamore Court questioned my identity when I called to ask if they'd share their memories of Roger Mallory. "Listen, I'm sorry to bother you so close to supper time, but I had a couple quick follow-up questions. Do you mind?"

"I don't mind at all." I hear what sounds like a whisk on a stainless steel bowl. "What can I do for you?"

"Well, I ran across a piece of information that I wanted to corroborate with you. But I also wanted to see how you'd feel about my using it."

"Oh? This sounds interesting."

"Well, it's awkward. You just tell me if it's none of my business, all right? I'm not out to embarrass anyone."

"I can't imagine. What is it?"

"It has to do with your husband, actually. James?"

"Ha." Is it my imagination, or does the whisking get louder? "We don't refer to him by that name here. Here we call him the son of a bitch. What about him?"

"Before you left Clark Falls, Roger helped you file a missing-person report? On the son of a bitch?"

"Good grief." The whisking pauses. "I'd forgotten all about that."

"I understand that Roger helped you recover child support." Myrna Webster seems like a very nice person. She doesn't deserve to be manipulated this way. "Is that right?"

More whisking, then the sound of water running in a sink. "Well, not entirely."

"No?"

"There was child support, if you want to call it that." Plates clatter together. "The son of a bitch left a college bond for ten thousand bucks on each of the boys' pillows when he left."

"Really."

"He must have been planning that for a while." Myrna snorts in my ear. "It sure as hell wasn't money *I* knew about. But the minute I saw it I knew we'd never see the son of a bitch again."

"I see."

"I never told Roger about that. He'd liked James. And James..." Myrna pauses again. The silence on her end of the line seems vaguely grudging. Finally she sighs. "My husband was a son of a bitch, but he cashed in vacation days at work to go help when they were looking for Brandon. I know that always meant a lot to Roger."

I proceed as carefully as I can. "Listen, this has nothing to do with my story. But if you don't mind my asking, why did you report him missing?"

"I guess it won't seem to make a lot of sense, explaining

it now," she says. "But back then, after what happened to Brandon..."

She stops.

"Mrs. Webster?"

"I'm sorry. I still get a little choked up."

"Please, don't be sorry."

"You know, I used to babysit Brandon. He and my oldest were the same age, and my youngest was only two years behind. I can't help thinking about that sometimes."

"Of course."

"They played together, all three of our boys. Ran all over those woods, rode their bikes all over town. Brandon must have slept over at our place every other weekend the summer before he..." She stops again. "Well."

"I'm sorry to bring all of this up." I'm not lying about that. It's not easy to feel very good about myself, playing games with this woman, but I think I can find a way to live with it. I don't think I can find a way to live with this burning in my gut.

"I don't think either of them have ever really gotten over it. My boys." Her voice seems to tighten. "I suppose I was fibbing before, when I told you I couldn't afford to keep up the house after the son of a bitch left. The truth is, I just couldn't live there anymore."

"That's certainly understandable."

"And my sons. I think it did them good, getting away from that house. Those woods."

"I can only imagine."

"Anyway." She seems to pull her thoughts back from the same woods she's remembering for me. "Please don't put this in your story, but the truth is, I filed that report more for Roger's sake than for myself."

"For Roger's sake? How so?"

"He seemed so concerned," she says. "The way James just up and disappeared, without a word to anyone... well. Roger had his own experience with that."

"Yes. I suppose he did."

"He wanted me to be sure nothing had happened to the son of a bitch." Myrna clears her throat. "I guess I thought that if I filed the report, like Roger wanted me to, he could put it out of his mind. Maybe he wouldn't have to worry about it anymore."

"I see."

"I'm glad you called," she says. "I wouldn't want Roger to hear all this from a newspaper story after all these years. He's such a good man."

I don't have the heart to dispute this. "I'm glad I called too."

"Seems like you can't believe half what you read anymore," she says.

"Thank you again, Mrs. Webster. I certainly appreciate the information."

"You have a merry Christmas, Ben."

40.

ALL THE WAY ACROSS TOWN, Myrna Webster's voice hounds my thoughts. *My husband was a son of a bitch. But he cashed in vacation days at work to go help when they were looking for Brandon.*

Surely what I'm thinking can't really be possible. And yet I can't shake the memory of something Roger told me, that day he took me to the hemlock grove.

One theory went that he might have made himself part of the search. That's what Roger had said. *He could have joined the volunteers... used the search tracks to hide his own.*

According to the dates in Myrna's police report, James Webster didn't abandon his family until long after Brandon Mallory's disappearance. More than two years had passed since the boy's body had been found in the woods behind Sycamore Court.

There were other theories, Roger told me. *None of those ever checked out either.*

I stop at a drugstore on the corner of Fifth and Van Dorn. I find what I'm looking for in the electronics section, near the cameras and computer discs and batteries. I stand in line and pay at the register, return to my car and drive on.

Surely what I'm thinking can't be possible. And yet I can't help remembering our first Saturday morning in Clark Falls. The day after Darius Calvin broke into our house, a sheep in wolf's clothing.

I imagine Roger walking across the circle to invite us to the emergency meeting of the Ponca Heights Neighborhood Association—all the while knowing that our wolf was a phony, a masquerade he'd arranged himself. *Just wanted to make sure you knew you were welcome.*

I imagine Roger crossing the same circle eight years ago. When Myrna Webster and her two sons still lived there, after her husband James had deserted his unit.

He wanted me to be sure nothing had happened to the son of a bitch.

Surely what I'm thinking can't be possible.

And yet I can't stop thinking about the fact that there are four names of authority contained in the report Myrna Webster eventually did file on her missing husband.

One of them is my neighbor. Another owns the company that installed our security alarm after our break-in. Another belongs to the family of my neighbor's deceased wife, and the last is our own Detective Harmon.

Among these names, there's only one person left I can reasonably expect may not know me on sight. According to Debbie's research, I can find him in Room 242 at Clark Falls Mercy General.

"Can I help you, sir?" The nurse seems to recognize me, but she's not sure why. The name tag on her smock says Harriet.

"Ben," I tell her. "I'm a friend of the family?"

"Of course, yes. I knew your face was familiar. I'm sorry."

"How's he doing?"

Harriet offers a kind smile. "We're doing what we can to make him comfortable."

A youth group from one of the local churches is going from room to room, singing carols. At the moment, they're doing "O Little Town of Bethlehem" in Room 242.

"Is it all right if I step in when they're finished? I don't mean to stay long."

"Of course." Harriet touches my arm. "He might not recognize you. He goes in and out with the pain."

"That's okay. I just wanted to stop by."

"I'm sure he'll enjoy the company." She takes a last look at me, smiles again, then goes about her business. Meanwhile, the church group wraps up with a rousing four-part rendition of "We Wish You a Merry Christmas."

When they're finished, the carolers smile and pass their wishes to me as they file one by one out of the room. They're all wearing their scarves and hats and mittens, as though moving about a neighborhood, stopping on wintry doorsteps. One guy has sweat running down his face.

I wait for the last of them to clear the doorway, then step inside. The room is dark except for the flickering light of the muted television mounted on the wall. It's quiet except for the occasional beep from a machine beside the bed. The distant sound of the carolers starts up again in another room.

The old man in the bed looks like a pile of bones wrapped in tissue paper. His eyes are open, but he doesn't appear to be looking at anything. His mouth is slack.

Van Stockman's father has taken a hard ride downhill since I last saw him. Two weeks ago, the man was sitting up in his easy chair, growling at strangers. Eight years ago, he was still on the police force. He can't be more than seventy years old.

Is it cancer? Cancer and five other terminal diseases? Whatever is killing him, it's killing him.

"Captain Stockman?"

In the dimness, I can see him blink. After a moment, his head sags toward the sound of my voice.

I walk over to the bed. One of his hands clutches the railing. The other rests on his bloated stomach. Laced in his wasted fingers is a crucifix on a rosary. He looks up at me with dull, sunken eyes.

I nod. "Merry Christmas, sir."

He says something, but his voice is little more than a rasp. When I lean forward, he lifts his hand from the railing, gestures limply toward the roll-around table beside the bed. There's a drink bottle half filled with water, the words *Clark Falls Mercy General* stamped on the side. I put down my coat, pick up the bottle, and hold the straw against the old man's lips.

He sips. Some of the water slips from the corner of his mouth, following a crease in his neck all the way down to the pillow. I put the bottle back on the table.

Clair Mallory's father clears his throat. "You're the reporter."

"That's right." He knows me on sight after all. He just doesn't know who I am. "I'm the reporter."

He coughs. It sounds like a shovel blade scraping wet earth. His eyes move to the ceiling. Clods of mud shift in his chest as he breathes. "Hell you want?"

From my coat pocket, I take out the small digital voice recorder I bought at the drugstore on my way here. Ironically, it's exactly the kind of tool a legitimate reporter might use. Brandon Mallory's grandfather watches me. His eyes move to the small red light that blinks on when I press the record button.

"I'm here to ask you about a man named James Webster," I tell him. "He used to live across the street from your daughter."

Stockman looks at me.

"James Webster's wife reported him missing eight years ago. You signed off on the paperwork. Do you remember?"

His eyes seem to focus for a moment, then drift back to the ceiling.

"James Webster, sir. Thirty-four Sycamore Court. Right across from Clair and Roger. And Brandon."

I hear beads click faintly. The old man's rosary hand moves and falls still.

Surely what I'm thinking can't be possible, and yet, in this moment, I know that my darkest speculation is true. It's almost as if the old man has been waiting for me. For this.

"You remember," I say. "Don't you?"

Stockman exhales. His breath hitches and clogs on the way out. On impulse, I reach out and take his other hand. I stand by his bed, looking down at him, already half shrouded in hospital sheets.

His skin is cool. His knuckles feel like marbles under silk. Somewhere, in the physical connection between us, I can feel what this dying man needs. If the world were right, I'd be the priest from his church. Or even the hospital chaplain.

But it's only me.

"Tell me what happened to James Webster."

Stockman looks at the recorder. For a moment, he seems transfixed by its patient red light.

Beads click.

The crucifix moves: three weak taps, the cross barely lifting, dragging the soft fabric of the gown along with it.

"We put him in the woods," he says.

They say an old dog can sense when the end is near.

Maybe Gaylon Stockman has been clinging to the instincts that compelled him, as a young man, to swear himself into service of the common good. Maybe he realizes that he's tethered to a stake and looking his wolf in the jaws.

I tell myself that I've done him a favor. I've given him permission to cut himself free before the wolf tears into his belly.

The truth is, I've only tricked a frightened man into telling me a secret. His wolf is hungry.

The victorious warrior wins first.

"I made them wait," he tells me.

For two years, they knew what James Webster had done. Every volunteer from the search party had been interviewed as part of the original investigation, and Webster had been cleared along with everyone else. But then, at some point during that first terrible summer—after Brandon had been found and Clair Mallory had taken her own life—the neighborhood raccoons had gotten into the Webster family's garbage.

"God forgive what I did to that man," Stockman says, and at first I assume he's talking about James Webster. Then I realize he's talking about Roger. "But I made him wait."

The old man looks toward the opposite corner of the room while he's talking, as if watching an old dusty slide show over there. He can't speak more than a few words without running out of breath, and he clicks the morphine button like a ticket counter. At some point the pain steals his clarity; he begins to mix up his facts. He loses his place, repeats himself. Sometimes his oldest daughter is alive. Sometimes she's gone.

Brandon is always gone. Always twelve.

And it's always raccoons that get into the garbage.

That was how Roger found a school paper with Brandon's name on it. Sometimes it's a shoe, or a pair of underwear. Stockman tells this part of the story a handful of times, and each time, the damning evidence changes. But it's always the raccoons who find it.

For two years, they'd known. For two years, Roger had lived across our circle from the man he believed had murdered his son. Two years watching. Two years waiting.

"Rodge, he kept tabs on that son of a bitch." Stockman finds the strength to nod. "You can believe that. God knows he had to do something."

I hear Myrna Webster's voice: *He wanted me to be sure nothing had happened to the son of a bitch.*

"Couple years in the clear, the son of a bitch starts driving across town, middle of the day. Watching schoolyards. You see?"

What I see, when I close my eyes, are Pete and Melody Seward, walking up a slope, their faces like masks.

By the time he's finished talking, I would swear that the old man's face has changed. *We put him in the woods.* It's almost as if a mask has fallen away. Beneath, he looks almost at peace. His strength is spent, and he looks grateful to rest.

At least that's what I'm telling myself when I hear the door to the room close behind me.

I turn expecting a nurse and see my own folly.

Van Stockman must be off duty. He's wearing jeans and a flannel coat. He turns from the door, one hand still on the lever, eyes black beneath his brow.

The man beside him wears a suit and an overcoat. His tie is loose, collar unbuttoned. I can see the dull gleam of a gold badge on his belt. I don't need to see his face to know that I'm not the victorious warrior.

"Good news," Detective Harmon tells me. "We found the guy who broke into your house."

41.

BEFORE CUFFING MY HANDS together in front of me, Harmon looks at Van Stockman.

Van Stockman is busy watching his dying father. After a minute, he looks at the floor. Shakes his head.

Harmon puts a hand on his neck. "Okay."

I feel like I'm floating. I wouldn't know my feet were touching the floor if I didn't look down. While I'm looking down, Detective Harmon snaps the cuffs on my wrists and squeezes until they bite.

"Am I under arrest?" My voice sounds distant and muffled in my ears, as if I'm underwater.

"Something like that." He grips the chain connecting the handcuffs together and applies subtle pressure. The pain brings me straight back to Earth, almost all the way to my knees.

Harmon leads me a few steps and stops at the door. He pockets my voice recorder, turns to Van Stockman, and says, "Take your time."

Van Stockman hasn't stopped staring at me. He looks like he wants to do things. Things that will make Timothy Brand look like he tripped on a flower and fell into a pile of pillows.

"Van."

Stockman finally breaks the glare.

Harmon nods at him.

With that, Van Stockman takes a long breath and lets it out slowly. He turns and approaches the bed.

"Pop," I hear him say, taking the old man's hand.

I hear a buzz, like an insect trapped in cotton. Harmon holds my tether in one hand and digs in his coat pocket with the other. He flips open his phone, holds it to his ear. He listens a moment, then quietly says, "Okay."

I'm seeing the situation now. Numb is gone. Anger is back. When Detective Harmon closes his phone, I say, "I don't think you're supposed to use those up here."

He smiles. It's not so different from the smile I remember seeing in my living room five months ago, when he was helping us. He leans close and speaks softly in my ear. "More good news. Your wife is home."

The burn in my gut goes immediately cold. An instant chill works its way through me from the inside out.

Over by the bed, Van Stockman leans over the railing and kisses the old man's head. The old man pats his arm.

The son straightens. I see his knuckles go to his eyes. Van Stockman hangs his head and stands there a minute. Then he reaches out, steps back, and pulls the privacy curtain around the bed, between him and his father. His eyes are wet and red when he returns.

"Here's what's going to happen," Harmon tells me, going through my pockets while he talks. He takes my cell phone, my car keys, my wallet. "You'll walk out of here with your eyes down and your mouth shut. Your compliance will be full. You'll do that, and Sara will wake up tomorrow. Do we agree that's what's going to happen?"

I must be nodding my head, because Detective Harmon looks satisfied. He hands me over to Stockman. "You know what to do."

Silence.

"Van?"

Stockman lifts his chin.

"Call Roger. Tell him you're on the way."

The two men look at each other one last time. I consider the fact that Harmon didn't say anything about *me* waking up tomorrow.

Then Van Stockman takes me by the elbow and opens the door. Detective Harmon stays behind in the room.

The carolers are long gone from the floor. It's just us and the nurses, all watching and whispering as I'm led past their various stations. On our way to the elevator, we meet Nurse Harriet walking quickly in the other direction, on her way somewhere. She scowls at me as she passes, shaking a finger. *I'm not as dumb as you think I am, Mr. Family Friend.*

In a basement level of the hospital parking garage, where I see no security cameras, Van Stockman pulls me around a fat concrete support column. He pushes me against the passenger door of his Dodge Ram, holding me there with one elbow while he digs his truck keys out of his pants pocket.

I take a breath. "Listen."

"Fuck you just say?"

"Please don't hurt Sara—"

I see his head flash toward me. It feels like a cinder block landing in my face. Explosion. Pain. Darkness.

I wake up cold.

I can feel that my eyes are open, but I'm still in the dark. An enormous jolt tosses me, rattling my teeth. When the back of my head hits the ground beneath me, I bite my tongue hard enough to squirt blood. At first I think somebody's hitting me in the face again.

Then I sense that I'm in motion. I roll onto my side and feel some kind of corrugated metal beneath me. There's a droning sound all around, so loud that it almost seems quiet.

I lie back and work out that I'm in the bed of Van Stockman's pickup, locked under the lid. My hands are still bound. The center of my face feels pulpy and crusted, and I can't breathe through my nose. My coat and gloves are back at the hospital; I wonder if Detective Harmon thought to grab them from the bed rail after he finished smothering Gaylon Stockman, or dosing him with morphine, or however you go about putting an old dog down without raising suspicions.

The truck slows down and pulls to a stop. In a moment, the drone disappears. The lingering wake of silence seems louder than the drone.

Behind my head, a door opens, then slams. The truck bed rocks gently.

I hear footsteps scuffling on pavement, rounding the tailgate. A faint jingle of keys, the snick of a lock somewhere down by my feet. The sound of the lid latch releasing is an amplified thud in the space around me.

The lid begins to open, then closes abruptly. I hear the sound of another car passing. Where are we? If I can hear other cars, and we've never left pavement, surely we can't be especially isolated. For a moment, I feel what I know is an unreasonable glimmer of hope: maybe I've been pardoned. We're on a highway somewhere, way out in the country, where I'll be released into the wild.

The lid opens on a black December sky. It's snowing.

"Get out."

I struggle to one elbow, then to my knees. Looking over the side of the pickup bed, I recognize my surroundings immediately.

I've made it almost all the way home.

• • •

Van Stockman unlocks my left hand and snaps the empty cuff onto his own wrist. He drags a duffel bag out of the bed of the pickup and slings it over his shoulder. Something metal clanks heavily inside the bag.

Stockman locks the bed cover and sets the alarm on the truck. He looks both ways, up and down Sycamore Drive. Then, without a word, he heads across the open ground toward the refuge, pulling me along behind.

I look at the sky. White flakes fall out of the endless dark. While I'm busy looking up, I manage to trip over my own feet; Van Stockman doesn't slow down, and for a moment I wonder if he's going to pull my shoulder out of joint. I decide to keep my eyes in front of me from now on.

The snowfall thins as we enter the woods. Above us, the clouds are drawn across the sky like a tattered quilt; a bright full moon shines through a bare patch, casting the bare-boned forest in a silvery gleam.

The trail is too narrow to take side by side through the thicker timber. Stockman leads the way, never allowing a moment of slack. Each time I stumble, the steel cuff grates against my wrist bone. When I trip on a root and fall to my knees, he drags me along the ground behind him. My wrist is bleeding by the time I make it back to my feet.

Our cold snap appears to have broken. But it's still not a night for a stroll through the forest without a coat; while the work of keeping up with Stockman keeps me warm in the middle, my fingers and toes are numb. I can't feel my ruined nose, either, which may be a blessing. All I can hear is the sound of my breathing. The occasional creak of bare branches around us. The crunch of frosted leaves under our feet. The shifting clank of whatever Stockman is carrying in that bag on his shoulder.

Should I be saying something? Should I be making some sort of plea for my life? I can't imagine what good it would do, but still, there must be something more than quietly allowing myself to be led into the woods.

On the other hand, the last word I spoke, in the hospital parking garage, had prompted Van Stockman to flatten my nose with his forehead. I'm not a tough guy. It hurt a lot. Based on the look in his eyes at the time, I can only imagine that he'd been restraining himself.

The truth is, I'm scared of what this guy is going to do to me. Simple as that. I don't want to make it worse.

So I keep my mouth shut and stumble along.

Roger is waiting for us when we reach the clearing. He's dressed in a barn coat and heavy pants, standing at the edge of the hemlock grove. His hands are in his coat pockets. His hair is disheveled.

"Paul," he says.

There's a small battery-operated lantern near his foot; the dim yellow light is just enough to bring up the edges of the clearing, throw a few grasping shadows over the ground between us.

I clear my throat. "Hello, Roger."

Our voices seem unnatural in the stillness. It occurs to me that the last time I spoke to Roger, Brittany Seward was still alive.

Van Stockman uncuffs my hand from his and shoves me into the clearing. I hear a zipper behind me, then the sound of metal clanging against metal. I hear other sounds.

After a few moments, something heavy hits the ground by my foot. I look down and see a folding camp shovel nestled in the snow-flecked leaves. It's been unfolded.

"I didn't want this," Roger tells me. When he takes his hands out of his pockets, I see that he's wearing latex gloves. "This isn't what I wanted."

"Be sure and tell Pete that." Between my parched throat and shattered nose, I hardly recognize my own voice. In the clearing, the snow falls freely, and the flakes have gotten bigger.

I can feel them on my face. I see them collecting in Roger's hair, on his shoulders, in his eyebrows. If they keep falling, this clearing will be completely covered by morning. "Melody, too. Maybe after Brit's funeral you can pull them aside and tell them how their little girl throwing herself off a bridge isn't what you wanted."

Roger flinches at the mention of Brit's name. I've never seen him look quite like this. Unkempt. Vacant. He says, "I didn't create the situation."

For some reason, I don't feel scared anymore. Uncuffed from Roger's thug-in-law, I don't feel anything. "You brought James Webster out here too," I say. "Didn't you?"

Roger is quiet.

"Did you make him confess first? Or did you just go ahead and kill him?"

Behind me, Van Stockman says, "Shut up."

"How did you know, Roger? You couldn't just murder a man over something you found in his trash. Could you?" While I'm talking, Roger's expression seems to darken in the lamplight. "Brandon slept over there all the time, isn't that right? He could have forgotten things there."

"Things?" Roger stands like a golem in the snow, eyes hidden beneath his brow. After a few moments, he raises his chin and repeats the word curiously. "Things."

"I don't know, Roger." I'm thinking of what Gaylon Stockman told me from his hospital bed not an hour ago: a shoe. A pair of underwear. A homework assignment. "Nobody knows, now. Except you and your buddies. Right?"

Roger looks at me as though he's contemplating a stranger.

After a long silence, he finally says, "He told me that he didn't want to hurt his own boys."

"Actually, never mind," I tell him. "At this point it doesn't even—"

"Urges, he called them." If Roger's composure was lost when we arrived at this clearing, he's found it again. "See, he wanted me to understand. Said he'd done it so that he wouldn't accidentally hurt one of his own boys. He thought I'd be able to understand that, as a father."

Hearing this, I honestly don't know what I'm feeling toward Roger Mallory. Disgust? Pity?

Mercy?

I can sense Van Stockman standing directly behind me.

"And then after, he didn't want *my* boy to have to live with what he'd been through. That's what he told me." Roger gazes toward the hemlock grove. "Isn't that something?"

"It was your money, wasn't it?" I'm still hearing Myrna Webster's voice: *There was child support, if you want to call it that.* "Ten grand for each of them, that's what Myrna told me. College money. She said Webster left it on their pillows before he ran off. But he didn't run off, did he?"

Van Stockman's voice is cold on my neck. "I said shut the fuck up."

But I'm not talking to Van Stockman. I'm talking to Roger. I just wish I could say that I'm not scared anymore.

"Is that what they'll say about me? That I ran off?" Snowflakes are already collecting in the blade of the shovel at my feet. "Two people disappear from the same house? In eight years? I don't know, Roger. You could run into perception problems."

"He's right," a new voice says.

The sound startles both of us. Roger blinks, pivots in the direction of the voice. We look to the edge of the clearing together.

A bald man in a camouflage hunting coat emerges from the trees. I recognize him immediately.

Roger says, "John?"

John Gardner blows on his bare hands, rubs them together. "I was afraid you might start without me."

Roger glances toward the trees with a puzzled look on his face. *How did I not hear you coming?* "John, what the hell are you doing out here?"

"Van called me."

Roger fixes his gaze past my shoulder. "That right, Van?"

Behind me, I hear only silence.

"Come on, Rodge." The owner of Sentinel One Incorporated shakes his head. "You can't fly solo on this."

"Go on home, John. You don't need to be here."

The shovel at my feet is nearly covered in white. I imagine going for it, using it as a weapon; the thought makes my heart thud in my chest. How far behind me is Van Stockman standing? Could I make it past him?

How far could I get before they caught up with me?

Gardner steps fully into the clearing. "Bill Bell's the lead on this, isn't he?"

"You know he is, John."

"Well, I know he's not stupid. You make it so the professor here disappears without a trace, old Bill's bound to get curious."

"It's my mess," Roger says. "I'll pick it up."

"Not just yours, Rodge." Gardner puts his hands in his coat pockets. "Don't forget. It's mine and Nancy's. Van and the old man; Valerie too. Tommy Harmon, Carol, that little girl of theirs. Lotta folks with skin in this."

"I said I'll take care of it." This time Roger's voice is louder, harder, a bark swallowed up by the trees. He lowers his volume. "Just like I've been taking care of this place all these years."

"Roger..."

"I'll take care of it, John. Then I'll tend this ground the way I've been tending it. For all of us." Roger's gaze drifts back to the hemlock grove. "I don't forget what I owe."

"Rodge." Gardner's voice remains steady. "We've been friends a long time."

"Someday, they'll sell off these woods." Roger gestures all around us. "They'll come in and scrape off these trees so they can throw up their houses. They'll turn up this dirt."

"I'm asking you to listen to an old friend."

"God has any mercy," Roger says, "by then it won't be ours to worry about anymore."

Even under the circumstances, part of me feels something akin to compassion for Roger. Part of me tries to imagine what our house must mean to him. The rest of me is thinking about that shovel.

When I look up, John Gardner is watching me. His eyes flicker briefly over my shoulder. I can still sense Van Stockman back there, waiting.

"Go on home now," Roger says.

Gardner shakes his head. He appears to contemplate his old friend for one last moment, then finally sighs and says, "I tried."

"All right, then."

"Rodge?"

"Yep."

"I'm sorry."

Roger nods once. "I'll come by in the morning."

When Roger turns, Gardner extends his arm. As if by magic, his hand has dressed itself in a glove and produced a gun. I don't know how he's performed this trick; his hands were bare when he put them in his pockets, and they've been there all this time.

The gun bucks. There's a flash.

I jump at the bang, a sharp ringing sound that echoes out into the cold woods.

A wad of matter leaves the side of Roger's head. His head bobbles a moment; his expression freezes as it is. He collapses to the ground like his strings have been cut.

By the time I see what I'm seeing, it's over.

"Jesus," Van Stockman says.

I turn and look. He's standing with his mouth open, one hand on his brow, staring at Roger's body in the snow.

Gardner says, "Go easy, Van."

Stockman shakes his head slowly. He looks past me, toward Gardner. "Lieutenant?"

"Lotta guys with skin in this." Gardner stoops and picks up his spent cartridge from a small hole in the snow between his boots. "Guys with families. You did the right thing. Tommy agrees."

Stockman seems slow to absorb what he's hearing. "Harmon? You telling me that son of a bitch *knew* this was the—"

"We did the right thing."

"I thought you were gonna *talk* to him."

"You heard me talking. There's no talking to Roger." Gardner's eyes seem sad. "Not anymore."

Stockman rubs his forehead. "He always listened to you."

"He didn't listen when I told him he ought to call in Bill Bell on that goddamned schoolteacher in the first place. Did he? But I trusted his judgment. We all did." Gardner thumbs a lever on the gun, lowers the weapon to his side. "And after the schoolteacher, it's been one goddamned thing after another."

"Yeah, but—"

"He'd lost it, Van. None of us wanted to see that. And now here we are."

"Jesus." Stockman takes a deep breath through his nose. "Here we fuckin' are, huh?"

I hear a sound near Roger's body, and at first I think he's moved. Then I see the syrupy puddle spreading slowly through the snowy leaves around his head. His blood looks black in the dimming moonlight.

Gardner leads me aside by my dangling handcuff. "Get square, Van. We've still got work to do."

Stockman steps nearer to Roger's body and bends at the waist, hands on his knees. He shakes his head, gazing at Roger's lifeless profile as if wondering whether to wake him up or let him sleep. "Christ on a bike."

I look down. Gardner is holding my empty cuff by the tips of two fingers. Just two fingers. That's all. The shovel is two feet away, an irregular shape in the snow.

My breathing quickens.

It would take only one good yank to get free. I could go for the shovel. Or I could forget the shovel and just run like hell. Maybe if I'm lucky...

The sky cracks open, and my mind goes blank. I can't see anything for a minute. I've closed my eyes reflexively.

When I open them, I see Gardner lowering his gun from the back of Van Stockman's head.

"And you haven't been helping," he says.

Stockman falls forward. His body hits the ground like a sack of grain. I stand where I am. Stunned.

Gardner turns and smiles at me. "Hope the neighborhood patrol didn't hear that, huh?"

He lets my cuff drop, lifts his coat, tucks his gun away behind his back.

I move without thinking. On my knees, in the snow, I grip the frigid handle of the camp shovel, pull it toward me.

"Deep breath, Professor. Try to keep it together." Gardner's voice is casual. He doesn't seem the least bit concerned that I've flung myself out of reach. Of course not. He has a gun, I have a small folding shovel. He says, "Don't pass out on me."

He thinks I'm going to be sick, I realize. Has he even noticed the shovel?

"Just slow down and breathe. Count to ten."

My heart is pounding against my ribs. My back is to Gardner. All at once, I'm afraid that I might actually pass out on him.

I take Gardner's advice.

One. Two. Three. Four.

"Okay." A firm hand grips my shoulder. "Up we go."

Five. Six. I find my feet.

"Good." The hand goes away. "Keep coming."

I stand. Seven.

"Now let me see your—"

I turn and swing with all my weight, aiming for the sound of Gardner's voice. Apparently, I've been deemed such a nonthreat that he's not even looking at me while he's talking. He's looking at the bodies a few feet away.

He's in mid-sentence when the bottom of the shovel blade catches him above the ear. The sound is a hollow, metallic *thonk*, like a frying pan striking an unripened melon. The impact rattles up the shovel and into my hands.

Gardner doesn't even see it coming. His eyes seem to jitter in place, then glaze.

Does he fall? I don't know.

I'm already running.

42.

SARA.

As I crash blindly through the trees, away from the clearing, into the thick of the refuge, that's the only thought in my mind. I'm begging God to let her be safe, even though I haven't said a prayer since I was a boy. I don't know if I remember how to do it properly. I don't even know which direction I'm running.

All I know is that I need to get to Sara before "Tommy" does. Detective Harmon. He's already paid a visit to Darius Calvin, that much I know. Harmon told me himself. *Good news. We found the guy who broke into your house.* And Harmon's still out there.

A branch whips me in the face, cutting through the panic, bringing the dark woods into focus all around me. Snow falls through the bare trees. I try to listen. All I can hear is the sound of my own wheezing.

I crash on. When branches rake my flesh, I keep going. When I stumble, I keep going. When I fall down, I get up and move.

When fatigue overtakes me, I pause against the base of a tree and try to listen again. Blood roars in my ears. My breath fogs around my head.

Behind me, all is quiet.

Panting, rough bark at my back, I think of the day I called on Detective Harmon in his office. John Gardner was there. I remember the way they'd looked at each other when I came in; I remember wondering what they'd been talking about.

I think I know now.

None of us wanted to see it.

John Gardner, Detective Tom Harmon, Van Stockman and his father. Roger Mallory. Five men bound by the same grim secret. Only two of them left standing now.

At what point had Gardner and Harmon reached the conclusion their founding member had become their greatest liability? Was it Timothy Brand? Darius Calvin? Was it Brit Seward? Was it me?

The exertion of running has caused my nose to start bleeding again; I can taste the coppery slickness on my lips. I'm getting cold. I need to keep moving. But I've caught my breath, and my head feels clear.

I realize that I don't need to get to Sara. I only need to get myself out of these woods. Back out into the world, where people can see me. If I can do that—

I freeze at the sound of a snapping twig. My heart leaps, and my throat tightens. A few feet away, branches clatter in the darkness. I lunge from my spot.

I make it about five steps before Gardner drags me down.

• • •

"Gotta hand it to you," he says, hauling me to my feet. "That was a good shot."

Droplets of blood fall from my nose, spattering the snow. I look down and see my own footprints. I understand, all hope draining away, that he's tracked me from the clearing like a wounded animal. I couldn't even hear him coming.

Gardner is bleeding himself, from the gash in his scalp I managed to produce, but it looks as though he'll make it. His ear and neck are streaked and glistening, the collar of his camouflage hunting coat darkened and wet. Holding my spare cuff in one hand, he scoops up a handful of snow and presses it against the cut I gave him with the shovel. He smiles. "Almost didn't know my own name for a second there."

"Your name is John Gardner," I tell him. "You murdered Roger Mallory. And Van Stockman. James Webster."

He looks at me. His mouth turns up.

"I guess that's one theory." Gardner tosses what remains of his bloody snowball to the ground, lifts his coat, and locks my free cuff to his belt. "Brace yourself, Professor."

Before I can brace myself, Gardner uses both of his hands to crimp the cuff on my arm as tight as it will go, just above the knobs of my wrist. There's a bolt of pain. A hatchet blade biting into the bone. I almost can't think of my own name for a second.

"Cooperate," Gardner says, "and I'll loosen that a little. When we're finished."

Even if I had the will to resist, I now have little choice but to cooperate. The pain of the overtightened handcuff is incredible; every movement makes the hatchet in my arm wiggle and twist. My revolution is over. My compliance is full.

Back in the clearing, Gardner works with surprising efficiency for a guy with an English professor attached to his hip. He kneels us down beside Roger's corpse, strips the latex gloves from Roger's hands, and puts them on his own. Hands covered, he goes to work on his gun. He releases the magazine. Replaces the two rounds he's fired with gleaming new bullets. He slides the magazine back into the grip and chucks it into place.

He lifts Roger's limp left hand and presses the gun into it. Holding the gun and Roger's hand together, he fires two shots into the woods, aiming at nothing in particular. I can smell the gunpowder.

We stand up. Gardner reviews the situation. He looks at the corpses on the ground. He makes an imaginary gun out of his left hand, points it at Van Stockman. Then he points his finger to his own head.

Apparently satisfied, he produces a small flashlight, searches the ground, finds a glint of brass in the snow. He pockets the empty casing from the bullet he spent on Stockman earlier, just before I bolted.

I'm with him every step of the way.

"You can go ahead and believe what you want," John Gardner tells me as we trudge through the timber. He now wears thermal gloves on his hands, a wool cap on his head. He's traded his small flashlight for a high-powered spotlight, which he retrieved from the base of a tree along the way. "But those are friends of mine back there."

I'm only half-listening. Although he's addressing me, Gardner doesn't seem to be talking to anyone in particular. I feel like I'm dreaming, but I'm not.

"Rodge and me, we came up through the academy together." Gardner moves a bare limb aside with his arm, lets it snap back behind us. "And Vanny, hell—his old man was my training officer. I know that kid since he was yankin' off to the swimsuit issue."

My teeth are chattering. I can't stop shivering. My wrist is bleeding again.

"You think I feel *good*? Leaving them back there that way?" Gardner might as well be talking to the trees. "Let me tell you something. If that's what you think, you're wrong as hell."

We keep moving. For a few minutes, Gardner seems to have said all he wanted to say. Then he shakes his head. "I didn't create the situation."

He shines the powerful spotlight beam along the ground in front of us, making sure I watch my step. It's almost as if he's trying to make my walk comfortable. Though I can't help noticing that he hasn't offered me a turn with his gloves.

"I mean, goddammit, all these years," he says. "And now all of a sudden you just couldn't know *what* the hell Rodge was apt to do next. Unless maybe you wanted him to listen to a little goddamn reason. You could just about bet he wasn't apt to do that."

New-fallen snow crunches underfoot. I can hear it, but I can't feel my feet anymore.

"And Vanny, Christ. You'd think Rodge had him on a leash."

The timber seems to be thinning in front of us. The snowflakes seem to be getting bigger again.

"Meanwhile, here's me and Tommy Harmon. Hell, *I* was *his* T.O. Now he's got a nice wife. A little girl who needs her daddy. I just got my first grandson." Gardner sighs heavily. "You tell me what we're supposed to do."

I can see an opening in the tree line ahead.

"You want to talk about James Webster, I'll tell you one goddamn thing," Gardner says. "Almost ten years we planted that short-eye son of a bitch out here. And *nobody's* come near finding him before now."

We finally come out of the woods, a mile beyond the clearing. The moon is long gone. The ground is white.

As we enter open ground, Gardner finally stops and looks at me. "Listen, Professor. I know this probably won't mean much. But the truth is, if I thought we could let you go, I'd—"

Something warm spatters my face. Dimly, I recognize that I've heard a bang.

Without a word, John Gardner is suddenly on the move, pulling me back. He drops the spotlight; the beam swings up and stabs the sky. For a moment, I think that we're retreating back into the woods. Then Gardner pulls me straight to the ground on top of him.

The impact jars my broken nose, filling my eyes with water. I can't see for a minute. I feel Gardner's stubble on my neck.

I blink. Little by little, my vision clears. Gardner and I are still on the ground together, still face-to-face. His eyes are open.

There's a hole in his cheek.

Hands pat me down. I feel a throb in my arm, followed by a flood of pain. Then a trickle of relief. My cuffs are gone.

I push myself up, off Gardner's body, and scramble to my feet. In the cast of the spotlight beam, through the falling snow, I see Detective Harmon pointing a gun at my face.

"Quiet," he says.

I say nothing. I think nothing. Snow falls. I stand.

Still holding the gun on me, Harmon keys a mobile radio and says, "David 42, Central, immediate backup on Branch Road, two miles north of the twelve-mile marker on old Route 20. Armed suspect on foot inside LH State Wilderness. All available units, K-9, over."

For the first time, I'm able to make out dark shapes in the distance behind Harmon: two vehicles parked along the side of the snow-covered road. Only the lead vehicle has snow on the windshield. I look down at what I presume must be its owner.

John Gardner's eyes are still open. His wool cap is missing. He looks like a camouflaged snow angel with a red halo.

Beep. Crackle. "Central, David 42. Repeat your position, Tom."

I look at Detective Harmon. His hair has gone white with snow. His gun hand hasn't wavered.

He keys the radio and pumps urgency into his voice, keeping his eyes on me. "Shots fired, shots fired! Ten seventy-eight on Branch Road, two miles north of the twelve-mile marker, old Route 20, suspect down. Repeat, shots fired, suspect down."

Beep. Crackle. "Copy, David 42. Units responding. Sit tight."

Harmon lowers his weapon.

For the second time tonight, he tells me, "Here's what's going to happen."

Protected Wilderness

43.

HOW DO WE TELL A CONVINCING LIE?

By sticking as closely as we can to the truth.

The facts are these:

- On the night of December 20, retired Clark Falls police lieutenant John G. Gardner murdered CFPD Sgt. Van Stockman, along with retired CFPD Sgt. Roger Mallory, at the site Maya Lamb, in a lustrous career moment, dubbed "Hemlock Hill."
- From that same site, in the weeks following the slayings, forensics personnel retrieved and identified the remains of James Martin Webster, former resident of 34 Sycamore Court.
- After executing Roger Mallory and Van Stockman, John Gardner manipulated the scene to create the appearance that Mallory had shot Stockman in the back of the head at point-blank range, then turned the gun on himself.

- After manipulating a deathbed confession out of retired Clark Falls police captain Gaylon Stockman, I had become Van Stockman's prisoner.
- I had then become Gardner's prisoner.
- Gardner subsequently was shot and killed by Lieutenant Detective Thomas J. Harmon, who took me into protective custody and delivered me to the care of Clark Falls Mercy General Hospital.

These are the facts, and none of them are in dispute. If you were to print them on index cards and lay them out on a conference room table, they would portray the truth, which is this:

More than two years after Brandon Mallory's remains were discovered in a shallow grave in the Loess Hills State Wilderness, four men—Gaylon Stockman, Van Stockman, John Gardner, and Roger Mallory—had taken James Webster to the same spot in the woods and buried him deeper.

But the facts don't tell the whole story.

I tried.

Maybe I should have started at the beginning. Instead, I started by expressing to Detective William Bell, and a hospital room full of other officials, my belief that Lieutenant Detective Thomas J. Harmon—in addition to being the fifth member of the James Webster posse eight years previously—had personally caused the death of Gaylon Stockman, as well as the death of a man named Darius Calvin, whose details they'd find in the employee records at Missouri Valley Medical Shipping & Warehousing Incorporated.

For my efforts, I received temporary arm restraints and a long-acting sedative.

Later, Detective Bell explained that Darius Calvin and Captain Gaylon Stockman were, in fact, both alive. He explained that it was Detective Harmon himself who had taken Darius Calvin into custody, acting on information he'd gathered in his own investigation. Furthermore, Calvin had corroborated my every claim regarding the break-in at 34 Sycamore Court on July 12.

Gaylon Stockman expired peacefully in his hospital bed two days after the Hemlock Hill killings.

Class, can you see how these points undermine my reliability as a narrator?

I'll concede that we're considering a convoluted story, one that features a large cast of characters, a time span of nearly ten years. And yet, in all of that, there exists only one fact which differs from the reported truth:

Detective Thomas J. Harmon shot first. And then he used his radio. That's the way it really happened, not the other way around.

It's a three-minute plot hole in a ten-year story. Of course, it's to be expected that a man in my traumatized state may have misperceived the exact sequence of events. As for Detective Harmon's claims that he pieced the whole thing together by connecting the attempted burglary at our address with a missing-person report he himself had taken eight years previously?

There's not a person left alive on Earth who can prove otherwise.

Such a person asks himself: if the lie is so close to the truth, is there really a meaningful difference?

In the end, Brit Seward's death does not go unpunished. A wolf in schoolteacher's clothing does not go unpunished. James Webster, a probable monster-in-training, doesn't live to repeat himself, as the experts say such monsters will.

Harmon gets a commendation.

My charges are dropped.

It's still the raccoons who get into the garbage.

Isn't it?

They buried Brit Seward the morning after Christmas. Sara and I wanted to be there, but we couldn't bring ourselves to intrude.

I went to the house and packed up a box of Brit's favorite books. I put the box on Pete and Melody's doorstep, along with a letter I'd written to each of them. If I'd been Pete, I think I would have thrown away my personal letter from Paul Callaway without opening it. But I left it for him anyway.

Sara and I spent the rest of the day together, some in Douglas Bennett's office, most in his guesthouse. We talked all morning. About Brit. About Melody. About Darius Calvin.

It got cold in the afternoon, and we started a fire. Bennett had a subscription to the Sunday *New York Times,* and he'd left the recent edition on the stoop for us. Sara took the business pages. I took the Book Review.

At one point, I dozed off reading and woke to find her watching me from the small couch on the other side of the room. The logs were still crackling in the fireplace. The fire was warm. She looked pretty in the light.

After a long, quiet minute, she said, "I wonder if I'll ever be able to trust you again."

I didn't know how to answer.

"Of course, you appreciate the irony," Douglas Bennett told me, a month after the national media had left town. They'd all wanted interviews, but I'd kept my word. Maya Lamb had the exclusive. She wasn't long for Clark Falls.

"I'm a professor of English literature," I said. "You'll need to tell me the specific irony we're speaking about."

"All these cameras of Mallory's actually helped save your bacon," Bennett said. "Legally speaking."

It was true. The possession of Timothy Brand's pornography had been a sticking point in my case—at least until Roger's surveillance footage showed Roger himself entering our empty home on half a dozen occasions. Not only our home but, at one time or another, the homes of everyone else in the circle.

Back when the tech guy from the university first set me up to log on to the campus network from home—a lifetime ago, it seemed—the same tech guy had installed, as a standard policy, some kind of security software that kept a log of all activity on my computer. Because he'd also given me a password, all activity theoretically came from me alone. But Douglas Bennett's experts, using date- and time-stamp information from Roger's video archives, had been able to place Roger in our house on the day and time certain digital photos first appeared on my hard drive.

Bennett had made plenty of hay with these findings, particularly in combination with my own sloppy habit of recording online passwords on sticky notes, which could be found in the materials the police had confiscated as evidence when they'd searched my office. When it came to building a trial-worthy criminal case against me, the county prosecutor's office, finally, had found cause enough to reconsider its charges.

"Ah," Bennett said. "Okay, here we go. Watch."

I leaned forward and watched the open video window on Bennett's computer screen. When he clicked the play button, I immediately recognized what I was looking at: Trish and Barry Firth's house. I watched.

Bennett played the video clips on a loop, each a snippet of footage from a different night. Each night, the same thing happened.

"You've got to be kidding."

"I thought you'd like that." Bennett seemed pleased. "There's a dozen more just like it."

All I could do was stand there, shaking my head. "Unbelievable."

"Just goes to show you."

"Just goes to show me what?"

"Hell if I know," Bennett said.

I pointed. "Play that again."

Bennett complied happily. Once again, I watched the video footage of Barry Firth exiting his front door, disappearing out of the right side of the frame—the direction of Michael Sprague's house—and returning with a Proposition 42 yard sign under his arm. Ben Holland's fight, it seemed, hadn't been with Roger after all.

"Absolutely unbelievable."

"I'll have Debbie cut you together a highlight reel," Bennett said.

I'll bet I watched that disc Debbie made me a hundred times before sending it to Michael. He called and said, "You've got to be kidding." *Just goes to show you,* I said.

We finally sold the house, at a loss, in April.

One Saturday afternoon, as I was packing up books, I saw a safety tip from the Clark Falls Police Department on the television in my office. *Make sure your kids know their full name, address, and telephone number,* the male uniformed officer said. *And remember,* the uniformed female officer added, *even young children should know how to use a telephone, and how to dial 911 in case of an emergency.* The commercial was paid for by the New Clark Falls Coalition of Neighborhood Patrols.

I immediately stopped what I was doing, found the address I'd written down months ago on a scrap of paper and tacked to my bulletin board. I couldn't count the number of times I'd contemplated that address; one last time I debated the idea, then decided that I couldn't stand the debate any longer. I took the address with me to the garage, got in my car, and drove.

Detective Harmon lived in a quiet cul-de-sac lined with shade trees in one of the older subdivisions on the east side of town. A nice house, big but not gaudy, with shutters on the windows, a basketball hoop in the driveway, and tasteful landscaping all around. A pretty blonde woman answered the door. The color drained from her face the moment she saw me.

"I'm Paul," I told her, though it was obvious she knew my name already. "Is Tommy home?"

Before she could respond, a man's voice said, "It's okay, hon. Go on out back with Becky."

The woman looked worried, but she stepped away.

Detective Harmon took her spot in the doorway. He wore faded blue jeans, an old Iowa Hawkeyes T-shirt, and a pair of moccasins. He waited for his wife to withdraw beyond earshot, looked me over like a stray dog, then said, "Go home, Paul."

I didn't move from my spot on his stoop.

Harmon seemed to expect that I wouldn't be smart enough to follow instructions. He brought me inside and took me up a flight of carpeted stairs to his study on the second floor, where he pulled the door closed behind us. He turned me around, kicked my feet apart, and frisked me from ankle to collar. Then he sat on the edge of the desk and crossed his arms. "I guess you wouldn't be here," he said, "if you hadn't convinced yourself you had some kind of reason."

"I just want to know one thing," I told him.

Harmon's face remained passive, promising nothing.

"The night we met. When you came over to our house, and you asked all your questions, and told us we shouldn't worry, and put on the whole cop song and da—"

"I remember," Harmon said.

"Did you know?"

"Did I know what?"

"About Darius Calvin."

Harmon looked at me.

I looked back. "All that time you were sitting there in our living room, did you know?"

Harmon seemed to study the carpet for an answer. After a moment, he looked up again and said, "I don't expect you'll believe me, but no. I didn't. Not then."

"You're right." I shook my head. "I don't believe you."

"I knew about the schoolteacher," he said. "And how Roger had handled that situation. And when I caught the call to Sycamore Court the night of your break-in, I had a bad feeling." He spoke calmly, informally. We might have been neighbors. "Later, after your golf club went missing, and I saw Van's signature on the property sheet, we had a private chat, Van and I." He sighed. "That's when I found out about Darius Calvin."

"The day I came to your office," I said. "John Gardner was there."

"I remember."

"You knew about Calvin then?"

Harmon nodded. "We knew then."

"But you didn't do anything about it."

"We talked to Roger. John and I. Thought he listened." Harmon shrugged his shoulders. "Few months later, I hear about another call to where? Thirty-four Sycamore Court. Again."

I thought of Roger's video cameras. The day I'd stood with the police in his driveway.

"And we talked to Roger. Again." Harmon nodded purposefully, in case I wasn't listening. "Couple weeks after that, you were arrested. Gardner actually heard the call before I did, not that it matters. Caught it over his personal scanner at home." Another shrug. "Anyway. Detective Bell was on his way to your place by the time I heard about it. And fifty-six hours later, we were fishing that girl out of the river."

I stood there. Harmon waited impassively. I wanted more. But I didn't know what, exactly, I hoped to get.

"I suppose I should thank you," I finally said.

Harmon raised an eyebrow. "Thank me for what?"

I almost couldn't bring myself to say it. "For saving my life."

After a long, quiet moment, Harmon chuckled without seeming amused. "If that's what's been hanging you up, consider yourself clear," he said. "I was protecting my family. You happened to benefit."

I told him that I didn't understand.

"John Gardner was a friend," he said. "But I knew him well enough to know one thing for sure: if any of this mess had splashed back on him—then, or a year from now, or ten years down the road—he wouldn't have taken it alone."

I watched Harmon's eyes while he spoke. They revealed nothing to me. I said, "So you murdered him."

"I protected my family." Harmon uncrossed his arms and

leaned on his hands. "If I was a murderer, Paul, you wouldn't be here now. In my home."

Was he making a threat? Or a simple observation? I didn't know. I didn't care.

"That night in the woods," I said. "Gardner told me he'd been your training officer."

"He was," Harmon said.

"Was James Webster part of your training?"

I imagined that I saw a muscle twitch in his jaw, but I couldn't be sure. Thinking back, I realize that it might have been just that: my imagination.

"You said you wanted to know just one thing," Harmon reminded me. He stood and crossed his arms again. "Your meter's up."

I looked out the window. Down below, on a flagstone patio in back of the house, I saw Harmon's wife picking flowers with a little girl. The girl was maybe six or eight years old. Except for the wheelchair, she looked very much like her mother.

Harmon came over and closed the blinds.

Without thinking, I said, "How was your daughter injured?"

"She wasn't."

As he escorted me out of his office, I noticed a plaque from the Spina Bifida Association of America on the wall.

Later, I looked up spina bifida on the Internet. It's a heartbreaking condition that occurs in various forms, in various levels of severity, and while every case involves a malformation of the spinal cord, no two cases are ever the same.

In the United States, nearly seven children in every ten thousand are born with it. There are preventative measures, things you can do to reduce the risk, but there isn't a cure. Apparently, there's not one damned thing you can do about it.

I visited Brit's grave before we left town. Sara had been there, but I hadn't yet. The inscription on her headstone read:

Unable are the Loved to die
For Love is Immortality.

I didn't recognize the quotation, but according to Brit's marker, it came from a poem by Emily Dickinson. I've always preferred prose to poetry, and it had been years since I'd looked at any Dickinson.

I stayed there for quite a while.

Monday, December 31—10:35 p.m.

TWO YEARS LATER

44.

MY WIFE, SARA, AND I are attending a New Year's Eve party at her department chair's home when Charlie Bernard notices that Sara hasn't been drinking all evening.

He lowers the skewered cocktail shrimp he'd been preparing to attack, looks back and forth between us, and says, "Surely you must be shitting me."

I look at Sara. She smiles and says nothing.

Charlie, for his part, has been drinking on pace. I've been working on a little scotch and water and keeping my eye out for the lobster balls. "Keep it under your hat, Charlie. We're superstitious."

"Well, I'll be damned." He raises his glass. "I heard on the radio the experts say we'll have fourteen thousand people per square mile in the Boston metro area within five years' time. But I'm sure you two know what you're doing."

"Thanks, buddy. That means a lot."

Later, I catch him whispering something in Sara's ear. I see her smile and pat his cheek. *Thank you, Charlie. We're very happy.*

Still later, Charlie and I smoke cigars outside. It's a nice night. Clear sky, not too cold.

"Someday, my son," he tells me, "I'll instruct you about protection."

I tell him there's only so much you can do to be safe in this world.

Charlie is snoring in a chair the next time I see him. At some point, someone turns on a television, and we watch the ball drop in Times Square. Michael and Ben call Sara's cell phone from Clark Falls to wish us both a happy New Year.

We wish them the same, kiss at midnight, and drive our old friend Charlie home.

ACKNOWLEDGMENTS

Special thanks are due to the First Annual Box of Wine Writer's Summit Invitational for its assistance in the writing of this novel. Thanks to David Hale Smith and Shauyi Tai for ground control.

Thanks also to Detective Craig Enloe of the Overland Park Police Department for answering sudden, left-field questions with grace and generosity. Verisimilitude relating to the practice of law enforcement is due in part to his efforts, and miscues are wholly my own.

Finally, heartfelt thanks to Danielle Perez, Nita Taublib, and the ace Bantam Dell team for their faith and support. Double thanks to Danielle Perez for holding my feet to the editorial fire (and for the ample on-hand supply of editorial ointment).

ABOUT THE AUTHOR

Sean Doolittle is the author of four previous novels: the Barry Award–winning *The Cleanup*, *Rain Dogs*, *Burn*, and *Dirt*. He lives with his wife and children in the Omaha, Nebraska, area, and his Web site is www.seandoolittle.com.